UNSETTLED SPIRITS

UNSETTLED SPIRITS

DAISY GUMM MAJESTY MYSTERY, BOOK 10

ALICE DUNCAN

Book and cover design by eBook Prep
www.ebookprep.com

April, 2019
Paperback ISBN: 978-1-64457-065-4
Hardcover ISBN: 978-1-64457-066-1

ePublishing Works!
644 Shrewsbury Commons Ave
Ste 249
Shrewsbury PA 17361
United States of America

www.epublishingworks.com
Phone: 866-846-5123

For Sue Krekeler and Lynne Welch, two of the best beta readers any author ever had.

ONE

My family and I, along with Sam Rotondo, welcomed the New Year, 1924, as we welcomed most new years. We walked from our tidy bungalow on South Marengo Avenue in Pasadena, California, to Colorado Boulevard and watched the Tournament of Roses Parade. No Rose Queen was crowned for 1924, although I don't know why. The day was chilly, but bright and sunny. We knew the press would publicize the parade, and that people all over the United States—and, for all I know, the world—would envy us our gorgeous weather. Roses in January? Must sound grand if you're buried under six feet of snow in Maine or New Hampshire. The parade was lovely, and my family and Sam enjoyed it greatly. We always did.

The only thing Sam and I knew that the rest of my family didn't was that Sam and I had recently become an engaged couple. I still cringe when I recall Christmas of 1923, when Sam attempted to bestow an engagement ring upon me.

Sam must have anticipated my possible reaction, because he took Spike, my late husband's black-and-tan dachshund and probably the smartest dog in the universe, and me to the front porch. There Sam and I sat on the front porch steps, bundled up against the nippy weather. Spike bounded off to chase leaves and, if he was lucky, the neighbors' cat Samson.

Sam reached into his pocket and withdrew a little box. "See if you like this," he said, handing the box to me.

Drawing back slightly, I took the box, opened it, and saw displayed therein a yellow-gold ring with an emerald set in what looked like a nest of rose leaves. It wasn't elaborate; it was, however, possibly the most beautiful ring I'd ever seen in my life.

So what did I do? I clutched my left hand, still bearing the plain gold band my late husband, Billy, had given me on our wedding day in 1917, to my heart and burst into tears.

Sam said, "It's all right, Daisy. I know it's probably too soon." He sounded resigned.

"I-I-I'm sorry, Sam," I blubbered, feeling like an idiot. "It-it's beautiful, but—" I couldn't go on.

Sam put his arms around me and rocked me like a baby. "I understand, Daisy. When you agreed to marry me, you told me you weren't ready yet. Take all the time you need."

After a minute or two I recovered my composure and glanced up at Sam from what I knew were swollen red eyes. Unlike the heroines of romantic novels and motion pictures, I don't look good when I cry. My skin gets all blotchy, and my eyes get red and puffy. "I'm sorry." I sniffled, and Sam reached into another pocket and produced a clean handkerchief. I took it with a shaky hand and said, "Thank you."

As I mopped my eyes and cheeks and felt foolish, Spike began barking like a bad dog, which was most unlike him. My bleary gaze couldn't quite locate him, so Sam rose from the porch steps and went to look for him.

"Here he is," he called a moment or so later. "He's just wishing Pudge a merry Christmas."

Pudge Wilson, son of the neighbors to the north of us, hove into view with Spike frolicking at his feet. Sam walked stolidly beside the boy and the dog. Sam never frolicked.

"Merry Christmas, Pudge," I said, trying with all my inner strength to pull myself together. I realized I still held the jewelry box and quickly stuffed it into a pocket of my coat.

"Merry Christmas, Miss Daisy," said Pudge. He shyly handed me a wrapped parcel. Pudge was about twelve years old by that time, and he'd been sweet on me for years. He was a nice kid; and I have absolutely no idea why people called him Pudge, because he was about as big around as a toothpick. He also had a ton of freckles and a delightful smile.

"Thank you, Pudge," I said. "You shouldn't have given me a present."

"I made it in Boy Scouts," said Pudge proudly. I guess he was too young to notice the signs of distress on my face. At any rate, he didn't comment on them. "Anyhow, your family always gives us about six thousand cookies for Christmas."

This was true, although it was only because my aunt Viola Gumm, widow of my father's older brother, lived with us, and she was the finest cook in the entire City of Pasadena, if not the whole U.S. of A. So I took Pudge's package, smudged where dirty little-boy fingers had pressed the paper, and opened it to reveal a piece of bark with something—it looked kind of like a horse—burned upon it.

"You did this yourself?" I tried to sound astonished and gratified.

"Yep." Pudge straightened and beamed at me. "It's made by heating an iron rod and burning the wood." He pointed at the image. "That's a unicorn. I thought you'd like it, because unicorns are kind of magic."

"How very thoughtful. Thank you so much, Pudge." I rose and gave him a hug, which succeeded in embarrassing him nearly to death and sent him scampering back home.

Spike wanted to follow him, but I called him to heel. Because Spike had been to obedience school three summers prior to this Christmas, he heeled. Bless the dog.

I sat again, and Sam and I surveyed my present from Pudge. "Do you think that's supposed to be the unicorn's horn?" I asked, pointing to a burned line that looked as if it were protruding from the animal's nose.

"I guess so. I thought unicorns had horns on their heads, not their noses."

3

I shook my own head. "Darned if I know where their horns go, but this was thoughtful of Pudge."

"Yes, it was," agreed Sam. "You see? I'm not the only one who loves you."

That started me off again, until Sam said, and curtly too, "Cut it out, Daisy. For God's sake, if I'd known you'd carry on like this, I'd have waited to give you the ring."

"I-I-I'm sorry!"

Sam rolled his eyes, something he did a lot in my presence.

Perhaps some sort of explanation is called for here. I am Daisy Gumm Majesty, and at the time I burst into tears that Christmas on our front porch after seeing the ring Sam had so thoughtfully acquired for me, I earned my living (and most of my family's) by working as a spiritualist-medium to the wealthy folks who lived in Pasadena. There were a lot of them. Pasadena was at that time a rich-man's town, and if it weren't for the fact that rich people required people like my family and me to work for them, we'd have been living elsewhere.

As for Sam Rotondo, he was a detective for the Pasadena Police Department, and a widower of some years, his wife having died of tuberculosis. He and she had moved from New York City to Pasadena in the vain hope the milder climate would help her condition. It didn't.

Sam and I would probably never have met if it weren't for the evil Mr. Eustace Kincaid, who was at the time married to Madeline Pinkerton. Mrs. Pinkerton had been my best client for more than half my life. This was partly because I began my career at the age of ten when Mrs. Pinkerton gave my Aunt Vi an old Ouija board, and I'd flummoxed my family by pretending to be able to use the thing. Aunt Vi was so impressed, she told Mrs. Pinkerton, for whom she worked as cook, and Mrs. Pinkerton had taken me under her wing. Therefore, by this, my twenty-third year, I was sought after by most of the well-off matrons of Pasadena, California, who wanted me to chat with their dead relations for them.

But I see I've veered off-course. To continue, I somehow—and it wasn't my fault, no matter what Sam says—got embroiled in catching Mr.

Eustace Kincaid in his dirty dealings. And the reason Mrs. Pinkerton is no longer Mrs. Eustace Kincaid is because after her first husband's villainy was discovered, she divorced him. Divorce was generally frowned upon back then, but I guess the high society of Pasadena let Mrs. P get away with it because Mr. Kincaid, although he tried, was unable to ruin the bank he ran. Mind you, this was mainly because Mrs. Pinkerton's son Harold had a...Never mind. I'll get into Harold later.

A year or so after her divorce from Eustace Kincaid, she married her longtime friend, Mr. Algernon Pinkerton, another fabulously wealthy Pasadena person. I'd always liked Mr. Pinkerton, a roly-poly, pink-cheeked, jolly gentleman, although I didn't much care for his nickname, Algie, because it sounds like...well, like algae, and that stuff is icky. But that's not the point.

Do I believe in communication with people who have crossed from this life to another one? Good heavens, no! I'm not stupid. Well, and neither are most of my clients, but they can afford to be whimsical and at least pretend to believe in communication with the dead. Heck, if I really could talk to spirits, I'd be chatting with my late husband every day. I only wished I could. Instead, I'm a middle-class widow woman with a family to support, and I made a whole lot more money as a spiritualist-medium than I could make doing any other sort of work available to females back then.

Actually, my mother, Peggy Gumm, worked as the head bookkeeper at the Hotel Marengo, which was an impressively good job for a woman at the time. However, if she were a man doing the same work, she'd have been paid a whole lot more money.

As I've already mentioned, my aunt, Viola Gumm, worked for the Pinkertons and was a spectacular cook. She cooked for the family too, and we were happy about it. Naturally, if she were a man, they'd call her a chef, and she, too, would make a whole lot more money. Does this seem fair to you? Me, neither.

My father, Joe Gumm, used to be a chauffeur for rich folks until he suffered a heart attack and was forced by his health to retire from that work.

Therefore, our family was supported by its women. I have an older brother named Walter and an older sister named Daphne, but they didn't live with us. However, at the time of the ring fiasco, Walter, Daphne, their spouses and their children were all inside our bungalow, having gathered for a magnificent Christmas meal prepared especially for us by Aunt Vi. Things were quite jolly inside the house.

But back to the front porch, where things weren't particularly jolly. Sam's churlish comment dried my tears, and I dug in my pocket for the ring box. "I'm not sure what to do, Sam," I told him in a mournful whisper. "I do love you, but it's only been a couple of years since Billy died, and I loved him *so* much. Not more than you, but in a different way." I pleaded with him with my watery gaze. "Do you know what I mean? I know it sounds silly—"

"No, it doesn't," said Sam, interrupting me. "I feel the same way. Billy was the love of your life. Margaret was the love of my life. No other woman can ever take her place."

Well! I liked that!

Can you tell I was a trifle irrational during this conversation? I mean, I'd just told Sam that, in effect, I could never love another man as I'd loved Billy, but I felt insulted when he said pretty much the same thing about his late wife Margaret. You figure it out; it's beyond me.

By the way, my Billy was a casualty of the Great War. The fighting didn't kill him instantly, but the forever-cursed Kaiser's poisoned gas had burned out his lungs, and at the time of his death, he still carried shrapnel in his legs. He took his own life, although our extremely kind family physician, Dr. Benjamin, had written the cause of his death as an accidental overdose of the morphine syrup Billy had to take because of the hideous pain with which he lived.

Anyhow, Sam must have noticed my indignation, because he heaved a huge sigh and said, "You know Billy asked me to take care of you after his death, don't you?"

He meant, of course, that before his death, Billy had asked Sam to take care of me if he died, but I'm not here to quibble. Anyhow, I knew what he meant because...

"Yes." I sniffled once more. I'd overheard the conversation during which Billy had asked Sam to care for me after he departed this earth. I hadn't meant to listen in. It just worked out that way. "But if you're marrying me just because—"

"Damn it! You know that's not the reason. I love you. I don't love you the same way I loved Margaret, because she was my first love. We were both innocents and believed we'd be together for the rest of our lives. I'm sure it was the same with you and Billy. Hell, weren't you only seventeen when you guys married?"

"Yes."

"Well, then. You're not a child any longer, and neither am I. I'm almost thirty years old, for God's sake. I love you. You said you love me. But don't forget that I also said we could be engaged for however long it takes for you to adjust to the idea before we marry. You needn't take the ring. I'll keep it."

He reached for the box, but I tucked it in my lap, slapped my other hand over the one holding the ring, and said, "No!" I swallowed and said, "May I keep it? I'll just...keep it in a drawer or something."

"For Pete's sake," muttered Sam.

"I know. But...I love the ring. And I love you. I'm just not quite ready to wear it. That sounds ridiculous, doesn't it?"

"Well..."

"But it's the truth!"

"Whatever you want to do with the ring is all right by me, but if you decide not to marry me, I want it back."

"Of course," I said, thinking melancholy thoughts about Billy, lost love, found love, and the symbols of love. Was I pathetic, or what?

Sam said, "I mainly just wanted to know if you liked it. My father designed it." Sam's family owned and ran a jewelry store in New York City.

After another pathetic sniffle, I said, "I love it. Your father is very talented."

"You don't mind that it's not a diamond?"

"I don't even like diamonds. The emerald goes better with my hair." I

7

suppose that sounds silly, but I had dark red hair, and I cultivated a pale, ghostly, wafting persona that fitted my position as a spiritualist-medium to perfection. Emeralds and rubies were my all-time favorite gems, but I wouldn't dare wear a ruby, which might be taken as bright and sprightly and...well, red. My job required me to be sober and pallid. I never wore red. Emerald green, on the other hand, had a sort of mystical air about it. Or maybe it didn't, but I'd wear an emerald before I'd ever wear a ruby.

"That's what I thought, too." I could tell Sam was trying not to laugh at my hair comment.

"But I...I can't give up Billy's ring, Sam. Not yet, anyway. I'm sorry."

"No reason to be sorry. You can just keep this one until you're ready."

At that moment, the front door opened, and Daphne's children raced outside.

"Aunt Daisy! Aunt Daisy! Come and play the piano for us. We want to sing Christmas carols!"

So Sam and Spike and I returned to the bosom of my family, the entirety of which barely fitted into our snug bungalow, and I walked to the piano and played Christmas carols for my family. I've always been glad my folks made me take piano lessons when I was a kid.

TWO

January 1, 1924, fell on a Tuesday. The week following that colorful parade day progressed at a slow, dignified, Pasadena-like pace. I had no séances to perform for anyone, no tarot cards to read, no nothin', probably because most of my clients were recovering from their Christmas and New Year's celebrations.

As for my family, my mother and aunt resumed their duties at their different workplaces, and I went to the library and picked up books for everyone to read. My favorite librarian, Miss Petrie, had taken some time off, so I had to search the shelves for reading material on my own—Miss Petrie liked to put aside books for my family and me to enjoy. Pa and I walked Spike every day, and Sam came to dinner most evenings. In other words, our lives were as normal as normal could be.

Then came Sunday, January sixth, when the elderly widow, Mrs. Theodore Franbold, dropped dead right after taking communion at our church. My family attended the First Methodist-Episcopal Church on the corner of Marengo and Colorado, and Mrs. Franbold's demise provided a whole lot more excitement than most of our Sunday services could offer. Not that I wanted people dropping dead in church; I only mention the matter as interesting.

9

At our church, we take communion once monthly, on the first Sunday of each month. I sang alto in the choir, and we choir members sat in a space reserved for us on the chancel. We were served communion separately from the rest of the congregation, so I couldn't rush to see what had happened when I saw Mrs. Franbold keel over right in front of Mr. Grover Underhill. Rather than trying to help her or catch her, Mr. Underhill jumped out of the way, plowing into several other people and nearly felling a couple of them. I frowned, thinking this behavior was typical of him. He was a certified meany, as far as I was concerned. Not that I knew him well, but what I did know of him, I didn't like. Poor Mrs. Franbold. Just her luck to be standing next to Mr. Underhill.

Squinting, I saw the folks around Mrs. Franbold steady themselves after being bumped by Mr. Underhill and gasp when they saw the reason for his ungentlemanly behavior. A few seconds later, I saw several people, including Sam Rotondo, who had taken going to church with us even though he'd grown up in the Roman Catholic Church, gather around the fallen woman. I lost Sam in the crowd when he knelt, probably to organize things and see what he could do for Mrs. Franbold.

A general buzzing ensued. Mr. Underhill looked irritated, as if he didn't approve of people collapsing in church. Lucy Spinks, a soprano who was engaged to marry an older gentleman named Albert Zollinger, whispered in my ear, "What do you think is happening?"

As much as I squinted, I couldn't see much because there were so many people in the way, so I said, "I'm not sure. It looks as though Mrs. Franbold fell down."

"Oh, dear. Poor sweet thing. I hope she didn't break anything."

"Me, too."

A scream erupted, and I winced, as I'm sure the rest of the choir did, also. This time, I decided to heck with convention and stood in an effort to discover who'd screamed. It was then I saw Miss Betsy Powell, who had been assisting with communion, cover her face with her hands and give out short, sharp, piercing shrieks. Little communion cups littered the floor around her. The trustees would never get the grape juice out of that carpet. At that point I guess our minister, the Reverend Merle Negley

Smith, decided to abandon his position behind the communion wafers and assist the afflicted, because he hurried down the chancel steps and rushed over to Miss Powell. She had by this time broken into noisy sobs, and Pastor Smith gently guided her out of the church via a side door. Another gentleman, Mr. Gerald Kingston, held out a hand as if to help Pastor Smith, but neither Pastor Smith nor Miss Powell seemed to notice his good intentions. Poor Mr. Kingston was left, looking unhappy, staring after the pair.

"What's the matter with whoever that is?" whispered Lucy.

On tiptoes, trying to see around the lectern used by our lay speakers, I said, "I'm not sure. Maybe Mrs. Franbold is dead or having a fit or something. It was Miss Powell who was screaming. There's grape juice all over the floor, because she dropped the tray of communion cups she was holding. I think Mr. Underhill bumped the tray out of her hands. He didn't even try to help Mrs. Franbold. Now it looks as if Miss Powell is crying hysterically. Pastor Smith is leading her away from the mess." Darn, but I wished people would get out of my line of vision!

"Why would she scream?"

"Maybe she's not used to seeing people fall over in front of her at communion?" I shrugged.

"Maybe."

Mr. Floy Hostetter, our choir director, also abandoned the chancel then, and rushed over to the crowd clustered around Mrs. Franbold. Lucy and I exchanged a speaking glance, but we both decided not to add our presence to what was already a chaotic scene.

Suddenly Sam Rotondo stood, rocklike in his solidness. His voice rose over those of the masses. He didn't holler. He didn't have to. "Everyone, please take your seats. I'll handle this."

Nobody moved.

"Take your seats," said Sam in a voice I doubt anyone could ignore. He sounded like a general giving instructions to a firing squad.

The well-behaved congregants of the First Methodist-Episcopal Church on the corner of Marengo and Colorado in Pasadena seemed inclined to obey him, because everyone straggled back to their seats. This was probably a good thing, although communion hadn't ended yet, so many of the sittees were as of that moment un-sanctified. Or something like that.

After a brief conference with Sam, Mr. Hostetter trotted back to the chancel, climbed the steps, and walked to the preacher's pulpit. He held up his hands, and all murmuring stopped. I sat down. Darn it, I wanted to know what had happened!

"Dear ladies and gentlemen, please remain seated for a moment or two more. Mrs. Franbold has been taken ill, and some kind fellows are assisting her out of the sanctuary."

What he meant was that Sam and Dr. Benjamin were picking the woman up off the floor and aimed to take her somewhere else. My guess was that they would go to Mr. Smith's office, where there was a convenient couch. Lying on a couch had to be more comfortable than lying on the floor of a church sanctuary. Of course, at that point in time, no one knew for sure that the dear woman was dead. Well, I kind of did, but that's only because stuff like that seems to happen in my vicinity. Not necessarily people dropping dead but, as my father once told me, "Strange things happen around you." I'd resented his words at the time, but he was right, whether I resented his saying them or not.

After another few minutes, during which Sam and Dr. Benjamin, each with one of Mrs. Franbold's arms draped over their shoulders, escorted the woman from the sanctuary, Mr. Hostetter said, "Er...We shall resume communion at this time." He glanced frantically around the church. "Um, may we have a couple of volunteers, since our minister and Miss Powell are indisposed?" He then turned, gestured to Lucy and me and said, "Miss Spinks and Mrs. Majesty, perhaps you might be of service now."

Lucy and I looked at each other, shrugged, and went to take over the giving of communion in place of Mr. Smith and Miss Powell. Communion isn't difficult to assist with, since all you have to do is have one person hold out a plate with communion wafers on it, and then another person offer each congregant a little glass cup filled about halfway with grape juice. Folks eat the wafer, drink the juice in the cup, and then—if they're doing it right—kneel prayerfully at the front altar or go to their seats. That day, the Communion Committee rushed to gather together more half-full communion cups, and I held the tray, still a little juicy from Miss Powell's earlier mishap. I regret to say my mind often wandered when it was supposed to be contemplating the state of my soul.

It sure wandered that day, and not just because I was trying to think of how to get grape juice out of a church carpet. I could hardly wait for the service to end so I could ask Sam what was wrong with Mrs. Franbold. If she was dead, how'd she die? If she was merely sick, what had made her sick? Had she suffered an apoplectic stroke? Heart attack? Perhaps she'd been ill and had come to church with walking pneumonia, although that sounded far-fetched. If a person is *that* sick, he or she should stay home, sleep and drink lots of hot tea with lemon and honey. At least that's what my mother always made me do when I was sick. Oh, and she'd give me cod-liver oil, too.

The mere thought of cod-liver oil made me shudder.

Lucy asked, "Are you all right, Daisy?"

"Fine, thanks." I decided she didn't need to know my innermost thoughts.

After communion was over, the congregation, led by Mr. Hostetter, began singing our final hymn of the day, "O For a Thousand Tongues to Sing," which is a nice hymn. It's also the first hymn in every Methodist hymnal I've ever seen, although I'm not sure why. It was written by Charles Wesley, so maybe that's the reason, the Wesley brothers having begun Methodism in the 1700s.

Because Pastor Smith hadn't returned by the time the hymn was finished, Mr. Hostetter gave the final benediction and bade the congregants Godspeed.

Fortunately for us, Lucy and I didn't have to pick up the leftover communion stuff. Ladies from the Communion Committee did that. So we both hightailed it to the choir room, removed our choir robes, hung them up, and hurried to Fellowship Hall, where tea and cookies would be served.

My family never stayed long at fellowship because Aunt Vi always had a delicious meal cooking for us at home. Therefore, I rushed around asking people if they knew what had happened to Mrs. Franbold. Nobody knew. And Sam, darn him, didn't show up at fellowship.

"We'd best be getting on home," Ma said not ten minutes after I'd appeared in Fellowship Hall. "Do you suppose Sam is still busy with Mrs. Franbold?"

"Don't know," said Pa.

"Probably," said Aunt Vi. "That poor woman. How old is she, anyway?"

"I don't know," I said. "Old. Well, elderly," I amended when I saw my mother's black look aimed at me. She expected her daughter to be polite and courteous all the time, even though her daughter—me—was all grown up and earning a living. I sighed. "Maybe he's in Pastor Smith's office. I'll go look."

"I'd like Sam to come to dinner," said Aunt Vi. She loved anyone who loved her cooking, and Sam lavished praise upon her every time he dined with us. Not that she didn't deserve his accolades, but I suspected him sometimes of going overboard just so she'd ask him to dinner more often.

"Right. I'll be back directly." And before anyone could stop me, I hurried out of the fellowship hall and to the pastor's office, which was just up the hall a few feet. I knocked softly on the closed door and wished curtains hadn't been drawn across the window.

A few seconds elapsed, and then I nearly leaped out of my skin when the door suddenly opened, and a scowling Sam glared down at me. He took up most of the doorway, so I couldn't see past him.

"What?"

"Aunt Vi wants to know if you're coming to dinner with us," I said, deciding not to bellow at him for his rudeness. We were, after all, in a church.

"I don't know yet."

Well, wasn't he just a load of joy and helpfulness? "But what should I tell Vi."

His scowl intensified. "Tell her I don't know yet."

Oh, boy. How friendly. "Sam, what happened to Mrs. Franbold?"

Before Sam could tell me it was none of my business, I saw a hand descend upon Sam's shoulder, and Pastor Smith said, "Perhaps Mrs. Majesty can help console Miss Powell, Detective."

So. Miss Powell needed consolation, did she? I wondered why. Rather than ask, I said, "I'll be happy to help." It wasn't even a fib. If I could get into the pastor's office, maybe I could finally learn what had happened to poor old Mrs. Franbold. And why whatever it was had so upset Betsy Powell.

Sam, who knew me very well, made a perfectly hideous face, which only I could see, and said, "She only wants to nose around."

"I do not!" Very well, that was just a tiny little stretcher. I also wanted to be helpful.

"I do wish you'd step aside and let her in, Detective Rotondo. Miss Powell is terribly upset." Pastor Smith sounded rattled.

After heaving a sigh about the size of Mount Wilson, Sam said, "Very well. Come in. But sit with Miss Powell and don't get in the way."

"I won't get in the way," I told him in a voice that clearly conveyed my irritation with him. Get in the way, my foot.

"Right," said Sam, unconvinced.

Nevertheless, he stepped aside, and I entered the pastor's office. I was surprised to see a couple of uniformed police officers standing at the sofa that held Mrs. Franbold. I shot a quick look at Sam and whispered, "Is she...?"

"Yes. She is. Now go comfort that other lady."

Oh, my. Poor Mrs. Franbold! What could have happened to her?

Betsy Powell sat sobbing on an overstuffed chair not far from the minister's desk. I walked over and knelt beside her. "Miss Powell? Betsy, please tell me what's wrong. Is there anything I can do for you?"

She lifted her head, and I saw that she, too, failed to look good when she cried. Her eyes were swollen almost shut, her face was red, and she was gasping and sobbing and generally looking like a mess. I feared she might faint if she kept that up.

Putting an arm on her shoulder, I said, "There, there. That's enough now. You needn't cry. Poor Mrs. Franbold was an elderly woman, and

15

she's now in a better place. If God decided to call her during commu-nion...Well, what better time to do it?" I thought that was kind of a nice way of putting it, but Betsy only gasped loudly and sobbed harder.

"No!" she cried, her words thickened with tears. "No! It wasn't her time! Oh, oh, oh!"

Perfect. Now what was I supposed to do? I'd heard that one could cure an hysterical person by slapping the person's face, but I didn't think church would be a good place to do that. Therefore, I shook Betsy's shoulder rather hard.

"That's enough now, Betsy Powell. Get hold of yourself. This is no time and no place to get the galloping glooms." Don't ask me why I used those words. I think I'd read them in a book or something. "This is Pastor Smith's office, and I'm sure he has better things to do than listen to you have fits while he's trying to deal with the death of a long-time congre-gant. Now buck up." I spoke sternly, for me. I generally try to convey a gentle waftiness, but I was dealing with hysterics here, so I believed firm-ness was called for.

Evidently Betsy Powell wasn't so sure, because she stared at me for about thirty seconds, and then crumpled into a faint. Oh, goody. Just what everyone needed: another body to contend with.

But no one else seemed to mind. In fact, Pastor Smith actually said, "Did she finally pass out? Thank God."

Sam said, "Thanks, Daisy. She was driving us nerts."

Dr. Benjamin said, "She fainted? Excellent."

Well, there you go. I'd been mean, and everyone appreciated me for it.

"What happened to Mrs. Franbold?" I asked after making sure Betsy still breathed. She did.

"Don't know," said Sam. "That's why the uniforms are here."

"Oh. I wondered why you'd called the cops."

Sam gave me a frown I don't believe I deserved. "Any time there's a sudden, unexpected death, it's a good idea to get a medical opinion. Dr. Benjamin is the one who suggested we call the uniforms."

"Really?" Still kneeling, although my knees were beginning to object, I turned to Doc Benjamin. "Why's that, Doc?"

He didn't answer me for quite a few seconds, and his lips pursed in and pooched out, as if he were determining whether or not to answer my question. I held my breath and slowly got to my feet, making sure Betsy Powell was firmly attached to her chair and wouldn't slither out of it.

At last, the doctor looked at me and said, "From the signs, it looks to me as if Mrs. Franbold might have taken or been given something that might have caused a violent reaction. I may well be wrong, but it's best to check these things out."

As luck would have it, Betsy Powell woke up in time to hear Dr. Benjamin's words. She let out a screech that could probably have been heard in Illinois. Fortunately, she fainted again instantly.

THREE

"You mean, she might have been given something like poison? How could she have been poisoned?" asked Aunt Vi as we gathered around the dining room table and I told my family what had transpired in Pastor Smith's office.

That day our dinner, which we took right after church on Sundays, was a pot roast with potatoes, carrots, celery and little pearl onions. Aunt Vi's pot roast was one of the more delicious dishes on the face of the earth.

"I don't know." I glanced across the table at Sam, who'd joined us. "Sam? Why did Doc think the woman was poisoned?"

"Beats me. He mentioned poison, and I called the department to send some uniforms in. He might be mistaken. The medical examiner will run tests to find out what happened."

"That's terrible," said Ma, a sensitive plant, if a not-very-imaginative one.

"It's terrible that she dropped dead in church," I said. "But how could she get poison there?"

"We don't know she was poisoned, and if she was, we don't know how," said Sam as if he wished I'd drop the subject. In a pig's eye.

"Maybe Betsy Powell poisoned her," I opined, thinking about how Betsy had reacted to Mrs. Franbold's collapse. She'd reacted again when she'd heard Dr. Benjamin mention poison. Hmm. Was that a clue?

"Daisy!" said Ma, who didn't approve of her daughter suggesting ugly things at the dinner table.

"Well, she was sure upset. I don't think she'd be that upset if Mrs. Franbold had just dropped dead, unless she knew something the rest of us didn't. Well, and she also spilled grape juice on the church carpet. Maybe she was worried about that."

"Oh, dear," said Ma. "Grape juice stains terribly."

"I thought the same thing," I told her.

"Peroxide," said Aunt Vi as if she knew what she was talking about. "Peroxide will get wine and grape-juice stains out of most things."

Wine and grape-juice stains? Vi's late husband, Ernie, had enjoyed imbibing. Maybe that's why Vi knew about peroxide's stain-removing capabilities.

Still and all..."But I can't imagine why spilling communion cups could have led to her hysteria."

"You can never tell," said Sam. "Some women cherish their hysterics."

I was about to argue with him, but then I remembered Mrs. Pinkerton. Mrs. Pinkerton might be said to cherish her hysterics, I guess, although she didn't seem to enjoy them much. Neither had Betsy Powell.

"Do you know Miss Powell well, Daisy?" asked Pa, buttering a biscuit. Aunt Vi also made the best biscuits in the world.

"No. Not well. I see her at church. She's not in the choir, although I think she's on a couple of other committees, because sometimes I see her on Thursday evenings after choir practice." Glancing again at Sam, I asked, "Do you know how old she is?"

"Who? Miss Powell?"

"Yes."

He shrugged. "The uniforms probably managed to take a statement from her after she woke up from her second faint. From the looks of her, I'd say she was in her forties, maybe?"

"Hmm. Never married," I mused. "That's kind of unusual, isn't it? I mean, she's not ugly or anything."

"Daisy!"

Oh, dear. I'd annoyed my mother again. "Sorry, Ma, but she's a nice-looking woman, and most nice-looking women get married when they're young, don't they?"

"Maybe women her age," said Sam. "Nowadays, though, there aren't that many young men still alive to marry them."

That was the truth. The Great War had cut down almost an entire generation of young men. We in the United States were luckier in that regard than were Great Britain, France, and Belgium, but a whole lot of our young men had been wiped out, too, thanks to Kaiser Bill's determination to rule the world. Too bad nobody'd poisoned him.

This sad truth was also why Lucille Spinks had agreed to marry Albert Zollinger, a widower some years her senior. Not that Mr. Zollinger wasn't a nice man, but still, there were precious few younger ones for Lucy to choose from. Dismal thought. Back to Betsy Powell.

"She's nice enough," I said. "Kind of sweet. You know the kind. Brings flowers or cookies to people who are sick and stuff like that. I thought men liked sweet women."

"Maybe she's just boring," said Sam.

My mother didn't yell at him, which I believe to be unfair considering his statement was worse than my earlier one had been. But there's never been any justice in this old world, and I don't suppose there ever will be.

"Will you know more tomorrow, Sam? I mean, will you have a report to read or something?"

He shrugged as he took another biscuit from the basket. "I don't know. Depends on what the autopsy report shows. If they do an autopsy."

Ew. Dinner-table talk didn't generally include autopsies. But as long as Sam had brought up the subject and Ma hadn't objected..."If Dr. Benjamin thinks she was poisoned, surely they'll do an autopsy on her, don't you think?"

"Probably," admitted Sam. "That doesn't mean I'll get to read it. Or want to read it, for that matter."

"But Sam!" I cried. "The woman dropped dead in our church! We all want to know what happened to her."

"I know. I know. But the Pasadena Police Department can't afford to take everyone's nosiness into consideration when they're dealing with a case. You should understand that by this time, if anyone should."

Pa snickered.

Ma nodded.

Vi smiled.

I considered heaving a biscuit at Sam, but restrained myself. Which was a good thing. My mother would probably have hauled me onto her lap and spanked me if I did anything that childish.

While I was trying to think of a suitable retort that would let Sam know what I thought of his attitude without incurring my mother's wrath, the telephone rang. We all sat at attention and stared at each other as we listened. It was our ring.

Since basically every telephone call we received in our family was for me, I got up from the table, said, "Excuse me, please," and went to the kitchen, where our phone hung on the wall. As I walked, I contemplated what this telephone call might mean.

Had Stacy Kincaid strayed from the narrow pathway allotted her by the Salvation Army, which she'd joined after a distinguished and disgusting career as a hellion? If she had, Mrs. Pinkerton might be telephoning me in a State. Could Harold Kincaid be calling to ask me out to luncheon? That was a pleasant thought. Could Mrs. Bissel have another ghost, or spirit, in her basement that required exorcising? I'd exorcised one ghost for her; I expect I could do it again if necessary, although the last one had been relatively easy to deal with, mainly because it wasn't a supernatural being but a runaway girl.

I'd just decided my money would have to be on Mrs. Pinkerton and was praying madly that she wasn't in hysterics—I'd had enough hysterics for one day—when I reached the telephone. I lifted the receiver and spoke into the mouthpiece, giving my regular line in my purring spiritualist's voice: "Gumm-Majesty residence. Mrs. Majesty speaking."

"Oh, Daisy! I'm so glad you're home!"

Mrs. Pinkerton. But she didn't sound distressed. I gave a silent sigh of relief. "How do you do, Mrs. Pinkerton?" I asked, still in my best low, purring spiritualist's voice.

"I'm fine, thank you."

Boy, that didn't happen often.

"Did you enjoy your stay in Santa Barbara?" I asked her. The Pinkertons had spent the Christmas season in Santa Barbara, California, a pretty town on the coast some miles north of Pasadena. I'd never been there, but I knew it was a gorgeous place—and expensive—because otherwise the Pinkertons wouldn't have gone there. Plus, I'd seen pictures.

"Oh, my, yes. Santa Barbara is *so* lovely, and the Miramar By the Sea is *such* a special place."

I just bet it was. Bet it cost an arm and a leg, too, although money didn't matter to the Pinkertons of this mean old world.

"I'm so glad you had a good time," I said, sparing Mrs. P my opinion of expensive resorts I couldn't afford to visit.

"Oh, yes, it was beautiful. The ocean is...so vast, don't you know."

"Indeed, yes. It must have been quite pleasant to stay there." And look at the ocean. Well, and they probably did other things, too, but I didn't know what.

She sighed into the phone. "Oh, it was. But I'm calling to see if you'd be interested in handling the fortune-teller's tent at a charity party I'm going to be giving early next month. You know you're always the first one I think of when it comes to all things spiritual." She honored me with one of her tittering laughs.

"I'd be happy to do that, Mrs. Pinkerton. What's the cause?"

"The Pasadena Humane Society," said she.

"Oh, that's an excellent cause! I'll be even happier to do it than I was before." I didn't generally joke around with my clients, but some imp of humor must have invaded my voice box at that moment.

Fortunately for me, Mrs. Pinkerton only laughed. "Oh, yes. I know how much you love that dachshund of yours. Mrs. Bissel will be there, and Pansy Hanratty, too. They're both big supporters of the Humane Society."

They were both big, at any rate. But I adored both women. Mrs. Bissel was probably my second-best client, and much easier for me to deal with than Mrs. Pinkerton, mainly because she never had hysterics. Well, and she'd also given me Spike. Mrs. Hanratty was not only the mother of the current, number-one, top screen idol, Monty Mountjoy, but she also had taught Spike's obedience training course.

"When do you plan to have the party, Mrs. Pinkerton?"

"I looked at my calendar, and I think most of my friends will be back in town by the second week in February. How about Saturday, February ninth? Will that fit in with your schedule?"

Of course it would. My schedule didn't have so many events on it that I even had to check. Nevertheless, in an effort to make Mrs. Pinkerton think I was busier than I was so she'd appreciate me more, I said, "Let me check my appointment book, and I'll be right back with you." I allowed the receiver to dangle for a moment, making sure it didn't hit the wall and cause permanent damage to Mrs. Pinkerton's eardrums. When I picked it up again, I said, "That date will be perfect, Mrs. Pinkerton. When would you like me to appear, and will you be providing the tent?"

"Oh, wonderful! You should probably arrive about seven-thirty so you can get yourself set up. The other guests will be invited to arrive at eight. And yes, Harold is making the tent. You know Harold." She spoke of her son fondly, as was only his due.

And I certainly did know Harold. He was, in fact, one of my very best friends. "That's wonderful. I'm sure he'll make a most...colorful tent." If I knew Harold, he'd dig up every arcane symbol from every occult group or religion he could think of and plaster them all over the fortune-teller's tent for his mother's party. Very artistic, Harold. He worked as a costumier at a motion-picture studio in Los Angeles.

I wanted to ask her if her no-good, evil daughter would honor us with her presence, but I didn't. Sufficient unto the day, and all that. Besides, if

Stacy had back-slid, Mrs. Kincaid would be wailing at me. Nevertheless, I hoped Stacy would stay away from the party.

"That sounds good. I'll be looking forward to it."

"Um...Daisy?"

Oh, dear. What did she want now? Bet I knew. "Would you like me to wear a Gypsy costume? Or perhaps one in keeping with the party's theme? Probably a Gypsy would be better, since Gypsies are associated with spiritualism. I'll be happy to do that." I did it every time any of my clients hosted a charity ball or party, in fact.

"As long as you don't think wearing a costume beneath your dignity, dear. Everyone knows you're the best spiritualist-medium in Pasadena, so I don't think appearing as a Gypsy would damage your reputation any."

"No, I don't think it would. I've done such things before, if you'll recall."

"Yes, I know. But I always...I don't know. Hesitate. Do you know what I mean? Because you're *so* important to me, and you help *so* many people with your gifts, it seems...Oh, how to express it? Unseemly, somehow, to ask you to dress up in a silly costume."

"I'll make sure my costume isn't silly," I assured her.

"That's why I hope you'll be a Gypsy and not some kind of animal."

"No animals. I promise. A Gypsy will do quite well, I think."

"Good. I knew you'd be able to think of just the thing to wear to such a party. The guests, you see, will be arriving in various animal costumes."

Good Lord. In that case, I *knew* my dignity wouldn't be assailed. I'd be telling fortunes for dogs and cats and horses and pigs, for Pete's sake. It was the guests whose dignity I'd worry about, if I were Mrs. P.

Thank everything on earth and in heaven, I'm not.

We ended our telephone call cordially, and I sauntered back to the dining-room table, took my seat, and told everyone about Mrs. Pinkerton's planned charity party.

"She's holding it to raise funds for the Pasadena Humane Society," I told my family and Sam. "Which I think is a noble goal, although her guests will be dressed in animal costumes, which will probably look silly. On some of them, anyway."

"*Animal* costumes!" Ma cried. "Whatever for?"

"Good question," muttered Sam.

"I suspect because the party is being held as a benefit for the Pasadena Humane Society, and the Humane Society cares for dogs and cats that need help. I read in the *Star News* a couple of weeks ago that they've even taken in desert tortoises and a goat once and a couple of sheep and a parrot." I eyed Sam speculatively. "If Mrs. P invites you, you ought to come in an ape costume."

"Thanks," grumbled Sam.

"Maybe someone will show up in a skunk costume," said Pa.

"Joe!" said my mother, giving him the evil eye instead of giving it to me for once.

"It'll be interesting to see the costumes, at all odds. I'm looking forward to it."

"And you'll do what? Read tarot cards?" asked Vi. "Mrs. Pinkerton admires you so much, I'm surprised she asked you to work at such a...I don't know. It just sounds undignified to me."

"Well, at least I won't be the only one who looks undignified. Heck, I get to dress up as a human being anyway. I always dress as a Gypsy for these sorts of things. Mrs. P isn't the only one who asks me to perform at charity events."

"Why don't you have to dress as a hippo or an elephant or something?" asked Sam.

"Because *I* will be manning—or womanning, I suppose—the fortune-telling tent." I shot him a good glare. "And don't you *dare* tell me fortune-telling is illegal, Sam Rotondo. This is for a good cause, and I won't be making money telling fortunes."

"But you'll be making money," he said.

I squinted at him from across the table. "Mrs. Pinkerton will be paying me to play a role, Sam Rotondo. I've *never* told fortunes!"

He had the gall to laugh at me!

"I just love to wind you up and watch you tear into me," he said.

Everyone laughed. Except me. Blasted man. And he wanted me to marry him? Well, we'd just see about that.

FOUR

Mrs. Franbold's funeral was scheduled for Friday at ten a.m. at Morningside Cemetery. Pastor Smith told us choir members that Mrs. Franbold's family didn't want a big, fancy funeral service at the church, but rather a more sedate service at the cemetery itself. We choir members practiced the hymn, "Abide with Me," to sing at the gravesite. Nice hymn, if kind of boring. Don't tell anyone I said that, please.

The timing was all right by me, although it meant neither Ma nor Aunt Vi could attend, since they both had to work during the day. I drove Pa in our Chevrolet, and wasn't surprised to see Sam's big, black Hudson parked near the gravesite. When he saw me parking the auto, he walked over to open my door for me. He let Pa fend for himself.

"You here in an official capacity?" I asked, hoping to get the scoop about whether or not Mrs. Franbold had been poisoned.

"Sort of," he said.

"Very informative," I muttered as I straightened my skirt and prepared to walk to the gravesite, which was conspicuous because a blue tent had been erected over it, although I didn't know long it would last, as a fierce wind howled that cold January day.

"Don't pick on Sam," my father said with a chuckle. "He was there when the poor woman died, don't forget."

"Yes, and it wasn't pleasant," said Sam.

I peered up at him, squinting because the sun shone brightly that day in spite of the frigid wind. "I thought you were used to dead people by this time."

"I'm not accustomed to people dropping dead at my feet," he said, sounding grumpy.

"She didn't drop dead at your feet. She dropped dead at Mr. Underhill's feet, and he didn't even have the grace to catch her, but let her fall, plunk, right onto the floor. You had to walk clear across the sanctuary to get to her body."

"Yeah, well, Doc Benjamin and I are about the only two in that congregation who know what to do when a person collapses like that."

"Hmm. I guess so. So that's why you're here, right? To scope out the crowd and decided who did her in?"

"Good God," muttered Sam.

"But..."

"Leave Sam alone, Daisy," said Pa. "He has his job to do, just as you have yours."

"Aha! So you *are* here in an official capacity!"

"Partially." Sam took my gloved hand, put it on his bent elbow, and he and Pa and I walked to the flapping blue tent. "We still don't know what caused the poor woman's death."

"Oh." Don't ask me why, but I was disappointed. I mean, I truly didn't want to think that anyone would murder poor old Mrs. Franbold, but a natural death was so boring compared to murder.

"Disappointed, aren't you?" said Sam. He knew me so well.

"Of course not," I lied. Then I changed the subject. "There are lots of people here," I said, gazing at a crowd that was larger than I'd anticipated, the weather being what it was. "Are all these folks related to Mrs. Franbold?"

Sam nodded at a cluster of three people, two women and a man, all of whom appeared upset and miserable. "Those are her children. The kids on the folding chairs are her grandchildren." I was surprised to see a row of gloomy-looking young adult men and women, one of whom dangled a baby on her lap. Mrs. Franbold must have been older than I'd thought.

"Oh, my. I didn't even know she had children and grandchildren. I'm sorry for them."

"Yeah. They were caught by surprise by their mother's sudden death."

"So you *do* think she was poisoned?"

Sam hesitated for so long, I was sure he wouldn't answer my question, but he surprised me. "Not sure. An autopsy was performed, and there were indefinite signs of some kind of alien substance in her stomach, but doctors don't have test results back." He shrugged. "We may never know for sure, although Doc Benjamin suspects that if anything deadly was used on purpose, it was probably cyanide."

"Cyanide! But she must have been poisoned if there was cyanine in her system."

"Not necessarily," said Sam. "Lots of things, including apple seeds and apricot pits, contain various poisons."

"Piffle. She wouldn't have been munching on apricot pits," I said, feeling my brow crease. Instantly I smoothed it out. Nobody wanted to hire a wrinkly spiritualist.

"No, but it's also contained in almonds and other things. If she inhaled it—and don't ask me how she could have done it, because I don't know—it might have killed her almost instantly. But we just don't know at this point."

"Don't people who are poisoned by cyanide have a pinkish cast to their skin?" I asked.

Sam rolled his eyes. "Not always."

"Hmm. Too bad." It was then I spotted Betsy Powell, clad all in black, sobbing into a black handkerchief. Mr. Gerald Kingston held her arm, trying against major odds to bring her comfort. Big help she was going to be during the hymn, not that she had to sing. That was the choir's job. "Has anyone figured out why Miss Powell was so upset by Mrs. Franbold's death and the prospect of her having been poisoned?"

"No," Sam snapped.

I sighed.

Pa chuckled.

But by that time we were at the gravesite. Pastor Smith nodded graciously at us, and, because I'm not merely a good spiritualist-medium, but am also a friendly person, I walked to Mrs. Franbold's children, who gazed at my approach with varying degrees of unhappiness.

"Good morning," said I, which it clearly wasn't for this group. But tradition holds with such inane comments. "I'm Mrs. Majesty, and I knew your mother from church. I'm so very sorry for your loss." I held out a hand, not aiming for any one of Mrs. Franbold's children specifically. A tall, gaunt woman in what looked like an expensive fur coat, took my proffered hand.

"How kind of you to come, Mrs. Majesty. Mother spoke of you often. I'm Vivian Daltry. My mother, my children, and I saw you in the recent production of *The Mikado* at the church. I must say you made an excellent Katisha."

Well, glory be! I had no idea Mrs. Franbold had brought her daughter and grandchildren to see *The Mikado*. I think I was flattered. "Thank you. It was an...interesting experience, singing in an operetta."

"I'd have been scared to death," said Mrs. Daltry.

"I was, at first. I'd never sung solo before, but it was fun after a while," I told her.

"Yes, I heard there were some...problems unrelated to the production that had to be solved."

"Indeed." And that was putting it mildly. "But I wanted you to know how much I liked Mrs. Franbold, and I'm awfully sorry she was taken from you so suddenly." I figured that might give them the opportunity to tell me if she'd been sick.

No such luck.

"Thank you," said Mrs. Daltry, letting go of my hand and bringing a white hankie to her eyes. "It was a terrible shock. I don't think she ever suffered a sick day in her life. And then, poof! She was gone, just like that." After sniffling and wiping her eyes, she said, "Please let me introduce you to my sister, Katherine—Katherine Peterson—and my brother, Charles Franbold."

"How do you do?" said Charles, taking my hand briefly and shaking it.

Katherine shook my hand, too, but she seemed too upset to speak. Her nose was red and her eyes continued to leak. As soon as she released my hand, she wiped both nose and eyes with a damp hankie.

Very well, it seemed to me that if someone had indeed done in Mrs. Franbold on purpose, her children didn't appear to be, on the surface anyway, the likely culprits. I'd take my oath all three were genuinely grieved.

Stuffing his hands into his pockets against the cold, Charles said, "I guess it wasn't exactly unexpected, although she never showed any signs of illness or weakness. She was eighty-seven years old, after all." He gestured to his two sisters. "Heck, we're all in our fifties, and my daughter has a daughter of her own." He gestured to the seated bunch of young adults. I noticed a man standing behind the woman with the baby. He seemed to be staring at the little girl with doting eyes. I got all misty for a moment.

"Charles," said Katherine, at last finding her voice and jarring me back to attention. "There's no need to announce our ages. I'm sure Mrs. Majesty isn't interested."

Actually, I was, but I didn't say so. Instead, I said, "I guess she led long and full life. Still, it's a shock when someone suddenly...well, dies like that. And in church. It was quite distressing to the entire congregation."

"I can imagine," muttered Charles.

"And it happened during the communion service?" said Vivian, making the statement a question.

"Yes. I fear Miss Powell, who was assisting with communion that day, was quite unsettled by your mother falling over like that. Miss Powell dropped the tray she'd been holding, and communion grape juice went everywhere."

"Oh, dear, did they ever get the stains out? Grape juice leaves such an awful stain." Vivian again. A practical woman, she.

"My aunt suggested we try peroxide on the stains, and that seems to have done the trick fairly well. At choir practice last night, I checked the carpet. You could barely see a stain left."

"Hmph," said Charles. "I hope they tested the carpet."

Both of his sisters turned to stare at him. He frowned at them. "I don't care what you think. Mother might have been old, but she was in perfect health."

"Yes," said Vivian as if she'd heard it all before. "You believe Mother was poisoned. But who would do such a thing to her, of all people? She was a wonderful woman." After sniffling once more, she turned to me and said, "Can you think of a single soul who would want our mother dead, Mrs. Majesty?"

"No, I certainly can't. From what I knew of her, she was a kind and well-loved woman."

Katherine sobbed into her hankie, and Vivian blew her nose. Charles just stood there, looking gloomy.

"Well, I don't want to take your time. I only wanted to offer my condolences," I said and turned to go. Vivian stopped me with a hand on my shoulder. My shoulder, by the way, was draped in a black velveteen cloak, which was not merely fashionable, but which kept me almost toasty on that cold, windy day.

"Wait, Mrs. Majesty. Mother told us you are a well-respected spiritualist-medium. Is that correct?" asked Vivian.

"Er, yes, I am." I tried to look modest. "At least my clients seem to be happy with my services."

"Do you think you could perform a séance for us? To see if we can get in touch with Mother?"

"Vivian," Charles said sharply, "that's about the most ridiculous thing I've ever heard. A séance? Nonsense."

I didn't consider my business nonsense, although I didn't tell Charles so. Anyhow, if he was the one who thought someone had poisoned his mother, wouldn't he *want* to know who did it? Not that a séance would tell him because I can't really communicate with spirits, but *he* didn't know that, darn it!

Rather, I said in my most soothing voice, "It often takes a soul a while to get settled on the Other Side"—whatever that is—"so you might want to wait a few weeks before holding a séance for your mother."

"Oh." Vivian was clearly disappointed. "I didn't realize that. I don't scoff at spiritualism as Charles does. And if he's right, and someone did poison our mother, I'd certainly like to know who it was."

"Vivian," said Katherine, "I don't think here is the place to discuss this. Anyhow, it looks as if the minister is about to begin the service."

Glancing at the elaborate coffin sitting on planks over a hole in the ground, I saw Katherine was correct. In fact, Pastor Smith had taken to glancing at us, and at his watch, and at us, in a way that let us know he wanted to get the show on the road. So to speak. I walked over and took my place with the choir.

So, as the frigid wind blew, folks shivered, and whole lot of people, including Betsy Powell, wept copiously, Pastor Smith performed a grave-side service, and poor Mrs. Theodore (her first name was Vivian, which I guess accounted for her oldest child's name) Franbold was laid to rest at Morningside Cemetery in Altadena, California. The choir did an admirable job with "Abide With Me," considering our vocal chords were frozen and we were singing *a cappella*.

As folks dispersed after the rite, and in spite of the cold, I decided to visit my Billy's grave.

"Is that all right with you, Pa?" Pa had a bum ticker, and I didn't want him exerting himself too much. But as long as I was at the cemetery, I felt almost compelled to visit Billy's grave.

"Why don't you go back to the Hudson, Joe," Sam suggested. "You can be warmer in there, and you won't have to walk so far." He cleared his throat. "I'd kind of like to visit Margaret, too." Sam's late wife had been laid to rest not far from Billy.

"Fine with me. You two go on ahead. Don't rush. I'll be nice and warm, thanks to the hat and coat Daisy gave me at Christmas."

I smiled. I was darned proud of that hat and coat, which Pa had left in the Hudson, because it wasn't correct funeral attire, being made of a bright plaid fabric. But he was right in that both garments were warm as anything. That's because I'd lined them with a double layer of flannel. I'd considered using fur, but the notion of an animal giving its life to keep a Pasadenan warm didn't seem proper to me. It might be different if we lived in Siberia. Or even Massachusetts with the rest of our family. Heck, cold for us was maybe forty-five degrees, which was probably the temperature that day, except the wind made it feel colder.

"Sure you don't mind, Pa?" I asked for the heck of it. My father never minded what other people did as long as they weren't performing evil deeds.

"Sure," said he.

"Thanks, Joe," said Sam, taking my gloved hand in his gloved hand.

"Thanks, Sam," I said, thinking I didn't deserve this kindness after the scene I'd made at Christmas. Oh, well.

"I haven't been to Margaret's grave for too long," said he, making me feel not quite so unworthy.

"I visit Billy pretty much every week. It's too cold for flowers, but..." I allowed my voice to trail off. Generally when I visited Billy's grave, I talked to him, very softly. Not that I expected him to answer, but because talking to him made me feel somewhat better about whatever was worrying me.

Of course, what worried me that day, besides the possibility of a woman having been poisoned in our church, was the relationship between Sam and me. I'd like to tell Billy that I still wasn't sure if I should marry Sam. Naturally, I couldn't say those things if Sam stood at my side and listened.

Billy's grave lay under a spreading oak tree in a very pretty part of the cemetery. Morningside Cemetery is lovely anyway, considering what it's used for. That day the lawns weren't bright green, as they'd been the June day when we'd buried Billy, but were sort of yellowing, in keeping with the season. The oak tree's leaves, after turning red in autumn, had turned brown and remained mostly brown and on the tree. A few leaves had dropped, but mainly acorns littered the ground on Billy's grave. His headstone was beautiful. I'd thought long and hard about what I'd had inscribed thereon: "Sacred to the memory of William Anthony Majesty. Beloved husband of Daisy. July 12, 1897-June 10, 1922. Rest now as you could not in life. *The Good Die First.*"

When Sam and I had met by accident over Billy's grave a year or so prior, he'd asked me about that "The Good Die First" thing. Well, I'll tell you, as I told Sam then. It's from a Wordsworth poem, *The Excursion*, which is actually part of a longer work called *The Recluse*. The entire sentence is, "The good die first, and they whose hearts are dry as summer dust, burn to the socket." I'd made up the part about him resting now as he couldn't in life, because it was the truth. My parents didn't approve, but I didn't care. My husband; my husband's grave; my husband's gravestone; my money. So, pooh. Besides, it was the truth. He'd taken his life because he couldn't rest in peace in the body he'd been given at birth. The Germans had murdered him, actually. I believe I've mentioned that before. Sorry to repeat myself. You can tell it was an important fact of my life.

I heard Sam heave a huge sigh beside me as we stared at the headstone and the acorn-littered grave. I heaved a sigh of my own.

"Want me to brush off those acorns?" asked Sam.

I thought about it. "No, thanks. I think they're perfect there." I hesitated for a minute, afraid I'd cry, and then said, "Poor Billy."

Sam repeated, "Poor Billy."

After standing and staring at my husband's last resting place for what seemed like too long, the weather being what it was, Sam and I moseyed a few yards up a small incline and stared at his wife's grave. Sam hadn't been as creative as I when instructing the stonecutters to commemorate Margaret's headstone. He'd only given her name and the years of her birth and death. That was all right. Sam had loved her; she'd known it; and life goes on.

We walked back to the Hudson. I don't know about Sam, but I was depressed and nearly frozen solid.

FIVE

During the third and fourth weeks in January, my own personal business picked up. Mrs. Bissel asked me to conduct a séance at her home, Mrs. Pinkerton asked me to visit with both the Ouija board and my tarot deck, and Mrs. Wright called me in a dither and asked me to drive over and consult Rolly for her via the Ouija board. Mrs. Wright wasn't a ditherer as a rule, so this surprised me. However, I took Rolly and went.

But wait. I haven't told you about Rolly yet, have I? Sorry. Need to take a quick trip off-topic here.

You see, at the height of the spiritualism craze after the Great War and the horrible influenza pandemic that followed hard upon its heels, people all over the world were mourning their lost loved ones. They flocked to folks who, like me, claimed to be able to get in touch with their dead relations. In order to do this, spiritualists required spirit controls. The spirit control, you see, would get in touch with the dear departed and pass messages back and forth across the Great Divide between life and death.

Yes, I know it's all hogwash. But that's how I earned my living, and I was darned good at it. I did, however, often wish I'd given my spirit control a more dignified name than Rolly. For that matter, I wish I'd given myself a name other than Desdemona. Everyone believed Daisy to be derived from Desdemona, but it wasn't. When I was ten years old and conjured Rolly out of whole cloth for the amusement of my family, I didn't give a thought to dignity or my future livelihood. And I certainly didn't know in my tenth year that Desdemona was a world-renowned murderee, or I'd have chosen a different pretend-name.

It probably didn't matter much. Most of my clients believed Rolly— who was, according to my story, an eleventh-century soldier in Scotland— spelled his name R-a-l-e-i-g-h. And maybe folks thought Desdemona was a keen name for a spiritualist. All I knew at the time all this unfolded was that it was far too late for me to change either Rolly's name or my fake one.

Actually, I was in some ways proud of Rolly. Most fake spiritualists used made-up Egyptian royal names as those of their spirit controls. At least Rolly was unique. Besides, when it comes to the people on earth, living or dead, the ratio of royalty to plain old folks (including soldiers) is heavily weighted in favor of the commoners. I mean, how many dead royal Egyptians can there actually *be* floating around on the Other Side, anyway?

But back to the main topic. As I said, my business picked up after the first-of-the-year doldrums. My first spiritualist session of 1924 was with Mrs. Wright, who lived in a magnificent mansion not far from where the Pinkertons lived, on Orange Grove Boulevard. Back in those days, Orange Grove was nicknamed Millionaire's Row, and the Wrights and Pinkertons didn't let the nickname down.

The Wrights were a wildly wealthy family that had made its fortune producing and selling chewing gum. I know. But somebody has to invent stuff like chewing gum, I guess, and the Wrights did. And then proceeded to make vast amounts of money manufacturing and marketing it. Mrs. Wright was normally a calm, organized person, who had never dithered at me before.

However, the day she telephoned and asked me to visit her, she was in a state almost big enough to rival of one of Mrs. Pinkerton's, if not quite hysterical enough to warrant a capital S. Therefore, I was curious as I parked my family's Chevrolet in front of the Wrights' massive home. The housemaid who answered my ring at the door filled me in. I vaguely knew her from high school, although she was a little younger than I, and we hadn't run around in the same circles, if you know what I mean.

"Good morning, Violet," said I to the housemaid, dropping a little of my mystical aura so she wouldn't be intimidated.

The notion of anyone being intimidated by me darned near made me laugh. However, I'm better at my job than that. At that moment, I was clad in a hip-length green velvet coat with an unfitted bodice that fastened at the waist and shoulders with pearl buttons I'd bought at Nelson's Five and Dime. Under the coat, I wore a dark brown mid-calf dress that was simple but oh, so, dignified. Greens and browns were my favorite colors to wear, because of my hair.

Which made me think of that beautiful ring Sam had given me. It would have gone smashingly well with my costume that day. However, the ring was buried under the unmentionables in my underwear drawer. I did wear the juju Mrs. Jackson had made for me. Mrs. Jackson, mother of Mrs. Pinkerton's gatekeeper, was a real, live, New Orleans Voodoo mambo whom I'd met the year prior. She claimed the juju would bring me luck. At that point, I was still waiting.

Anyway, back to the Wrights' front door. Violet Donaldson, the housemaid in question, said, "Morning. Mrs. Wright's in the front parlor." She turned to lead the way. I wondered where the Wrights' butler was. The Wrights' butler, Evans, was nowhere near as superior a specimen of butlerhood as was Mrs. Pinkerton's Featherstone, but he played his role well.

"Where is Mr. Evans today?"

My question stopped Violet in her tracks, and she spun around, her face pale. "Don't ask me! I think that's the problem. Nobody knows where Evans is. Mrs. Wright has been having spasms all morning long."

"My goodness. I'm so sorry."

"Huh. You'd be a lot sorrier if you worked here." She brightened fractionally. "Say, maybe that's why she called you in. Maybe she wants you to use your magic to find Evans."

"I don't use magic," I said in as repressive a voice as I could muster.

But really! Evans was missing? How exciting! I hoped nothing horrid had happened to him.

"Well, whatever you use, try and find Evans, will you? He organizes everything and everyone's duties. The whole household is up in the air without him."

"I'm sorry. When did he go missing?"

"Last Friday. But I can't talk any more. Here's the front parlor."

I'd been in the Wrights' front parlor at least a dozen times before, so I knew where it was, but I thanked Violet anyway.

When I entered the room, it was to find Mrs. Wright in a deep discussion with, of all people, Mrs. Pinkerton! Oh, dear. What did this mean? Mrs. Pinkerton saw me first. She leaped up out of her chair—quite a feat for so large a woman—and rushed at me. I braced myself for the blow, but she surprised me and stopped before she hit me. That didn't happen often.

"Oh, Daisy, I do hope you can help poor Vera! Evans has *vanished*!" Vera, in case you wondered, was Mrs. Wrights' first name.

"My goodness," I said in my staid, spiritualistic voice.

"But do come on in, Mrs. Majesty," said Mrs. Wright, also standing. She didn't lunge at me, thank God. Mrs. Pinkerton was the only one who did that on a regular basis.

I wafted across the floor in my practiced, spiritualist's glide, and sat on a chair near the two from which the women had risen. They sat, too. "Now," I said in order to get things going and to preclude Mrs. Pinkerton taking charge of the conversation, "what's this about Evans?"

"He's gone," said Mrs. Wright. "Vanished." She lifted her arms in a helpless gesture.

"Into thin air," supplied Mrs. Pinkerton in a dramatic whisper.

Interesting. "Did he take his personal belongings with him?" I asked, trying to be practical. Heck, maybe the guy had become sick of butlering and lammed it out of Pasadena for greener pastures. If there were any pastures greener than those in Pasadena; I wasn't sure about that. Pasadena was a pretty place.

"No. That's what's so strange," said Mrs. Wright. "All of his personal belongings are still in his room. But he left on Friday to go to out for a bit, and nobody's seen him since then. I'm terribly worried about him."

"Hmm. Have you been in touch with the police department?"

"The *police?*" Mrs. Wright pronounced the word kind of like Mrs. Pinkerton did; as if the police were foreign and unpleasant beings that had no place in her vicinity, and the very word tasted nasty on her tongue. I suppressed my sigh.

"Oh, I don't think it's a police matter," said Mrs. Pinkerton.

"A man is missing, and you don't believe you should tell the police? It's been what? Today is Tuesday, so he's been missing for nearly four days. Don't you think you should call the police and tell them this? Perhaps something terrible has happened to Evans. Perhaps he dropped dead on the street or something. Perhaps he's lying now on a cold marble slab in the morgue." I didn't know if morgues had cold marble slabs, but it sounded good. The two women both gasped, so I guess I got my point across.

"Oh, dear!" said Mrs. Pinkerton, covering her mouth with her hand.

"Good gracious," said Mrs. Wright, doing likewise.

Rich folks. Gotta love them. "Does Evans have any family to whom you might drop a line? I don't believe you're doing Evans any favors by not taking his disappearance seriously."

"Oh, but I *am* taking his disappearance seriously," cried Mrs. Wright, this time slapping a hand to her bosom. "The household can't even *run* without Evans overseeing things! Everything is at sixes and sevens, and nobody knows what to *do*."

"I can't even imagine trying to get along without Featherstone," whispered Mrs. Pinkerton, who also thought Featherstone was a peach, although I'm sure her reasons for thinking so were different from mine. Featherstone even had an English accent. How much more perfect can a butler get?

"Well, then, does he have any family?"

Mrs. Wright and Mrs. Pinkerton exchanged glances, and Mrs. Wright looked at me. "I...don't know. I haven't gone through his things."

Oh, for Pete's sake. "Why not?" I really wanted to know. Heck, if Sam disappeared, I'd break down his cottage door—he lived in a little cottage in a court on South Los Robles Avenue—and rifle through everything I could pick up if it would help me locate him.

"It...I don't know. It seems so intrusive somehow."

Mrs. Pinkerton nodded vigorously. As for me, I was getting more than a little bit tired of the both of them.

"Mrs. Wright, it's entirely possible that Evans got hit by a car or something. Perhaps he's languishing in the Castleton Memorial Hospital with a severe case of amnesia. Perhaps he collapsed with a heart problem. You need to talk to everyone who knows him, and to the police, if you truly want to find him. And if he *does* have family somewhere, I'm sure they'd like to know he's missing. Or maybe he's with them. Unless you get in touch with *someone*, how are you going to find out where he is?"

The two women exchanged another glance or two, then Mrs. Pinkerton said, "I knew Daisy would know what you should do, Vera. She's so wise for a woman of her tender years."

Oh, boy. I was glad neither my mother nor Sam was there to hear that. They'd both have doubled over laughing. Anyhow, an idiot would know to call the family and/or the police when someone vanished. Common sense was a faculty most of my extremely wealthy clients didn't need to have, I reckon, because they had enough money to hire other people to think for them.

"I suppose you're right," said Mrs. Wright, doubt plain to hear in her voice. "Still...the police?"

"If you don't have information on how to get in touch with any of his family members, then yes, you should call the police," I said, and firmly too.

"I have it!" cried Mrs. Pinkerton, going so far as to clap her pudgy hands. "*Daisy* can do it! You know that policeman fellow, Detective Ro... Ro...Whatever his name is, don't you, dear? You can ask *him*!"

She'd known Sam for as long as I had, yet she claimed never to remember his name. And she'd even thrown a party for him not long back. Well, the party was for me, too, but honestly. "Detective Rotondo generally works on homicides, Mrs. Pinkerton. I don't know if he'd be the correct person upon whom to call about handling a missing-person case."

"But he could direct you!" Mrs. Pinkerton was sure proud of herself for thinking of Sam, even if she refused to learn his name.

Mrs. Wright seemed happier, too. "Oh, my, that would be so kind of you, Mrs. Majesty. Would you mind awfully?"

Darn it anyhow! What was it with these rich people refusing to do the least little thing for themselves or their servants? But I knew upon which side my own personal bread was buttered, so I smiled spiritualistically and said, "Of course. I'll be happy to talk to Detective Rotondo for you, Mrs. Wright."

She thanked me profusely, and then I got out the Ouija board. Rolly conveniently manifested himself through my fingers, and he spelled out (did I mention he was a poor speller? Well, he was, mainly because I was ten when I thought him up, and it was too late to change his illiterate status now) the same advice I'd given Mrs. Wright. Mrs. Pinkerton sat by, staring at the planchette moving across the board, her hands clasped, in awe of my mysterious ability.

After Rolly was through dispensing advice via the Ouija board, Mrs. Wright asked for a tarot-card reading, so I dealt out a five-card horseshoe pattern, and interpreted the cards precisely the way I'd had Rolly interpret his advice.

When I was finished with Mrs. Wright's reading, Mrs. Pinkerton said, "Oh, my, Vera, it looks as if Daisy was absolutely correct. You need to go through Evans' room and see if you can find any relations of his to get in touch with. And the police, of course, although Daisy has kindly offered to do that for you."

I hadn't either. I'd been coerced into telling Sam about the missing Evans. I didn't point out Mrs. P's mistake.

"Thank you so much, Mrs. Majesty," said Mrs. Wright. "Madeline is right about you." Madeline was Mrs. Pinkerton's first name. "You're wise beyond your years."

Oh, brother.

However, she gave me a big wad of money and, since Mrs. Pinkerton begged me to deal out a tarot pattern for her, too, I went home that day fairly floating in mazuma. All in all, I considered my morning a success. I guess the evening was, too, although Sam, who came to dinner again, didn't seem to care much that the Wrights' butler, Evans, had disappeared.

Eyeing me with disfavor, he said, "What does she want me to do about it?"

I shrugged. "Tell the people in charge of missing persons, I guess." I had, after several minutes of questioning Mrs. Wright, determined that Evans' first name was Daniel, so I gave Sam that information, too.

"She does realize that calling the police means she and her staff will be questioned, doesn't she?" Sam had dealt with rich people before, and his experiences with them hadn't been as enriching as had mine. That's because wealthy people just *hated* to have police cars in their yards and uniformed officers in their houses. Besides, they didn't hand him wads of money, as they did me.

"Probably not." I couldn't help myself; I smiled. The notion of uniformed police officers invading the Wrights' mansion and questioning the personnel and family therein tickled my funny bone.

"It won't be any fun," said Sam, who seemed to know what I was thinking even when I wished he didn't.

"Not for you, it won't," I said. "I'd like to be a fly on the wall when they do it, though."

My mother said, "Daisy."

But my father and Aunt Vi both laughed.

SIX

The rest of that week passed peacefully enough. Ma, Pa, Aunt Vi, and I had piled the library books we'd read on the table beside the front door, so on Thursday, since I had no appointments, I decided to visit the library after Pa and I walked Spike. We had a lovely neighborhood to walk in. Marengo Avenue itself was lined with pepper trees that fairly dripped leaves and peppercorns at certain times of the year. In February, their branches still sort of dripped, but they weren't shedding anything in particular. Spike loved his walks and left little liquid remembrances of himself wherever we went.

When I got to the library my favorite librarian, Miss Petrie, was back on duty, and she was as delighted to see me as I was to see her. After dumping my stack of already-read books on the returns table, I scurried over to her little booth. Or whatever you call those things where reference librarians hang out. I guess one could call it a cubicle, but that doesn't sound any better than a booth. Oh, never mind.

"Oh, Mrs. Majesty, I've saved so many books for you!" Miss Petrie said with a big smile. She was...well, kind of homely, actually, with big glasses and mouse-brown hair, which she knotted in a bun on top of her head. I think she could be quite good-looking if she went to some effort,

43

but I guess she didn't feel like it. I couldn't fault her for that. Most days I didn't want to fix myself up, but I did it anyway for the sake of my image.

"Thank you! I always love the books you save for us. And so does my family. I've missed you."

"Thank you. I spent a couple of weeks with my parents in Oklahoma." She frowned. Originally from the Tulsa area, she still had family there. While I'm sure her parents were fine people, she also had some family members whom she'd just as soon everybody forget about. After having been peripherally involved with a couple of them, I didn't blame her. "The good side of my family," she added because she and I both knew about the other side.

"How nice. I'm glad my parents live here in Pasadena and I don't have to travel to see them."

"Hmm," said she, frowning slightly. "If I had your family, I'd probably wish they lived closer to me, too. But never mind families. Look at these." She bent down—she was sitting on a high stool—and hauled out a pile of books I was surprised she could lift, what with her being sort of skinny and all. She plopped them on the desk and smiled proudly.

"Oh, my goodness! Look at all of those!" I whispered, but I was delighted and whispering was a strain.

"There are several westerns for your father," said Miss Petrie. "And then I'm not sure you'll enjoy this one, but figured you might give it a try. It's *Sleeping Fire*, by Gertrude Atherton."

"Ah," said I, thinking nerts on that one. Not that I didn't appreciate Miss Atherton's creativity and so forth, but her earlier books hadn't been to my taste which, I guess, is low, because I prefer Mr. P.G. Wodehouse and other funny stuff like his.

She laughed softly. "You never know. You might like this one better than her last couple. But look here! Two new books by Mr. P.G. Wodehouse."

And, lo and behold, there appeared before my eyes *The Inimitable Jeeves* and *Leave it to Psmith*. "Oh, *thank* you!"

"And here's another one for you. It's a children's book, but it's truly darling. It's called *The Voyages of Dr. Doolittle*, by a fellow named Mr.

Hugh Lofting. Dr. Doolittle is a most interesting character, and he meets up with some fascinating creatures."

What the heck. "Thank you. I'll give it a read."

"I think you'll like it. And here are a couple of Edgar Wallace novels. We just got in his last Lieutenant Bones book, *Bones in London*, and I do believe we're going to be getting *Bones of the River* soon. It takes so long for books to travel from Great Britain to us, you know."

"Yes. I know. And there are so many good British authors, too." I decided there was no real need for the note of sadness in my voice. After all, some Americans wrote good books, too. As if to prove it, Miss Petrie lifted *One of Ours*, by Willa Cather. "Here. You might enjoy this one."

"Thanks." Truth to tell, and I know Willa Cather is an American icon these days, but I'd found her books a trifle flat. But please don't tell anyone that. My favorite American author was Mrs. Mary Roberts Rinehart—or she had been before she began writing books about the war.

"And I *know* you'll like this." And she lifted a book called *The Secret Adversary*, by Mrs. Agatha Christie.

"Oh!" I cried, perhaps a trifle too loudly, because Miss Petrie glanced around the library. More quietly, I said, "Is this another one with that little Belgian fellow in it? I loved *Murder on the Links* and *The Mysterious Affair at Styles*."

"Monsieur Poirot? No. This is one features a married couple, Tommy and Tuppence Beresford. They're spies. Of a sort."

"Oh. Well, I'll give it a try." I wasn't much excited by spy stories, but I expected Mrs. Christie would have given her characters and plot a nice twist or two.

"Here's another one I think you'll enjoy. It's *The Film Mystery*, by Mr. Arthur B. Reeves. It's not a new book, but we just got this copy in. I know you enjoyed his Professor Craig Kennedy books."

"Yes, I did. Thank you!"

"And here are two newish Edgar Rice Burroughs books for your father," said Miss Petrie in her normal librarian's voice. "I know he likes Mr. Burroughs." She set out *Tarzan the Terrible* and *Tarzan and the Golden Lion*.

"He might have read this one," I said, holding up *Tarzan the Terrible*, "but Pa probably won't mind rereading it. I love rereading books." A case in point was Mary Roberts Rinehart's *The Circular Staircase*, which I must have read a dozen times by that particular day.

"Speaking of that," said Miss Petrie as if she'd been reading my thoughts, "at last Mrs. Rinehart has left the war behind."

And she set *The Breaking Point* on the desk before me. I gasped and clasped my hands to my bosom. "Oh, I'm so glad! *The Amazing Interlude* about did me in. I'm so glad she's through with war stories." I had too many of my own that yet haunted me. I didn't need to read about anyone else's. "Thank you so much, Miss Petrie! These will keep my family and me happy for days and days."

"I've saved the best for last," said Miss Petrie, a gleam in her eye. Again, she reached under her stool where, I presume, a shelf had been built into the booth. She revealed her next selection with quite a bit of élan, for her.

"Oh, *thank* you!" I felt like gasping and clasping my hands to my bosom again, but restrained myself. There, before me in Miss Petrie's smallish hands, was *The Great Roxhythe*, by Miss Georgette Heyer, another British lady writer. I hadn't read many of her books, mainly because she hadn't written many, but I'd adored every one I'd read.

"You'll love it. It's really...wonderful." Miss Petrie sort of breathed the last word on a soft sigh.

I understood. Miss Heyer wrote the best, most thrilling, and most romantic books I'd read to date.

Whatever would the world be without books in it? I didn't even want to consider the possibility.

"Well, drop by any time," she said, in a wistful sort of voice. "Just to chat, if you feel like it."

I'd gathered for some time by then that Miss Petrie led a rather lonely life. But I loved chatting with her, so I'd be in again soon. I silently promised her that. Then I figured, what the heck, and promised her aloud, "I will." Then I scooped up my treasure trove of books and staggered to the check-out desk with them. Oh, happy day!

That afternoon, after I'd dusted and dust-mopped the house, carpet-swept the carpet, and set the table for dinner, I lounged on the sofa in the living room with Spike curled up on my lap and read. Miss Petrie was absolutely correct. *The Voyages of Dr. Doolittle* was charming. So, after reading that one, I sank more deeply into the sofa cushions and buried my nose and imagination in *The Great Roxhythe*. Oh, my. There I was, in Restoration England, in the very court of King Charles II. I was almost sorry when Vi came home, fixed dinner, and I had to put the meal on the table.

Not that dinner wasn't as delicious as ever, what with Vi teasing our palates with spaghetti and meatballs, a great big green salad, and some garlic bread she'd made with sourdough French bread (which she'd also made). Yum.

"This is so good," I managed to say between bites.

"The sauce is Sam's recipe," Vi told us.

"Speaking of Sam, where is he tonight?" asked Pa.

Everyone at the table looked at me. A trifle annoyed, I said, "I don't know. I didn't see him today. Anyhow, I'm not his keeper." I was engaged to marry him, but they didn't know that, darn it.

"Daisy," said Ma in a mildly reproving tone of voice. "I know the two of you sometimes have little tiffs—"

I sat up straight in my chair, dropped my fork and interrupted my mother, something I seldom do. "Little *tiffs*? The big galoot drives me *crazy!*"

"Piffle," said Ma. "I know the two of you are...Well, let's say you're friends." She gave the word a deeper meaning and I understood perfectly. Crumb.

"Huh," I said, reminding myself of Sam. Oh, well. I saw my dinner companions exchange a series of glances and knowing looks and figured I was doomed. So I just kept eating.

Along about the end of dinner—we all had seconds. Actually, I think I had thirds—a knock came at the door, and Spike went into his usual "a friend has come to call" frenzy, wagging his tail like crazy and barking fit to beat the band. Because Spike was so happy, I assumed the caller to be

Sam, and I was proved correct when I opened the front door and saw him there, looming and glowering.

"C'mon in," I told him, ignoring his ominous mood.

"Thanks."

"Want some dinner? There's plenty left, and it's delicious." We were generally through with dinner and cleaning up by the time Sam's knock came at the door. But as I said, we'd had seconds. And thirds.

He removed his hat, coat and scarf, hung them on the coat rack next to the front door, and said, "I didn't mean to come during dinnertime. I figured you'd be finished by this time." His stomach growled and he slapped a hand over it. If he'd been anyone else, he'd have been embarrassed.

"Dinner was especially good tonight," I said, ignoring his growling tummy. Poor guy. A bachelor had a rough time of it, I reckon. "Your recipe for spaghetti sauce."

He sniffed the air. Since the mouth-watering aroma of Italian sauce had permeated the air hours ago, he didn't require a large sniff. "Ah. Smells great."

"Come and have some."

"I didn't come here to eat," he said, sounding grumpy, which wasn't unusual.

"Pooh. You're hungry. We have food. Tons and tons of food. So come eat. You can tell us why you visited us as you dine."

"You sure?" He peered down at me as if he were truly concerned that we'd think he was taking advantage of our good natures.

"Of course! Come on, you big lug." And I dragged him to the table, where everyone greeted him with cheer and helpfulness. Ma had already set another place for him. Beside me. Any time I set the table when I knew Sam was to join us for a meal, I sat him across from me. My mother, the matchmaker. Bless her heart. I think I mean that in the southern sense. Or maybe not.

"So glad you joined us, Sam!" said Pa. "I wondered where you were, but Daisy said she didn't know."

Ma sniffed meaningfully.

"This is your recipe, Sam, so you really *should* eat it with us," said Vi, dishing out a lavish portion of spaghetti and meatballs for the family detective. I handed him the bread basket after he'd taken his plate, and Ma set a bowl full of green salad before him.

"Thank you very much. I honestly didn't mean to interrupt. I figured you'd be through with dinner by this time."

"Yes, yes. We know," I said. "We're kind of late this evening. But why are you here, if it's not to eat?"

"Daisy," said Ma. She would.

After swallowing his first bite of spaghetti, complete with half a meatball, Sam closed his eyes in rapture for a second, and said, "No, but I'm here about Evans."

"Who's Evans?" asked Pa.

"Who's Evans?" asked Ma.

"Did you find him?" asked Vi.

"Oh, Sam, how wonderful! Tell us all about how the Wrights reacted to a police presence in their grand home!" said I.

Sam scowled at me. But honestly, can you blame me?

"They weren't pleased."

"I can imagine." I couldn't help grinning.

"Who's Evans?" asked Ma again.

"Oh, is he the butler who disappeared?" said Pa.

"That's the one, all right," I told him, all but rubbing my hands with glee. "So, tell us, Sam. What happened to Evans? And what did the Wrights and their servants tell you?"

"We don't know, and not much," said Sam, taking a bite of garlicky sourdough bread.

I could tell he considered this a meal made, if not in heaven, at least as close as we mortals could get to it. I expect he missed the food of his childhood. Well, heck, I knew he did, because he'd told me all about the foodstuffs available in New York City. I still hadn't asked Vi if she knew any recipes for pumpernickel bread. As for falafel, curried goat, tandoori chicken, pizza pie, and the other delights Sam had told me about time out of mind, I'm sure I'd have to go to New York City to get any of those things. Maybe if we ever got married, we could honeymoon in New York. I'd wait to ask him, since I didn't want to start anything, if you know what I mean.

"So what happened?" I asked after I'd waited until he'd had another bite of spaghetti. He twirled his spaghetti with his fork sort of balanced on his spoon. I guess that's the proper Italian way of eating spaghetti, but I never tried to do it that way. In fact—Sam considers this akin to blasphemy—I often cut my stringy spaghetti noodles into smaller bites and scooped 'em up. Oh, well.

"The Wrights were aghast to see uniformed policemen at their door," said Sam, taking a sip of tea. His family probably drank red wine with their spaghetti, but that was in New York City. I got the feeling people didn't pay a whole lot of attention to Prohibition laws in New York City.

"I can imagine," I said, wishing I'd been there to see it.

"But nobody claims to know anything. Nobody claims to have seen Evans since Friday afternoon sometime. We searched his rooms. His clothes and other possessions were still there. We presume he took his wallet with him, and there's one suit of clothing missing."

"Which he was probably wearing," I said, bemused. What the heck had happened to Evans?

"Precisely." Sam stopped talking and ate some more. My parents and Vi and I all exchanged puzzled glances.

"What kind of shoes was he wearing? Do you know?"

"Nope. Nobody knows how many pairs of shoes or what kinds of shoes the man has."

"Did you ever meet Evans, Vi?" I asked.

"Nope. I don't meet the staff at other wealthy people's houses as a rule."

"I suppose not." I turned to Sam. "Did you check the hospitals and morgue and stuff like that?"

"Daisy," said my mother, but not forcefully. She wanted to know where Evans was, too.

"Yes, we did. No Evans."

"Hmmm. I wonder what in the world happened to him."

"We all do," said Sam.

My family and I quit pestering him after that and let him alone to finish his dinner, but Ma and I discussed Evans as we cleaned up the dishes. We came to no conclusions about what could have caused the man to fall off the edge of the world. How odd that he just left the house one day and vanished.

Sam and Pa played gin rummy in the living room.

SEVEN

Friday and Saturday passed peacefully enough. I had to visit Mrs. Wright again on Friday and soothe her with a tarot reading, since she'd been so upset about the police visiting her home. The weather remained chilly, so I wore my three-quarter length brown tunic dress with bishop sleeves gathered into black cuffs. The wide hip-level buckle belt was black, too. I'd stolen the buckle from an old dress of Ma's that she'd dumped into the rag bag for me to weave into a rug when I got around to it. I wore black beads over the dress and my Voodoo juju under it. Because I felt like it and it made me feel kind of glamorous, I also took along my black velvet cape.

Anyhow, the tarot told Mrs. Wright that everything was going to be all right. When she asked if anyone would ever find Evans, I told her that particular aspect of the future was unclear.

Did I know my job, or what?

"Oh, dear. Well, I hate to do it, but I suppose I'll have to call the agency."

"The agency?" I asked as I packed the tools of my trade into their nice cloth containers.

"The employment agency. We'll have to hire another butler."

Don't ask me why, but I was shocked. "Before you know what happened to Evans? What will you do with his things?" Boy, if servants were this disposable to rich folks, I'm glad I wasn't rich.

I don't mean that. But if I were rich, I wouldn't consider my employees the same as pieces of furniture. At least Mrs. Pinkerton had paid for Jackson's hospital care when he got shot by the KKK. That's the kind of rich person I'd be. Except I wouldn't be a nitwit. Oh, don't pay any attention to me.

"I have to have someone run the household. Things are in chaos without anyone at the helm. Evans is *such* a wonderful organizer. But I'll need to hire someone temporarily until he can be found." She shook her head. "I can't believe he'd just...leave like that, with no word or anything."

"And without his belongings," I reminded her.

She heaved a sigh. "Yes. I'm terribly worried about him."

That admission made me feel better.

So after I left the Wrights' mansion, I went to the Salvation Army to have a chat with Flossie Buckingham, a former gangster's moll. She married my school friend Johnny Buckingham, who went from being a dipsomaniacal wreck after the war to being a Salvation Army Captain. Flossie and Johnny made a perfect pair. What's more, they've both always credited me for introducing them. Which I guess I did, but I'd been trying to get rid of Flossie at the time. Not a flattering admission, but true. And it all worked out, so I suppose I could stop feeling guilty.

Naw. I feel guilty about everything.

However, Flossie greeted me with true joy and her son Billy, named after my own darling Billy, in her arms.

"Oh, Daisy, I'm so glad you could visit!"

"Ho, Day," said Billy, who was only about a year old. I thought his saying hello to me was both precious and precocious.

"Good day, Billy. So happy to see you happy."

Billy hid his head on his mommy's shoulder, and Flossie and I both laughed.

"Come in!" she said. "I want to show you what I'm sewing."

"Wonderful!" I'd taught Flossie how to sew, and Johnny had found a used sewing machine for her. It had a foot pedal, unlike my own (well, my mother's, but I used it) side-pedal White, upon which I made clothes for the entire family, including Spike, which he didn't appreciate.

So we walked through her little house to a back room that was probably a spare bedroom or something—Johnny didn't earn much as a Salvation Army guy, but he and Flossie didn't seem to mind—and which Flossie had turned into a sewing room.

"Look at these," she said proudly, pointing to a big pile of children's shirt-and-trousers sets.

"Good heavens, are all those for Billy?" My mind boggled as my eyes goggled.

With a laugh, Flossie said, "Oh, no. Not all of them. We have so many families in need these days. I make children's clothing for the Salvation Army, and people can buy them cheaply. Or we give them away."

"You're a saint, Flossie," I said, meaning it.

"Nonsense. It's Johnny who's the saint."

"You're both saints," I told her firmly.

She only laughed again.

"But Flossie, I have to tell you about Evans."

"Who's Evans?"

Sensible question. "He's the Wrights' butler, and he's gone missing. I guess it's possible that he went on a drunken spree, or something else might have happened to him. I thought if you knew about him, you could be on the lookout for him. He might come here for food or to dry out or something."

"Goodness. I'm sorry to hear about the man's missing status. Anything might have happened to him. Do you have a description of him? I can tell Johnny to watch for him."

Casting my mind back, I sought in its nether reaches to remember what Evans looked like. Should have done it before, but oh well. "Let me see. He's about five feet seven or eight inches tall. Not as tall as Johnny. He's kind of gaunt, but he looks healthy. Um...brown hair beginning to gray around the edges. Dignified. Well, he's dignified when he's on duty. I don't know what he's like the rest of the time. I've only seen him in his butler suit, so I don't know what he wears when he's on his own time."

Flossie and I exchanged a couple of looks, and I sighed. "I know. That could describe just about every other man in Pasadena, couldn't it?"

"Pretty much." Flossie smiled sweetly. "Do you recall any distinguishing moles or scars or anything like that?"

"No. He has good posture, I think. Or maybe he stoops a little. No, you'd better not add that part, because I'm not sure. Bother. Wish I'd paid more attention to him when I had the chance."

"You can't be expected to retain precise descriptions of everyone you meet in your life, Daisy," said Flossie, her gentle kindness making me feel good. "I'll give Johnny this description, and we can see what we can see."

"Oh," I said, suddenly struck by a memory. "He has a really healthy-looking complexion. As if he hikes or something. You know: tanned face, pink cheeks. Stuff like that."

"Hmm. He doesn't sound like a dipsomaniac from that description."

"You're right. He's probably not. In a way, that's more worrying than if he were. I mean, if he was on a rip-snorting drunk, Johnny might know where to look for him."

As soon as I said those words, I wished them unsaid, but Flossie burst out laughing, so I guess she didn't mind.

Billy reached out and grabbed hold of my velvet cape. He rubbed his pink cheek against it, and my heart melted. "Does that feel good, Billy?"

The kid nodded. I felt tears in my eyes and ruthlessly suppressed them. My Billy and I had wanted three children. That was before he came back from the war wrecked and unable to father children. I wondered if Sam...

But I didn't want to think about having children with Sam. Or anything else with Sam.

"Thanks, Flossie." My voice was a little froggy, so I cleared my throat and slapped my chest as if I felt a cough coming on. I managed to frighten little Billy into hiding his head against his mother's shoulder once more, and I sighed. "Sorry."

"Nonsense," said Flossie, as if she understood everything. She probably did.

I took off my cape and put it over Billy. He was startled at first, but then burrowed into it, kind of like Spike burrowed into the covers on my bed at night. Flossie and I both smiled, rescuing a maudlin moment from my stupid sentimentality.

"You know what would really help would be a photograph of Mr. Evans."

"Oh, of course." How silly of me not to have asked for a photograph of Evans. Not that Mrs. Wright decorated her home with photos of her servants. Still, one might have existed and been a useful tool if I'd had brains enough to ask for one. Oh, well. Sam had probably confiscated any existing photos of the butler.

"I don't have a photo. I should have asked for one. Every time I've seen him, he's been dressed impeccably and he stood regally erect. Good posture. Of course, I've only seen him when he's working. As I said, I don't know how he dresses on his afternoons off."

"Do you have any idea how old he is?"

"Oh, dear. I'm not good at guessing ages, but he does have graying hair. Maybe in his sixties? Fifties? My father is fifty, and his hair still is still brown, but both my mother and Aunt Vi are going gray. Evans' hair isn't all gray, though. It's mostly brown."

"Sounds like a distinguished gent," said Flossie.

"He looks like one," I said.

After we chatted for about forty-five minutes, I left for home. I walked in to find the house empty and the telephone ringing. I listened carefully. Our ring. With a sigh, I didn't even bother throwing my cape on the coat rack, but went straight into the kitchen and picked up the receiver. "Gumm-Majesty residence—"

"You needn't give the whole spiel," said Harold Kincaid. "I called to ask you to lunch at the Castleton. Emmaline Castleton and Del will come, too."

I glanced at the clock on the wall. Its hands pointed to twelve-fifteen. A timely call, indeed. "Thanks, Harold! That sounds like a nice respite on a gloomy day."

"What's gloomy about it?" asked Harold, avid for gossip.

"Well, the day itself is cold but clear, but I just came from the Wrights' home, and—"

"Oh. Evans," said Harold. "Old news. Mother babbled about Evans all last night during dinner. Your aunt outdid herself yesterday, Daisy, by the way."

"What did she feed you?" I asked, wondering if she'd fed the Pinkertons and Harold the same thing she'd fed us.

"Spaghetti and meatballs. Never eaten anything so delicious in my life. Not even in New York City, where all the best food is."

I smiled at the 'phone. "That's Sam's recipe. For the sauce, I mean," I told Harold proudly. Don't ask me why I was proud, but I was.

"You're joking!"

"Am not."

"Well, how about that. I don't suppose if I ask him politely, he'll give me the recipe?" Harold knew Sam didn't care for him and why.

So I might as well tell you about Harold Kincaid and Delray Farrington now. They were lovers. I know, I know. Some people consider people like Harold and Del to be evil somehow. After talking to Harold extensively—he was one of my best friends, after all—I've come to the conclusion that people are born either to be attracted to the opposite sex or to their own. It certainly isn't a choice. Why would anyone choose to be hated and/or jailed by people who only judged them by their one little idiosyncrasy. If that's what it is. I don't know. All I know is that neither Harold nor Del could help being what they are. Don't even try to argue with me about this, because I remain adamant in my position.

So there you go.

"You probably don't have to go so far as to ask Sam," I told Harold. "Just ask Vi the next time you see her. Or, heck, I can ask her and give the recipe to you."

"Spaghetti Rotondo. I think I'll open a restaurant and feature it as a specialty dish."

"Don't even think about it," I told him. "If Sam didn't kill you for it, I would." Then I laughed.

"Oh, very well. But let me pick you up in about thirty minutes, and we'll tootle off to the Castleton."

"Sounds great to me. Thanks, Harold."

"Any time."

I only wished.

All right, so now I'll tell you about Miss Emmaline Castleton. She was the daughter of Mr. Henry Castleton, railroad magnate and robber baron, who retired and spent some of his ill-gotten gains on a perfectly fabulous home in San Marino, only a mile or two south of Pasadena. The grounds are vast, there's a sculpture garden, a Japanese garden, and all sorts of other gardens. Miss Castleton had been engaged to marry a young man named Stephen Allison, who was killed in the war. We had a lot in common, Emmaline Castleton and me, even if we did come from vastly separate stratospheres on the economic scale.

Mr. Castleton also was a founder of the Castleton Memorial Hospital and the magnificent Castleton Hotel on South Oak Knoll Avenue in Pasadena. The man was made of money, in other words.

Pa and Spike, who'd gone out for a walk together as I'd been tarot-ing with Mrs. Wright and talking to Flossie, came home before I had to leave. I was as delighted to see Spike as he was to see me. I love dogs in general, but Spike was special. I love Pa, too, in case you wondered.

Harold was right on time. Because I didn't want Spike to feel slighted, I slithered out the front door while he was occupied in drinking from his water bowl in the kitchen, and walked out to Harold's Stutz Bearcat. Loved that car, and luckily, probably because of the weather, he had the top up. Good thing, or we'd have been blown to bits.

Harold hopped out of the machine and rushed to open my door for me. He bowed as deeply as any butler. "Enter, your Majesty."

"Cut it out with the Majesty jokes, Harold." But I giggled.

Grinning like an imp, he shut my door and hurried to his side of the car. When he got inside, he said, "But you have such a perfect name. It goes so well with your line of work, too. Desdemona Majesty. What could be more perfect?"

"I dunno. Being born to money?" If Harold could throw applesauce at me, I could throw some back at him, by golly.

"Maybe. Hasn't helped my idiot sister any."

"Bet it has. If she'd been poor from birth, she'd have been locked up years ago, and nobody would have bothered bailing her out."

After considering this unflattering comment for a second or two, he said, "You're right. Having money's better than not having it."

"As if you'd know," said I.

"Ah, but I mingle with peasants like you, and you keep my feet on the ground."

"Pooh. Harold, you're pip. You know that, don't you?"

"Absolutely."

And with a smile as big and wide as his tummy, Harold drove us to the Castleton. I reasoned from this that Del and Emmaline were expected to arrive at Emmaline's father's hotel on their own.

I was right. Del stood outside in the cold, his topcoat and hat keeping him warm, looking like the southern gentleman he was. I didn't see Emmaline until we entered the grand hotel. By the way, Harold drove up to the entrance and a liveried fellow ran up to him, bowed, and opened my door while another liveried lackey opened Harold's door and then got into the machine. Harold took my arm, we greeted Del, and we waltzed into the hotel without giving the Bearcat another glance. From this I deduced that the liveried fellows would park Harold's Bearcat for him and, when we left the hotel, would fetch it for him.

Whether Harold wanted to admit it or not, money talked. Loudly.

Very well, so I'd also visited Emmaline Castleton at her home, which was lavish. I'd been to her father's Castleton Memorial Hospital several times, but I'd never been to the Castleton Hotel before in the company of a Castleton. You'd have thought we were visiting royalty. That is to say, you'd have thought we were royalty visiting the hotel. Oh, you know what I mean.

A fellow in a black suit who looked vaguely like an undertaker, hurried to us as soon as our feet hit the red carpeting inside the building. "Miss Castleton's guests?" he inquired in a snooty voice.

"Yes, indeed," said Harold, who didn't let his money give him airs. He let his money give his servitors airs.

Am I being cynical? I suppose so. I apologize.

Anyhow, we were divested of our outer garments, asked if any of us would like to visit the "guest facilities," which, I assume, were the bathrooms, and when we all declined the invitation, he led us to the main dining room, which was a supremely fancy place, through that room, and to a private dining room, where he opened the door and bowed. Harold and Del let me enter first, as was only proper.

Emmaline had been seated at the beautifully set table, complete with a gorgeous flower arrangement in its middle, with her elbow on the table and her palm supporting her chin when we entered. As soon as the door opened, she got to her feet and headed to me with both her hands out.

"Daisy, it's so good to see you again," said she, beaming at me.

That was nice. "It's good to see you again, too, Emmaline." I beamed back at her. What the heck.

Harold rubbed his hands together. "What's on the menu today?" he said.

Del bumped him with a shoulder in a funning gesture one wouldn't necessarily expect from the extremely sober and proper Delray Farrington, who hailed from a fabulously wealthy family from New Orleans.

Which is kind of funny, because Mrs. Pinkerton's gatekeeper, Jackson, is also from New Orleans, only his family is black, so they probably were either owned by or waited on the Farringtons back in the day.

Oh, pooh. Forget I said that. Life isn't fair, never has been, and never will be, so it's almost not worth making note of the fact.

"But Daisy, I wanted to ask you about Mrs. Franbold," said Emmaline, taking my arm and leading Harold, Del and me to the table. "Was she really poisoned? At a *communion* service?"

To say I was surprised by this introduction to the luncheon table's conversation would be a major understatement.

EIGHT

Before I could say anything, which was a good thing since words seemed to have fled from my brain, Emmaline gave some instructions to the dignified man in black, who bowed to her and left the room. By the time the door shut behind him, my words had returned. All I had to do then was put them in some kind of coherent order.

"You *knew* Mrs. Franbold?" I asked, surprised. I didn't know Mrs. Franbold had toddled around in such exalted company.

Emmaline cocked her head in seeming surprise. "Her granddaughter, Vivian Daltry's daughter Glenda, is a good friend of mine. She's engaged to marry Barrett Underhill. Vivian's husband, Ralph, is one of Grover Underhill's partners in their fertilizer company."

My face must have shown my opinion of Grover Underhill, because Emmaline laughed. "Yes, I know. Mr. Underhill is a horrible person, but Glenda and Barrett are very nice, and poor Glenda was most cut up about her grandmother's death."

"Yes, we all were. I mean the congregation of the First United Methodist-Episcopal Church were. Was. Whatever the correct tense is. Mrs. Franbold was a sweet woman." Then, because I couldn't stop myself, I blurted out, "Do you know that when Mrs. Franbold fell over at church, rather than try to catch her, Mr. Underhill actually jumped out of the way? He bumped into a bunch of other people, too. In fact," I said because I'd just then thought of it, "I wouldn't be surprised if he's the one who knocked Betsy Powell's tray over and made her spill communion grape juice all over the church carpeting."

"Communion grape juice?" Del asked, as if he couldn't help himself either.

"Yeah. We Methodists don't drink wine. And don't ask me why, because I don't know. Probably because alcohol used to cause so many problems when the Wesley brothers were around."

"It still does," said Harold, with a wry grin. "In fact, now that we're in the midst of Prohibition, alcohol is causing more problems than ever."

"Yes," I said. "Those bootleggers are killing each other—and lots of other people, too—right and left." Something occurred to me then and I asked Del, "Say, Del, do you Roman Catholics still use wine in your communion services?"

"Yes. It's communion wine."

"They got a special dispensation from the Pope," said Harold, his voice snide.

"I doubt the Pope has much political sway here in the good old US of A," I said.

"You're right," said Emmaline. "But I think the Episcopalians use wine, too. I'm sure they've been granted special permission or something."

"True," said Harold. "Mother goes to that Episcopal Church on Euclid. I think the pastor is Father Learned, but Father Frederick is Mother's preferred priest. In fact, I thought she might marry him after she dumped my father, but she chose Algie. Which is probably the better choice, because I can't see Mother as a minister's wife."

I couldn't either. In fact, my mind boggled even as I tried to picture Mrs. Pinkerton as benefactress to a bunch of Episcopalians. Or anyone else, for that matter. Because I couldn't think of anything cogent to say, I muttered, "I like Father Frederick." Truth. He was a great guy, and, as nearly as I could tell, kindhearted and non-judgmental, although I'd never been to services at All Saints, which was the church Harold meant. In pursuit of information, I did go there one day and tried to speak to Father Learned, but he was stone deaf and I didn't get very far.

"But forget the Episcopalians," said Emmaline impatiently. "What else happened that day, and do you know if Mrs. Franbold was actually poisoned? It must have been dreadful."

"It was." I gave a little shudder as I remembered the chaos of that morning. "Did you go to the funeral? I didn't see you there." Not that I meant to be judgmental myself. I only wondered.

"No. I wasn't able to attend, although I spoke to Glenda before and after the service. I guess all of Mrs. Franbold's children were upset. As were her grandchildren."

"Yes, they were. I met Mrs. Franbold's children, but I'm afraid I didn't get to meet Glenda, and I didn't see the Underhills there, either."

Emmaline sighed dolefully. "I've been having a horrid time with my chest," said she, patting same gently. "The doctor said I had tuberculosis on one lung, so I had to go into hibernation for nearly a year. It was awful."

"Tuberculosis? Oh, my goodness. I'm so very sorry!" The only people I knew of who'd ever had tuberculosis were dead. Sam's late wife sprang instantly to my mind.

With a cynical smile of her own, Emmaline said, "Yes, it's been awful. But thanks to my father's money, I got the very best treatment. In fact, I do believe I had to go into isolation shortly after your husband's funeral. I actually left your house and went directly home and to bed." She sighed. "What a bleak, unhappy day that was."

It sure came flooding back to me just then. In fact, it flooded back so fast and so furiously that I lost my appetite. Dang. And I'd been so looking forward to that special luncheon.

Harold must have noticed my change in demeanor because he slapped me on the back so hard, all my sorrows flew out of my mouth in a big "Whuff!" I turned on him. "Harold Kincaid, what was that for?"

"You got the dismals. I saw you. So I drove 'em out."

"Oh, dear. I'm sorry I brought it up, Daisy. What a stupid thing for me to talk about."

But Harold's whack had cured me. "No, it's all right. Yes, it was a miserable time in my life, but life goes on whether you want it to or not. And with Harold around, I don't dare sulk or anything."

"Better not," said Harold.

"You might try to be a little gentler next time," said Del, frowning at his beloved.

"Being gentle with Daisy doesn't work."

"Harold Kincaid! What a mean thing to say!" Then Emmaline Castleton laughed. It wasn't a genteel laugh, but a big, happy, contagious laugh, and we all joined in.

After we'd quieted down, Emmaline bade us seat ourselves, and asked again, "So do you think Mrs. Franbold was murdered? Glenda is worried that she was poisoned. Evidently her uncle, Charles Franbold, believes she was. Glenda is afraid someone will think Barrett did it."

"Why would anyone think that?" I asked, interested. I still didn't have an answer for her on the poison issue, because nobody'd bothered to tell me. Darn Sam Rotondo. "And why would anyone want to kill Mrs. Franbold? I thought everyone loved her."

"So did I, but Glenda is frightened to death." Emmaline sat there with her lips pursed for a second before she said, "She's worried that someone wanted to kill Mr. Underhill but got Mrs. Franbold by mistake."

"My goodness. Why would anyone want to kill Mr. Underhill?" I asked, puzzled.

"Because Mr. Underhill is such a beast to work for. In fact, he's just a beast. Treats everyone with contempt."

"Even you?" I asked, incredulous.

"Well, no, but that's only because my father has more money than he does." Emmaline produced an admirable sneer.

"How very odd," I said. "I mean, that's kind of twisted logic, isn't it? That someone would have wanted to murder Mr. Underhill during communion and got Mrs. Franbold instead. Isn't that kind of...well, not very likely?"

With a shrug, Emmaline said, "There's no accounting for people's thoughts, I reckon. And I honestly *can* feature why almost anyone would want to kill Mr. Underhill. He's just awful."

"Except to you," said I.

"Except to me," said she. "Because of my father and his buckets of moolah."

Miss Emmaline Castleton knew all about how money could buy things, like respect from the disgusting Mr. Grover Underhill. Her father's money had even bought entry into the United States for two young German folks. This, in spite of the scene I made at her home when she asked me to help the German soldier who'd tried to save her Stephen's life. But I'd had a young German woman of my own to save, so I really had no business screeching at Emmaline. I'd screeched anyway, and had been heartily ashamed of myself afterwards. Emmaline, however, had been a peach about the whole thing. And, as I'm sure you've noticed for yourself, money talks. It did then, it still does now, and now the United States possessed two newish immigrants from Germany cluttering it up. Actually, Hilda, the woman I saved from deportation, was as tidy a specimen of human womankind as you could find anywhere.

Life is so strange sometimes.

Back to the luncheon table. The waiter and a couple of minions arrived with soup for all of us and little individual plates with bread, butter, and a dollop of something black on it. I stared at that black dollop in a teensy bit of dismay. I knew from reading that rich folks loved caviar, but I wasn't keen on trying fish eggs myself.

Harold, who always seemed to know what I was thinking, said, "Don't worry. It's an olive tapenade. It's good smushed on the rolls and butter."

"I'd never force anyone to eat caviar," said Emmaline with a grimace. "Can't stand the stuff myself."

"I'm like that with oysters," said Del. "Oysters are practically a staple in New Orleans." He shuddered delicately.

I'd never eaten an oyster, either, but I'd never admit it to this trio of privileged people. After surreptitiously watching Harold deal with a roll, butter and some olive tapenade, I did the same thing. "Oh, this tastes like those olives we had in Egypt and Turkey, Harold!" Those olives were nothing like their tame cousins we usually eat in the USA.

"Indeed," said Harold with a blissful grin on his face.

I dipped into my soup, front to back with my spoon as my mother had taught me, and took a sip. "This is delicious, too," I declared. Then I felt a little silly.

"It's one of my favorites," said Emmaline after taking a sip of her own soup. "It's green pea soup."

"Hmm. It's not like my aunt's split-pea soup. That's much heavier and has ham in it."

"Yes. This is made with fresh green peas. Chef Armand, the head chef here, made it up and won't let go of the recipe. He'd probably endure torture and still not reveal it."

"Sounds silly to me," said Harold.

"I don't know," I said after taking another bite of delicious, sweet, fresh-tasting green-pea soup. "It's his bread and butter. So to speak. If everybody knew how to make it, it wouldn't be special any longer."

"Precisely," said Emmaline. "I don't begrudge him his recipe, but I made him promise to leave a copy for me in his will."

"Good idea," I said, laughing.

"It goes really well with the olive tapenade," I said after trying a bite of roll, butter and tapenade along with a sip of soup.

"Well-chosen meal, Emmaline," said Harold. "Depending, of course, on what you serve us next."

We didn't have to wait long. A second after Del, who ate more slowly than the rest of us, probably because of his southern-gentleman upbringing, put his spoon on the plate beside his soup and sighed, a host of waiters swarmed in, swept the soup and bread-and-butter plates off the table, and set before each of us a plate upon which sat a wide goblet filled with a thick red sauce and with whole cooked shrimp draped over the rim of the goblet, tail ends facing us and front ends dipping into the sauce.

"Oooh," breathed Harold, his hands clamped over his heart. "Shrimp cocktail. I knew I liked you for a good reason, Emmaline."

"For my food, you mean?" asked Emmaline with a laugh.

"Yes!" Harold picked up one of the lemon quarters residing on his plate next to his goblet, squeezed lemon juice on top of the red stuff, and then he proceeded to pick up a shrimp tail with his fingers and dip it into the sauce. "Heaven," he said with something of a moan after he'd chewed and swallowed.

What the heck. I'd never had shrimp cocktail either, so I followed Harold's example, squeezed a quarter of a lemon on top of what I found out later was the cocktail sauce, and dunked in a shrimp. Harold was right. If it wasn't precisely heaven, it came in a close second place.

"Another of my favorites," said Emmaline emulating Harold and me (and Del, too, by this time). "But this recipe is easy to find in almost any cooking book."

"Is it really?" My head lifted, and my gaze landed on Emmaline. Perhaps I'd have to pay another visit to the library sooner than I'd anticipated, if any cooking book had this recipe in it. Although I wasn't sure where Aunt Vi would find shrimps. Perhaps Jurgensen's, the rich-folks grocery store in Pasadena would have them, but they'd also probably cost a lot. Well, I'd just have to think about how to get my hands on some shrimps.

After the shrimp cocktail had been downed by one and all, I was full. But that didn't stop the industrious team of waiters. They swept in and out again, and another team brought in steaming plates of chicken a la king. It was good. Not as good as Aunt Vi's, but I didn't say so.

Harold did. "I think Daisy's aunt makes a flakier crust than this on her chicken a la king," he said with a judicious expression on his face after he swallowed his first bite.

Emmaline laughed again. "She probably does. Chef Armand is good with soup, but his pastry chef should probably take lessons from your aunt, Daisy."

"I don't know," said I, feeling a trifle embarrassed. "I think it's delicious."

"It is, indeed," said Del.

He was forever trying to undo perceived damage done by his more outspoken lover, Harold. But everyone who mattered already knew Harold and never held the things he said against him. At least I don't think they did.

After we'd demolished the chicken a la king and a delicious pudding bristling with coconut and pineapple, we all sat back in our chairs, stuffed.

"That was wonderful. Thank you, Emmaline."

"You're more than welcome, Daisy. And I do hope you won't think I've invited you here under false pretenses, but I'm going to ask an enormous favor of you."

Oh, dear. I didn't like the sound of that. I said, "You are?" Trepidation was clear to hear in my voice.

"I am." Emmaline put her elbows on the table, folded her hands, and stared at me. "I would be ever so grateful if you'd poke into Mrs. Franbold's death. The family can't get anything out of the doctors or the police, and they *really* need to know how she died, for their own peace of mind. The poor woman's demise has put a hold on every aspect of their lives, particularly since Charles Franbold suspects something dire proceeding from the Underhill connection."

"He thinks Barrett Underhill had something to do with Mrs. Franbold's death?" I said, incredulous. "That would definitely put a damper on things, I reckon."

"Well, he hasn't directly blamed Barrett yet, but it's clear he thinks either Barrett or Mr. Underhill had something to do with Mrs. Franbold's demise, even if some sort of unintentional action on their part caused the woman's death."

"But what could either of them have done?"

"Underhill owns a fertilizer company south of town, Daisy," said Emmaline. "Fertilizer plants are fairly dripping with poisons, especially if they also produce pesticides, which Underhill does."

"They are? I didn't know that!"

"Pesticides are poisons, aren't they?" said Harold, as if he honestly wanted to know and wasn't making fun of me.

"Yes, they are. And I do believe lots of fertilizers use cyanide to one extent or another. I mean, the Underhill plant is basically a chemical plant. We're not talking about Irish farmers cutting peat to grow their gardens in," said Emmaline.

"Goodness," I muttered, wondering what she thought I could do to determine if an Underhill had done in Mrs. Franbold. "I'm not...Well, I'm not sure what I can do."

"Detective Rotondo would pitch a fit if you snooped into another one of his cases," said Harold with a wicked grin.

I allowed my chin to drop, feeling awful. I wanted to help Emmaline and the Franbolds, but if I did, Sam would be on me like that red paint the KKK had sloshed on Mrs. Pinkerton's gatehouse.

"It's because Emmaline hates you," said Harold, again being wicked.

"I do not! I know Daisy to be a kindhearted, resourceful woman. For heaven's sake, she's taken care of her family for years. That takes resourcefulness and intelligence. The fact that she's maintained her humanity in the face of so much inhumanity is something to take pride in."

"Thanks," I muttered. "I think."

"Can you just snoop a little bit?" Emmaline said in a wheedling tone. "I don't expect you to play private investigator or anything."

I heaved a heartfelt sigh. "Well, I guess I can ask questions of people, but if Sam gets wind of my poking around, he really will pitch a fit."

Ignoring the last part of my sentence, Emmaline smiled and said, "Oh, *thank* you, Daisy."

Nuts.

NINE

My snoopery began that very evening, when Sam joined my family for dinner. I was still full from lunch, so I didn't do proper service to Vi's admirable dinner of salmon croquettes served with a cream sauce. I wasn't a particular fan of croquettes—I'd been forced to teach a bunch of immigrant women how to fix them a couple of years prior, and I still hadn't fully recovered from the ordeal—but Vi's were delicious. Still, I only ate about three-quarters of one, all my asparagus, and dawdled over my dessert, which was a baked apple with cream.

"You aren't eating much, Daisy," said Vi, noticing my poor appetite and disapproving of it.

"I'm sorry, Vi. It's all delicious, but Harold took me to lunch at the Castleton today, and I'm still not hungry yet."

"Exalted places you dine in," grumbled Sam, digging into his third salmon croquette.

"Not my fault," I said. "I just happen to have exalted friends. Heck, Emmaline Castleton was the one hosting—or should that be hostessing—?"

"What difference does it make?" Sam growled.

"None, I guess." I sighed. "But she's a friend of Glenda Daltry, who's Vivian Daltry's daughter, and—"

"Who are the Daltrys?" asked Ma. Fair question.

"Vivian Daltry is Mrs. Franbold's daughter. If you'd been able to come to Mrs. Franbold's funeral, you'd have met her. She's a nice lady. I didn't meet Glenda, her daughter, but I'm sure she's nice, too. Anyway, Emmaline seems to like her. They're friends."

"What about them?" asked Sam, his voice not inviting frivolity, darn it.

"Well, you know that Charles Franbold thinks someone poisoned his mother on purpose, right?"

Sam set his fork and knife on his plate. They crossed each other, kind of like swords. I considered this a bad sign. He said, "Here we go again," in a voice that could have etched glass.

"We do not!" I cried, already feeling abused. "Emmaline just asked if you knew yet if Mrs. Franbold was poisoned. Or not."

"What difference does it make to her?"

"None, except that's she's friends with Glenda, and Glenda is engaged to marry Barrett Underhill, and he works at his father's chemical plant. Well, I guess it's a fertilizer plant, and Glenda is worried that someone will blame Barrett for Mrs. Franbold's death because chemical plants and fertilizer plants use a lot of poisons in their products."

Everyone at the table had stopped eating and was staring at me by the time I finished my explanation. I understood. It sounded lame to me, too. I lifted my shoulders and my hands in an "It's not my fault gesture." Didn't work.

"You are *not* going to get involved in another investigation, Daisy Majesty," said Sam, laying down the law. He always did that, and I generally ignored him.

"Do they know what did in Mrs. Franbold yet?" asked Pa, being relevant.

"Oh, I do hope she wasn't really poisoned," said Ma.

"Me, too," said I.

"Indeed," said Vi.

"The cause of Mrs. Franbold's death is still under investigation," said Sam formally. "Her death is being scrutinized by the Pasadena Police Department in cooperation with a couple of doctors. We don't need your help, Daisy."

"I know you don't, but if you ever figure out what killed her, will you please let me know? Just so I can tell Emmaline? So she can tell Glenda, and Barrett can stop worrying?"

"Why is he worrying that he'll be blamed if he's innocent?" asked my mother, who almost always used her common sense.

"I don't know," I admitted. "Sounds kind of fishy, doesn't it?"

"Yes." It was Sam who answered. "And I do believe I'll have to pay a call on Mr. Barrett Underhill."

"Oh, Lord, please don't tell him I sent you!"

"You didn't send me," said Sam. "I'm investigating a woman's death. We don't divulge who gives us our leads."

"Is it a lead?" I asked in a weak voice.

"Don't know yet." Sam reclaimed his silverware and dug into his dinner again.

That went well, didn't it? I'm being sarcastic, in case you couldn't tell.

The next day, Saturday, I drove Vi to work at the Pinkertons' mansion. Well, I also drove Ma to her job at the Hotel Marengo, but that was just up the street a ways. After I dropped Vi off, I toddled down to the Pasadena Public Library, hoping this was one of the two Saturdays per month during which Miss Petrie was on duty. It wasn't. That meant I was on my own.

So the first aisle I turned to was where the cookery books were shelved. I knew they were in the 600s, and it didn't take me long to find them. Hmm. Now where would one find a recipe for shrimp cocktail sauce? If the one in question were I, she didn't have the slightest idea. So I picked up a few cooking books and flipped to their tables of contents. I looked under "Appetizers," thinking that's probably where the recipe would be.

I'd gone through maybe six books and was about to give up when I picked up a huge volume called *The White House Cook Book*. If anybody should eat shrimp cocktail, I figured it should be the President of the United States. Sure enough, I found what looked like it might be a recipe for cocktail sauce made with tomato catsup, made mustard (whatever that was), and a few other things that might be suitable for dunking shrimp in, especially if you traded the made mustard for horseradish. I definitely tasted horseradish in the cocktail sauce Emmaline fed us. So I tucked the book under my arm and headed for the card catalogue to look up where the poisons might be hiding in the stacks. Since I couldn't find any card in the catalogue labeled "Poisons", I decided to look at "Forensic Science".

They were in the earlier 600s. Should have looked at the card catalog before I started my search. Oh, well.

The library is a fabulous place. I love it and would live in it if I didn't already have a home of my own. If I ever had an opportunity to go to school again in my lifetime, I'll study how to be a librarian.

However.

Because Sam Rotondo was a rotten, no-good beast, I didn't know what poison might have caused Mrs. Franbold's death, *if* Mrs. Franbold was poisoned. Sam had mentioned as Mrs. Franbold lay dead in Pastor Smith's office that Dr. Benjamin suspected cyanide. So I heaved a tome about forensic science off the shelf, after carefully putting the cooking book on the floor at my feet, and flipped to the table of contents. What I found was a whole lot of stuff about how to determine if a bullet came from a certain kind of gun. Or maybe a specific gun.

Not what interested me at the moment, although ballistics—which is what folks called this new discovery—was kind of interesting if, say, one were writing a murder mystery. I wasn't. I was trying to solve one, providing there was one to be solved. Oh, dear. Perhaps I should have looked at plant books. Most poisons came from plants, didn't they? Hadn't Sam mentioned apricot pits and stuff like that? So, after I stuffed the forensic science book back into its place, I traipsed back to the card catalogue.

At least looking up plants got me out of the 600s. All the way to the 500s. What a thrill. Fortunately for me these books weren't as huge as the forensic-science books had been.

And it looked as if I'd struck pay dirt! There they were, in all their glory: all the plants I'd read about in murder mysteries: belladonna, foxglove, apples. Wait a minute. *Apples?* My goodness. I didn't know that. Did you know that apple seeds were poisonous? Well, they are, but not very. Anyhow, it would be hard to poison a person with them, especially during communion.

Unless you pounded the seeds to powder and dumped them into the grape juice. But you'd still have a suspiciously thick inch or so of communion juice, and I doubt anyone would drink it.

Ah, and there were Sam's precious apricot pits. Good heavens above! Darned near everything we eat contains poisons of one sort or another. Potatoes? I guess I'd rather die eating potatoes than apricot pits. However, I got bored with my research before I found anything particularly useful in the plant section.

My best guess was still on cyanide, and it probably came from the Underhill plant. But how? And who did it?

I didn't have a single idea, although I hoped Emmaline was right, and whoever did it—if anyone did—wasn't Barrett Underhill.

Hmm. Did Betsy Powell work at the Underhill plant? I'd have to ask someone. If she did, and if she'd slipped some kind of poison into the communion grape juice, it might account for her outburst at church. But why would she want to poison nice old Mrs. Franbold? What if she'd made a mistake, and the juice meant for someone else had been consumed by Mrs. Franbold? That had been Emmaline's suggestion. But whom would sweet, spinsterish Betsy Powell want to poison?

Bother. I don't know how detectives like Sam ever solved their cases if they were all as indefinite and befuddling as this one. If it even was a case. Bother.

I picked up the cooking book and went to the fiction section. Someone had done library patrons a huge favor by placing detective and mystery novels in a section all to themselves. They'd done the same for westerns. So I prowled around the mystery section, picking out a couple of my favorites, *The Circular Staircase* and *The Window at the White Cat*, by Mary Roberts Rinehart; *The Thirty-Nine Steps*, by John Buchan;

The Moon and Sixpence, by W. Somerset Maugham (very well, this isn't a detective novel. I wanted to read it); and (back to the mysteries) *His Last Bow*, by Arthur Conan Doyle, mainly because I missed Sherlock Holmes so much. *His Last Bow* wasn't all that great, but it was Sherlock.

After that, I decided to check out a few of Edgar Wallace's books, even though I'd read most of them already. Boy, I really missed Miss Petrie when she wasn't there. She could always steer me in the right direction. But I struck gold! *Bones of the River* sat there on the shelf, staring back at me. This was one of the books Miss Petrie had mentioned as coming from Great Britain. If she'd been there, she'd probably have stuffed it under her desk for me. So I grabbed it, took my haul, and staggered to the check-out desk with my bounty. There's nothing so comforting as knowing you had plenty of books to read!

Oh, and in case you thought I was being unnecessarily greedy, I'd picked up the already-read-by-my-family books from the table beside the front door and returned them. So I was only exchanging books. In a manner of speaking.

I could hardly wait to get home and read!

TEN

However, lest you think I do nothing but snoop into other people's business and read books, before I sat Spike and me down on the sofa to read, I cleaned the house and set the table for supper. I even made my own lunch! I know that doesn't sound like a big deal to lots of people, but you mustn't overlook the fact that I can't cook a lick.

I can, however, fix a sandwich, providing there's anything to put between a couple of slices of Aunt Vi's good bread, and there was leftover ham in the Frigidaire. So I not only prepared my own lunch, but I also made a sandwich for my father. What's more, I served them both very prettily, with a sliced apple as an accompaniment. There. I'm not totally hopeless in the kitchen. It's only when I try to prepare something from scratch and have to apply heat that my culinary clumsiness asserts itself.

Pa was pleased. "Good sandwich, sweetheart." He was trying to make me feel better about being a crummy cook.

"Thanks, Pa. I guess even I can't ruin a sandwich."

He laughed, but he knew. My entire family and Sam Rotondo knew about the kitchen and me, and what mortal enemies we were.

Vi brought home our dinner from the Pinkertons' house that evening: a delicious and hearty lamb stew that she served with her light-as-air biscuits. She also served us apricot tarts for dessert, and I couldn't help but think about those apricots' poisonous pits. Fortunately for all of us, Aunt Vi had removed the pits before undertaking her pastry-baking. She made the flakiest crusts known to man. At least all the men I knew.

Sam didn't come to dinner that night, and his absence was felt. But when he telephoned later that evening, he said he'd been detained at the office. When I asked what had detained him, he said he'd had to look at a corpse in the morgue. Ew.

"Who was the corpse? I mean when it was alive?" I asked.

"Don't know yet. I thought it might be the missing Evans, but it wasn't."

"Oh." I paused for a second, digesting this. "How did you figure that out?"

"Description. This guy was in his late sixties. Looks as if he died from drinking bathtub gin, or something approximating it."

"Oh. How awful."

"Yeah. It was awful, all right."

"Um...What happens when a person drinks that stuff?"

"Lots of things. Generally, you'll go blind first, and then your liver and kidneys and stomach get torn to shreds. This guy's innards were almost not there any longer, and his skin was a bluish tinge." I heard a huge sigh come over the wire. "I swear, people will drink anything."

"That sounds ghastly. I wonder why folks drink that stuff."

"Can't get anything else, I suppose."

"Yes, but...Oh, never mind. I suppose some folks are driven to drink like some other folks are driven to...I don't know. Gamble, or something."

"Too true."

"I appreciate your looking into Evans' disappearance, Sam."

"You're welcome. However, this wasn't him. Or he. I forget which it's supposed to be."

"I don't suppose it matters."

"You're the one always correcting my grammar," he said. I think, although I'm not sure, I heard a smile in his voice.

"Nonsense. I am not. You missed a delicious dinner," I said, deciding not to be annoyed by his attitude.

"Didn't know I was invited," he said.

"You're always invited, Sam. You should know that by this time."

"Am I?"

"Of course you are."

"Well, thanks."

"You're welcome," I said, still holding on to my sweet temper, albeit with difficulty. How on earth would Sam and I ever get along if we were to marry?

No answer occurred to me, so after I replaced the mouthpiece on the cradle, I took my dog and my book and sat in the living room until I was tired enough to sleep.

The next day, the first Sunday in February, I felt a little creepy because it was last communion Sunday during which Mrs. Franbold had dropped dead. Nevertheless, after breakfast of ham and eggs and toast, my family and I (except Spike) walked up to the church. Right before I swerved to enter the choir room and assume my robe, Sam strolled up to greet us. I didn't linger, but bade him good morning, gave him a peck on the cheek, which surprised him as much as it did me, and went to do my duty.

Lucille Spinks was in an uplifted mood because her marriage to Mr. Zollinger was coming right up on the second Saturday in March. She'd asked me to be a bridesmaid, which I thought was nice of her. I'd volunteered to make all the bridesmaids' dresses, which she thought was nice of me, so we were in accord that warm first Sunday in February. Odd weather we have in Pasadena sometimes. It can be cold and foggy in July and August and warm as toast in February and March. That was one of the toasty February days.

Our anthem that morning was "Holy, Holy, Holy," which was an oldie but a goodie, and one we hauled out every now and then for Communion Sunday, as we did that day. As usual, the choir got served communion first and separately, and then the room full of congregants got in two lines and proceeded down the center aisle to take communion.

I noticed Betsy Powell was helping again that day, along with several other long-time church members.

With some displeasure, I saw Mr. and Mrs. Underhill standing in the line. I didn't dislike Mrs. Underhill; nor did I dislike the two Underhill girls, Miranda and Millicent, both of whom were adolescents, perhaps thirteen or fourteen or thereabouts. They seemed to be sweet girls. I'd never paid much attention to the Underhill clan until I'd witnessed Mr. Underhill allow Mrs. Franbold to fall to the church floor and then look grumpy about her demise. The rest of the Underhills seemed unexceptionable people, although I didn't really know them. Mr. Underhill appeared grumpy that Sunday, but he always looked grumpy, so there you go. The rest of his family seemed wary, unless that was my imagination, which sometimes fires up for no discernible reason.

But by gum, perhaps it *wasn't* merely my imagination making me acute that day, for no sooner had Mr. Underhill snatched up his communion wafer, stuffed it into his mouth, and gulped his grape juice than he started to convulse and then fall to the ground amid a chorus of gasps and shocked cries from the churchgoers.

"What's happening?" asked Lucy. She was supposed to wear spectacles but didn't most of the time, so she had to rely on other people to report interesting happenings to her.

Not at all shy, I stood to see what had happened to Mr. Underhill.

"Mr. Underhill collapsed," I reported to Lucy.

"Mercy sakes! Another one?"

"Indeed," said I, thinking this was ridiculous. Not that I didn't appreciate excitement as much as the next person, but to have two Communion Sundays in a row disrupted by a falling body was a trifle too much to endure.

"What do you think happened to him?" asked Lucy, pulling the edges of her eyes outward so that she could see better and squinting hard. I thought she'd look better if she just wore her cheaters, but I didn't tell her so.

"I don't know." I suspected poison, but I didn't let on.

But why did someone persist in poisoning the First Methodist-Episcopal Church's congregants on Communion Sunday? I didn't know, but I felt mighty unsettled by the notion. I liked my church, darn it, and I didn't think it was nice of someone to persist in killing its members.

A space had cleared around Mr. Underhill and I heard someone, probably his wife, cry, "Grover!" In the cleared space, I saw Mr. Underhill clutching at his throat and uttering gasping, unintelligible phrases or words. If he were a better-liked man, probably someone would have rushed up to help him, but evidently no one quite dared, which I considered an interesting phenomenon. When Mrs. Franbold fell, everyone except Mr. Underhill had raced to assist her, for all the good it had done.

But there were Sam and Dr. Benjamin. They didn't care how unpopular a man was; if he was in distress, they would try to help him. I saw them both kneel beside the writhing form of Mr. Underhill. Then I saw Mr. Underhill shake all over once and then lie still.

Goodness gracious. What did that mean? Actually, I thought I knew. The man was dead. His was a much more dramatic demise than Mrs. Franbold's had been. Interesting.

I squinted into the sanctuary. The lights were on, but the room was big, and folks had begun crowding around Sam and Doc Benjamin. Was Mr. Underhill's face a pinkish red? One of the books I'd checked into at the library had confirmed my notion that a victim of cyanide poisoning was liable to show a distinct pinkish coloring after death. Perhaps I was imagining the pinkening of Mr. Underhill's skin tone. My imagination takes off on its own quite often.

Sam stood and said clearly in his order-giving voice, "Everyone, please take your seats. Dr. Benjamin and I will assist..." His voice trailed off. Guess he didn't know what Mr. Underhill's name was. He continued. "We will assist this man out of the sanctuary, and then communion can recommence."

Pastor Smith stood back, holding the communion wafers and staring down at the now-unmoving Mr. Grover Underhill, his mouth agape.

Miss Betsy Powell, holding a tray of communion juice vials, again dropped same and started screeching. Oh, boy. She was *such* a help in an emergency. Mr. Gerald Kingston put a hand on her shoulder as if to calm her, but she continued to make dreadful howling noises.

"Good Lord, is that Miss Powell again?" asked Lucy.

"Yup," I said. Then, bravely daring, I slithered out of the choir's cubbyhole and boldly walked up to our choir director, Mr. Floy Hostetter. "Mr. Hostetter?"

He jumped a trifle and swirled around. "Mrs. Majesty!" He'd put his hand to his throat, and for only a second I worried that he, too, might have partaken of whatever had killed Mr. Underhill.

But no. He was merely alarmed and startled. As were we all.

"I'll be happy to help with communion if Pastor Smith needs to take care of Miss Powell again."

As Betsy Powell still screeched, this seemed like an apt suggestion. I stood there, angelically holding my hands clasped in front of me, and waited.

"Er...Ah...Oh, yes! Yes, that would be a grand idea." He peered out into the sanctuary, and sure enough, Pastor Smith was once again guiding Betsy Powell out a side door of the church. "Um...Can Miss Spinks assist you? I think we need more than one person."

I turned and gestured to Lucy, who squinted at me for a couple of moments, but then caught on. She slid out of the choir enclosure and rushed up to Mr. Hostetter and me.

"We need to help with communion again," I told her.

"Of course," said she, good girl that she was.

So Lucy and I descended the chancel steps and headed over to the communion tableau. Grape juice had stained the carpeting once more. I swear, if Miss Betsy Powell didn't owe the church a new carpet, I didn't know who did.

One of the people on the Communion Committee rushed out the other side of the sanctuary, probably to get more grape juice poured into more little glass vials, and Mr. Hostetter, Lucy Spinks and I renewed the communion service as Sam and Doc Benjamin once more carried a dead person out of the sanctuary headed, unless I was much mistaken, for Pastor Smith's office, where a sofa stood ready to accept another corpse.

What the heck was going on in my church? Whatever it was, I didn't approve.

However, we managed to get through the communion service, *sans* members of the Underhill clan, Detective Sam Rotondo, Dr. Benjamin, and Pastor Merle Negley Smith. And Miss Betsy Powell.

Naturally, as soon as the service ended, I practically raced to the choir room, tore off my robe and, not being as careful as usual, flung it on its hanger and stuffed it into the closet. I was sure I'd pay for my neglect later, when I had to iron out all of the wrinkles, but I wanted to get to Fellowship Hall and find out if anyone knew what had happened to Mr. Underhill. I also wanted to know if I'd imagined the pinkish tint to his complexion as he lay there, dead—I was sure he was dead—on the church carpet, splashed yet again by many vials of fallen grape juice. Betsy Powell must have nerves made of dandelion fluff.

My parents and Aunt Vi stood at the door of the hall as I rushed to the room. Ma held out a hand to me, and I skidded to a halt.

"Daisy, Sam asked if you could go to Pastor Smith's office. I guess they're having a terrible time trying to calm Miss Powell down."

Merciful heavens! Sam had asked for my help. Would wonders never cease?

"Thanks, Ma. You go ahead and have some cookies and tea and stuff, and I'll see what's going on in the pastor's office."

I turned and headed down the hall a few paces where the pastor's office door was. I heard my mother say in a tone that sounded like distaste, "I wish she didn't enjoy things like this so much."

Then I heard my father and Aunt Vi laugh, so I didn't despair.

When I got to the pastor's office door and tried the handle, I discovered some rat had locked the door. I suspected Sam, who might, in a fit of befuddlement, have asked for my help, but really didn't want it.

But as soon as I was about to thump on the door, it opened, and there stood Sam, scowling down at me.

I scowled back up at him. "You're the one who asked for me."

"Yeah," said he. "Come here. Thanks for coming. That woman is driving us nerts again."

Sam had actually thanked me! What a shock.

He stepped aside, and I entered the room. Sure enough, Miss Betsy Powell was having hysterics on the chair she'd occupied the last time she'd had hysterics in this office.

"Can you please do something to shut her up?" muttered Sam, hooking a thumb at Miss Powell.

"I guess so," I said. Then I sighed and looked at the sofa, hoping to discern if Mr. Underhill's skin had turned red. I was foiled in my effort by a positive hedge of uniformed officers, not to mention Dr. Benjamin and Pastor Smith. I cursed inwardly and moseyed over to Betsy. There I once more knelt beside her. "Miss Powell? Betsy? You need to stop this nonsense right now!" Sternness had worked before; I hoped it would work again.

It didn't.

Betsy surged around on the overstuffed chair and grabbed me by the shoulders. Darn it, she had grip like iron, and it hurt. "But it's a *judgment!*" she shrieked. "It's a *judgment!* It's all my *fault!*"

Very well, that was it for me. I smacked Betsy's hands away from my shoulders, held both of her hands in my own tight grasp and said in a voice that reminded me of my recent role as Katisha in Gilbert and Sullivan's operetta, *The Mikado,* "Stop wailing this instant, Betsy Powell!" I'd loved playing Katisha, who is mean, nasty, evil-tempered and cruel. I made my living being nice, so the part had been fun for me. It was fun now, too, although I'm probably a wicked sinner to admit it. "Everyone has too much to do already, and they've heard quite enough out of *you!* You're making a pest of yourself and interrupting people who are needed elsewhere. So shut your mouth right this second and be quiet!"

By golly, she shut her mouth, stared at me with wide, goggling eyes, and slumped into the chair. She didn't faint this time, more's the pity, but at least she stopped making a scene. She did commence to sob, but did so quietly. I waited until I was pretty sure she wouldn't kick up another fuss, then rose to my feet and tiptoed to the crowd gathered around the sofa.

A whole bunch of tall men stood in my way but I managed, by

discreet insertion of my short self under men's arms, to sidle up to the sofa. By gum, Mr. Underhill's face was pink as a cherry pudding!

"Cyanide," I whispered, forgetting in whose company I stood. Or crouched. I didn't quite dare stand up straight.

Didn't matter. All the male heads swiveled, and all the male gazes settled on me.

Dr. Benjamin spoke first. "We can't be sure of that yet. Not until we get tests done, but yes, it looks like cyanide poisoning."

A scream from Betsy Powell made me wince.

Sam said, "Damnation, get back to that idiot, will you? You're supposed to be calming her down."

"Don't swear in church," I grumbled, but I ducked under some more arms and marched to Betsy's chair. She'd begun uttering short, sharp yips of dismay, and I decided I—and everyone else in her vicinity—had taken enough of her nonsense. So I smacked her cheek, not too hard, but hard enough to jolt her.

"Mrs. Majesty!" she cried.

"Stop making that awful noise right this instant!" I replied. "People in this room are busy taking care of a sick man. They don't need you to shriek at them. Make another noise, and I'll smack you again." Was I mean, or was I not mean?

"But...But..."

"But nothing. You're not helping. In fact, you're interfering with the police and the medical people who are trying to figure out what happened to Mr. Underhill."

After uttering one long, soft, "Ooooooh," Miss Betsy Powell did the right thing and fainted.

And thank God for it, I say. Actually, so did Pastor Smith.

ELEVEN

Because we'd stayed overlong at the church, Aunt Vi's roasted chicken was a little dry, but nobody minded. We just poured gravy over the chicken and potatoes, and gobbled it up.

"So Dr. Benjamin thinks this was cyanide poisoning?" I dared ask Sam after Mr. Underhill's collapse in church had been talked about as Vi served our plates. I figured it would be safe to ask, since I didn't start the conversation about Mr. Underhill's untimely demise.

After frowning at me for a moment, Sam gave up his grump and said, "Yes. He's fairly certain Mr. Underhill died of cyanide poisoning. It was quick after the initial convulsions, and he turned that distinctive pinkish color."

"I thought so," said I in a soft voice. "But how'd he manage to take poison during communion?"

"We don't know, and don't you begin speculating, Daisy. We'll have enough to deal with without you interfering."

"I hadn't planned on interfering!" I said, hurt.

"Huh."

"It's awful that these things keep happening at church," said Ma, who didn't appreciate disruptions in the orderly flow of life. Not that I could fault her for her lack of an adventurous spirit, given the circumstances.

"It is awful," I concurred, mainly to divert Sam from scolding me. Then I dared say, "I don't recall Mrs. Franbold turning red after she died."

"That's because she didn't," said Sam.

"Oh. Do you know how she died then?" I asked, knowing as I did so that I was risking Sam's temper.

Sam said, "No," in an uncompromising and extremely testy voice.

"Daisy," said my mother. "Don't pester Sam. Just eat this delicious meal and be grateful our family is safe."

"Good idea," said Pa.

"*Very* good idea," said Sam.

Vi smiled at me, so I knew she didn't mind my curiosity, but I also knew I'd better curb my tongue for the sake of peace.

Drat.

The remainder of the week passed uneventfully. Mrs. Wright asked me to visit her again to consult with Rolly about her missing butler. Rolly didn't have any idea where Mr. Evans was, although he did assure Mrs. Wright that Mr. Evans' soul hadn't been spotted in the Great Beyond yet. I always hedged a bit about this sort of thing, mainly because I had no idea what had happened to a whole lot of people folks wanted me to chat with.

Perhaps that sounds odd, but it isn't. The Great War had killed thousands of young men, but often bodies were never identified, and some were never even found. I'd read articles about farmers trying to get their families' lives back to normal, only to uncover corpses, old weapons, and bones as they plowed fields. The souls attached to those corpses and bones were completely unknown unless some identification was plowed up with them, and that didn't often happen. It's pitiful to think about, but there you go. I expect thousands of mothers, fathers, lovers and spouses will never know what happened to their nearest and dearest, which is really a shame. It's bad enough to know your loved one was killed in a war, but not ever knowing for sure what happened to him must be worse even than that. Kaiser Bill has a lot to answer for. But that's not the point here.

The point is I told my clients who had missing, but not yet discovered and identified, kin that it often took a spirit some time to settle comfortably into the afterlife. Therefore, no one expected me to get in touch with the newly departed. Or the imprecisely or perhaps not-quite-yet departed, which was what Evans was at that point in time.

Mrs. Wright was unhappy with my indifferent results, but she coped and said she understood. That was a lot more than I did, but I didn't let on.

On a happier note, I was looking forward to Mrs. Pinkerton's charity ball, which was to take place the Saturday following Mr. Underhill's death. His funeral, by the way, took place on the Thursday after his demise. I didn't attend, since I hadn't known him and what I did know, I didn't like. Besides, I feared Betsy Powell might be there and screaming. Evidently my absence wasn't noticed, because I heard from no one regarding the funeral service or burial.

For the charity function, I made a charming Gypsy costume, not based on anything I knew about Gypsies—because I knew nothing except what little I'd read in issues of the *National Geographic*—but based on what people *thought* Gypsies wore. I gleaned my information, in other words, from books and the flickers.

I made myself a white peasant-style blouse and a multi-colored skirt. I sewed together different colored strips of cloth that had ended up in my bits-and-pieces drawer, drew the skirt together at my waist with elastic stripping I found at Nelson's Five and Dime, and wore it and the blouse with a bright red sash that dangled. For my head covering, I chose a blue, red, and yellow striped material. And, because I figured why not? I also wore the juju Mrs. Jackson had given me. I thought about tying Sam's ring to a tassel, but didn't quite dare, for fear I'd lose it.

I wore lots of cheap necklaces I found in various junk shops, mostly made of colorful fake beads. Well, the beads weren't fake precisely, but they weren't gemstones. I actually had a bracelet full of rubies, diamonds, emeralds, and sapphires, that had been given to me by a Russian count—at least he claimed to be a Russian count. You couldn't tell in those days. There were fake Russians running around all over the place. However, that bracelet was in a safe-deposit box at the bank and I'd no more wear it to a costume party than appear at the ball as Lady Godiva.

People always donated used clothing and so forth to the Salvation Army, and Flossie Buckingham helped me create my Gypsy costume. She also made up my face right before I motored over to Mrs. Pinkerton's house. She was a whiz at makeup due to her former life.

When Flossie was through with me, I'd never looked so exotic, ever. Whereas I generally cultivated the pale-and-interesting image, that night, I looked like a Gypsy queen in a motion picture, only in color. Vivid makeup, vivid clothing, vivid jewelry; I wouldn't have recognized me if I'd encountered myself walking down a street.

"You're a genius, Flossie," I said, admiring my Gypsy self. She'd used dark makeup on me and, except for my blue eyes and dark red hair, I could have passed for any Romany wench, providing no one cared about authenticity.

"I've had lots of practice," she said, laughing. It always amazed and gratified me that Flossie wasn't ashamed of her past. In fact, I do believe her own early years of poverty and unhappiness helped her understand and assist Johnny's Salvation Army flock.

"Thanks, Flossie." I sighed happily. "I'd better get going. Mrs. Pinkerton wanted me there early to approve the tent she had Harold set up for my fortune-telling job."

Another laugh from Flossie, this one joined by one from Johnny. I glanced up and saw him standing in the doorway, holding baby Billy and grinning from ear to ear.

"I've never seen you look more ravishing," said Johnny.

"Right," I said. "Ravishing. That's me."

Both Johnny and Flossie laughed. After a second, little Billy joined them. I darned near cried, which shows what a sap I am. However, that's nothing to the point.

After thanking Flossie another seventy or eighty times, I drove to Mrs. Pinkerton's place. Joseph Jackson, who had been keeping tabs on the Pinkerton family's gate for as long as I could remember, greeted me cheerfully and opened the black wrought-iron gate for me. I waved at him as I drove up the deodar-lined way to the roundabout in front of the mansion. I do believe I was more colorful than Jackson's mother that evening, and she was the most colorful woman I'd ever met in my life, what with her being a Voodoo mambo and all.

The family Chevrolet looked a lot better in Mrs. P's circular drive than my old horse-and-buggy used to, although it was nowhere near as grand as Harold's Stutz Bearcat. But I didn't care. I hopped from the Chevrolet's front seat, grabbed my spiritualist's bag—containing my crystal ball, my Ouija board and planchette, and my tattered deck of tarot cards—from the seat next to me, and walked up the massive front steps, across the massive front porch, whacked the brass lion's brass ring against the brass knocking plate, and smiled when Featherstone opened the door as if he'd been waiting just for me.

For the first time since I'd met him, more than half my lifetime ago, Featherstone actually did something uncharacteristic for him. He blinked at me. I gave him a finger wiggle. "It's just me," I trilled happily. "Desdemona Majesty, spiritualist-medium extraordinaire."

"Ah," said Featherstone, back in his role as the world's best butler. "Come this way, Mrs. Majesty."

So I went that way. This time Featherstone and I bypassed the drawing room, which was generally where Mrs. Pinkerton plagued me with her problems, and continued on to the back of the house, where a ballroom awaited us. Harold and his pals had outdone themselves! Colorful garlands hung everywhere, pictures of dogs and cats and even an elephant, a hippo, a rhino, several species of antelope, and a giraffe hung on the walls, having been painted by Harold, I assumed. He was an artistic gent, was Harold.

The room buzzed with staff setting up tables and chairs around the sides of the room. The center of the room was reserved for dancing. A balcony held a small band, the musicians of which were at the moment tuning their instruments. I beheld Jackson's son with his cornet. I remember having been shocked to see this same son playing in a jazz band in a speakeasy once, but he looked right elegant that evening. So did his band mates.

As luck would have it, Harold spotted me before his mother did. This was a break for me, since Mrs. Pinkerton had a habit of knocking me down whenever we met. Not that she meant to, but she was a large woman, I wasn't, and she was generally in thrall to some overwhelming emotion when she called on my services. So she'd run at me, and I'd try my hardest to brace myself against some piece of furniture, and so far she hadn't succeeded in toppling me over, but it had been a close-run thing a time or two.

"Daisy!" cried Harold. "You look utterly spectacular!"

"Thanks, Harold." Harold's opinion mattered to me more than most people's since he earned his considerable living as a costumier at a motion-picture studio in Los Angeles. Not that he needed the job; he had a tidy fortune all his own thanks to his family. But he adored his work, so he did it and earned mega-bucks.

He grabbed my hand. "Come over here and look at your tent! I did a simply smashing job of it. Del's setting up the insides right this minute."

"How nice." I tripped along after Harold, pleased to be there at that evening and for the sake of the Pasadena Humane Society. "Will Stacy be here?" I asked, fearing Harold's answer. If there was one person liable to clog up the works, it was Harold's irritating sister, Stacy Kincaid.

"Nope. You're safe. Actually, we all are," said Harold, whose opinion of his sister echoed my own.

"Oh, I'm so glad!"

"We all are. Well, except Mother, but she would be if she didn't have a blind spot where Stacy is concerned."

Yet another opinion shared by the both of us.

I stopped dead in my tracks when I spotted my tent. "Oh, Harold," I breathed. "It's a masterpiece!"

"Isn't it, though? I thought so, too." Modesty wasn't one of Harold's more prominent virtues.

Oh, but the tent was spectacular. Like my skirt, Harold had sewn different colors of cloth—in the tent's case, canvas—together, and he'd painted all sorts of animals, most of which wouldn't have been caught dead in the Pasadena Humane Society, on it. There were lions, tigers, antelopes, zebras, elephants, giraffes, okapis, gnus, water buffalos, crocodiles (or alligators; I couldn't tell which), and any number of other exotic species painted on the canvas sides.

Above the tent flap, Harold had painted a circle with all the symbols of the Zodiac emblazoned thereon, and underneath the Zodiac he'd painted the palm of a hand with some kind of mystical symbol thereon.

"What's that symbol mean?" I asked him, pointing at something that looked a little bit like one of Vi's cinnamon buns, but with more curls. I know pointing isn't polite. I was with Harold, so it didn't matter.

"Oh, my dear!" cried Harold. "You don't know how much research I put into that stupid symbol. It's an ancient Armenian Arevakhach."

"An ancient Armenian what?"

"Arevakhach," said Harold with satisfaction clear to hear in his voice.

"What's that?"

"An ancient symbol of eternity and light."

"Armenian, you say?"

"Absolutely. Took me forever to find it, too. I knew sort of what I wanted, but only the ancient Armenians had it."

"How in the name of gracious did you discover it?" I asked, honestly curious. Did Harold, too, spend a bunch of his time in libraries?

"Los Angeles Public Library," said he, answering my unasked question. "They have books on mystical symbols and stuff there."

"I haven't noticed any in the Pasadena Public Library, but maybe I haven't looked on the right shelf."

"Be serious, Daisy," said Harold, giving me an arch look.

After taking a second to think about it, I said, "Yeah. You're probably right. Pasadena would never stand for arcane symbols in its library."

"You've got it in one, my dear. Arcane symbols for my favorite spiritualist-medium are something else entirely. I'd go to any lengths to glorify you." He yanked on my hand again. "But come inside. I want you to see what I've done with your working space. He pulled back the tent flap, and I entered."

The inside was just as elaborate as the outside, but more intensely mysterious. I stopped stock-still. "Oh, Harold, it's perfect!"

"Darned right it is," said he, pleased by my reaction.

"Thank you, Harold! Thank you, Del!"

"Honored to be of service," said Del, bowing in a gentlemanlike manner. He was always a gentleman.

Harold and Del had hung the entire tent with dark red silk (real silk, according to Harold), and had placed a round table and three chairs in the tent's center, only toward the back. The chair in which I was to sit had its back to the rear of the tent, and looked kind of like a throne. Mind you, it was only an elaborate chair with an elegantly carved back that he'd snatched from another room in his mother's mansion, but it looked quite regal. He'd also thought to provide me with two plush pillows covered in deep crimson silk so my poor back wouldn't have to rest against the carved wood. Well, and also because the chair was deep, and my feet wouldn't touch the floor without some help from the pillows at my back. I guess he'd added the third chair in case someone came in with a friend.

"Luxurious," said I, grinning.

"Nothing but the best for you, my dear," said Harold, bowing deeply and gesturing me to my throne. "You'll notice that I set a small stand next to your chair, so that you can put the tools of your trade on it and select whichever one you want to use when you want to use it. Oh, and there's also the money bowl there."

"You've thought of everything, Harold. Thank you so much."

"You're more than welcome. My mother calls upon you to do the damnedest things. I figured you might as well do them in comfort."

"Thanks, Harold."

"There," said Del, climbing down from a short stepladder. "That's the last of the bows."

It was only then I realized that each of the silk dangling things was tied to the top of the tent with a dark red bow.

"Gorgeous. Thanks, Del."

"Any time," said he. I'm pretty sure he didn't mean it.

"Daisy!" came a piercing shriek from the tent's entrance.

Mrs. Pinkerton had found me. I turned and smiled spiritualistically at her. "Good evening, Mrs. Pinkerton. Harold and Del did a marvelous job with the tent, didn't they?"

"Oh, my gracious, yes!" said she, rushing up to me at full tilt. Fortunately for me, Harold stood at my back and steadied both Mrs. P and me when she hit. "It's so wonderful of you to do this, Daisy. And it's for *such* a good cause."

"It sure is," I agreed. "The Pasadena Humane Society does good work for the poor dogs and cats of the community." That sounded stupid. So be it. Mrs. Pinkerton wasn't the brightest candle in the box, so I doubted she'd notice. Harold, on the other hand, rolled his gaze to the top of the tent in a gesture of irony. Mrs. P didn't notice, and I didn't mention it. Del merely stood there and grinned.

"I'm so, so *very* glad you agreed to come this evening. Your costume is simply smashing."

"Thank you. So is yours."

In actual fact, Mrs. P had costumed herself as a massive gray kitten. I think she was supposed to be a little baby kitten, but she was a large woman. I presume Edie Applewood, my high-school chum and Mrs. Pinkerton's lady's maid, had drawn the whiskers on her cheeks. Her gray flannel costume came complete with gray flannel arms with paws attached to her hands by elastic bands.

"Did Harold make your costume?" I asked, admiring the tail Mrs. Pinkerton held in one of her paws and switched kittenishly. "It's darling."

"Thank you. Yes, he did." She beamed at her son, who beamed back at her. "But come to the dining room, Daisy, and get a little snack before the rest of the guests arrive. I don't want you to be hungry as you work."

"Thank you. I'll be glad to have something to eat."

"I'll join you," said Harold. And he did.

Del said, "I'll just recheck all the hanging pictures to make sure they're secure." Del didn't like to eat as much as Harold and I did.

"Thank you, Del!" said Mrs. Pinkerton, charging across the ballroom, making a sharp left turn, and bounding into the dining room. "Just take whatever you need, my dears. Make sure it will tide you over until midnight, when supper will be served. Then everyone can go home."

Mrs. Pinkerton's idea of a snack consisted of a selection of little sandwiches ranging in filling from Aunt Vi's ham and cheese, chicken, tuna-fish, or salmon; various olives and pickles; Aunt Vi's potato salad, Aunt Vi's Caesar salad, Aunt Vi's Waldorf salad, Aunt Vi's Jell-O salad, Aunt Vi's cheese straws, Aunt Vi's stuffed mushrooms; all sorts of things to spread on all sorts of crackers and breads; and about a billion different kinds of hors d'oeuvres—including shrimp with cocktail sauce! By golly, I do believe Aunt Vi had used the *White House Cook Book* I'd brought home to her in order to create this particular masterpiece. Aunt Vi's cock-tail sauce was better than that served at the Hotel Castleton.

Harold agreed with me when I said so.

By the time I got back to my spiritualist's tent, I was stuffed to the gills and wanted to take a nap. However, guests had begun to arrive, so I had to remain alert.

Remaining alert was not, I discovered, a difficult state to achieve and maintain.

TWELVE

For one thing, Harold followed me back to the tent, and we chatted amiably for quite a while before anyone else came in desiring my spiritualistic skills.

"So," said Harold, patting his tummy, which was rather large, "I understand somebody did in that awful man, Grover Underhill."

I'd been taking my tarot cards out of their cardboard box, but my head snapped up at Harold's comment. "You knew him?"

"Knew him and loathed him. Thought you knew that from Emmaline's luncheon. Everyone hated him. Does anyone know what happened to him?"

"Well, I don't know for certain, but Dr. Benjamin thinks he was killed with cyanide."

"Aha. A woman's weapon, poison."

I frowned. "Why just a woman? If you're going to kill someone in church, poison's a heck of a lot quieter than a gunshot. Anyhow, tell the Indians in the Amazon or wherever they live who use curare to kill their prey how much a woman's weapon poison is."

"Don't get miffed. I suppose you're right. Hmm. Underhill was such a devil, though. I should have thought someone could have figured out a more gruesome end for him."

"Was he really that awful? I didn't know him, although I didn't much like him when I ran into him in church and stuff like that. Well, church is the only time I ever saw him, actually. But he always wore a frown, and he treated his wife and daughters like dirt."

"He treated his son like dirt, too, and Barrett was doing everything he could do to save the Underhill Chemical Company from financial ruin. I hope to God Barrett didn't kill him. Might just kill Glenda, and she's a good kid. Not that, if he did kill his old man, he doesn't deserve a medal rather than jail time."

"Really?" Harold had me interested. "Underhill's company was in bad shape?"

"Yep. Barrett and I went to school together, you know. We're friends." He must have seen my lifted eyebrows, because he said, "Not *those* kinds of friends. Friends-friends. Like you and me. Barrett's engaged to Glenda Darby, for the Lord's sake, and it's not just for show. They actually love each other." Harold frowned. "I suppose the wedding will have to be postponed because that bastard got his just desserts."

"Harold!"

"It's true. Although why anyone would want to respect his memory is beyond me. Anyhow, according to Barrett, Underhill was running the business into the ground. He made poor business decisions and refused to listen to anyone who told him so. In fact, he used to berate Barrett on a regular basis, and all Barrett did was try to steer his father away from making disastrous investments."

"Oh. Interesting. I used to feel sorry for Mr. Underhill's family, although maybe I shouldn't."

"Definitely not. They're better off with him dead. Well, except for having to postpone Barrett and Glenda's wedding."

"That's not a nice thing to say, Harold Kincaid."

He squinted at me. "Since when have you known me to say nice things about ghastly people?"

"Never." I chuckled.

"Darned right. Hmm. How could you kill a man in church and not raise a ruckus, I wonder, unless you used poison?"

After giving the question a moment's thought, I said, "I don't suppose you *could* kill anyone in church without raising a ruckus. I mean, people notice when other people fall over and die in front of them. Two months in a row, somebody's died in church, and both deaths created a ruckus."

"I suppose so. But think of the possibilities. How about loosening the screws in a light fixture and having a ceiling light fall down and crush someone's skull."

I wrinkled my nose. "Ew. That would be bloody. And noisy."

"Yes, I imagine it would be. Or perhaps some woman he wronged—his wife, for instance—might stick one of those long hat pins in his ear and into his brain."

"Or stick it in the back of his neck and penetrate his spinal column. I read that in a mystery novel once. Someone could do that in a pew during prayers, and nobody'd even notice."

"That's good. Or, if you wanted to poison the buzzard and didn't want his death to be clean, you could use...What's that stuff called? Oh, yes. Strychnine. Doesn't that cause convulsions and spasms and so forth? That would be good, and it would entertain the congregation for longer than it took Underhill to die, from what I've heard."

"Well, he did have a convulsion or two before he died," I pointed out.

"Good," said Harold.

"A poisoned dart!" I said, my mind wandering back to South American Indians.

"Excellent. Good use of curare, or whatever that poison was you said. Or some other quick-acting poison."

"Ground glass?" I suggested, beginning to giggle.

"Good one! Or maybe someone could pour gasoline over him and light a match."

"But we don't want to burn down the whole church," I said, trying to stifle my guffaw.

Harold didn't bother stifling his. "I've got it! Wait until he steps outside and gun him down with a Tommy gun!"

"But you might hit other people."

"Make sure he's with a bunch of other miserable creatures just like him, and it won't matter."

"Vitriol!" I cried, recalling a Sherlock Holmes story.

"Wonderful!" said Harold, laughing louder.

"Harold!" trilled a large gray cat from the entrance of the tent. "I can hear you all the way to the door to the ballroom. Get out of this tent, and let Daisy get herself together. Guests are beginning to arrive." Mrs. Pinkerton smote her son lightly with her kitty-cat tail.

Wiping away tears of mirth, Harold said, "Sorry, Mother. Daisy and I were just trying to figure out the best way to murder someone."

"Harold Kincaid, sometimes I wonder about you," said his fond mother, smiling broadly and making her painted-on whiskers twitch.

"Sorry, Mrs. Kincaid. Harold and I got carried away there for a minute," I said, wiping tears of my own, being extremely careful not to mess up Flossie Buckingham's hard work on my face.

"Don't be silly, child. I know you two are great friends. But people *are* arriving, so I expect you'll be getting folks in your tent soon. Don't forget. A dollar for any kind of reading you do, and it all goes to the Pasadena Humane Society."

"Right," I said, sobering as quickly as I could. Once Harold and I got going, sometimes we were hard to stop.

"See you," said Harold. "Got to get into my own costume."

"What are you going to be?" I asked him.

"A hippopotamus. I wanted to wear a comfortable costume that wouldn't squish me."

He was, of course, referring to his rotundity, which seemed to be growing. I expect he also wanted another use for however much gray flannel he'd purchased to make his mother's cat costume. I wondered what Del would be. I'd suggest a giraffe if anyone were to ask me, because Del was so tall and lean, but no one asked me.

Shortly after Harold and Mrs. Pinkerton left my tent, I heard the band strike up a jolly tune, "I Wish I Could Shimmy like My Sister Jane," to which I had the music in the piano bench at home. I wasn't sure what a shimmy was, but I imagined it would shock the parents of the children who did it. Oh, well. Children were shocking their parents all day, every day, in those risqué times, and we all survived. Or most of us did, anyway.

The band was good. After "I Wish I Could Shimmy," they rolled on in to "You Can Have Him, I Don't Want Him," another catchy tune.

After that I kind of lost track, because people started lining up outside my tent. So I put on my spiritualist's persona and went to work with vigor. I saw fortunes in the crystal ball for people who wanted money, and love in the tarot cards for people who were looking for same, and answers to puzzling questions via the Ouija board for those who asked them. The dollar bills began to spill over the top of the glass bowl Harold had provided for them, and I wished he'd come back and relieve me of them. Besides, I wanted to see him as a hippo.

Before I got that pleasure, however, I had to continue performing. Among the first folks to avail themselves of my skills were the two Underhill girls, Miranda and Millicent, both of whom were dressed as milkmaids. Well, I don't suppose people *had* to dress as animals. They both looked nervous as a couple of frightened cats, so I smiled to let them know I was on their side, whatever side that was.

"Good evening," I said, purring. Someone had to keep the cat theme going.

"Um..." said one of them.

"Uh..." said the other.

"Are you Miranda and Millicent Underhill?" I asked kindly.

"Y-yes," said one of them. She pointed to her chest. "I'm Millicent."

"And I'm Miranda," said the other one.

Couldn't prove it by me. They looked very much alike. Therefore, after offering my condolences on the loss of their father, to which they didn't respond, I asked, "Are you twins?"

"Yes," said Millicent. I think it was Millicent.

"I'm terribly sorry about your father's death," I said again, trying my best to appear sorrowful. In truth, my curiosity was avid. I mean, it had been less than a week since the father of these girls had dropped dead of cyanide poisoning in church, for Pete's sake, yet they were both here at a party. Yes, it was for a good cause, but still...

"Thank you," said Miranda (I think). "He was...Well, we're not in deep mourning."

I could tell that from the milkmaid costumes, but I didn't say so. Rather, I asked, "May I help you? Do you have a knotty problem you need solved?"

I smiled, but the two of them clutched each other's hand and stepped back a pace, as if they'd been choreographed. What did this mean? I couldn't even hazard a guess.

The two girls exchanged a worried glance and then walked haltingly up to my table. They shuffled in front of me for a second or two before I said, "Please, why don't each of you take a seat and tell me what's troubling you? I might be able to help you." I might not, too, but I didn't point that out. They sat, though, which was the important part, because they couldn't escape as easily as if they'd continued to stand.

Miranda (I think) licked her lips and glanced again at her sister. "Um...Anything we say here will be confidential, won't it?"

"Of course. My business is always conducted with the utmost confidentiality." Unless one of the girls confessed to murder. I didn't point that out, either.

They again exchanged glances. I was getting a trifle bored with the both of them.

My boredom ceased instantly when Millicent (I think) said, "Can you tell us if our mother killed our father?" Then they both shrank back in their chairs and looked as if they wished she hadn't said that.

Although my mind boggled, my spiritualist's pose didn't alter one iota. I was a consummate professional, I tell you. "You believe that to be a possibility?" I asked as I reached for my crystal ball. I'd used the cards with the customer before these two.

"No," said one.

"Not really," said the other.

Another exchange of glances, and then one of them blurted out, "But Father was so *awful* to Mother and the rest of us, I wish she had!"

Two heads bowed as if they'd both confessed to unmentionable crimes. Interesting. And what they'd just said also explained why they hadn't reacted a whole lot to my condolences. Shoot. Even his children had hated the man!

"Try to calm down, Miranda and Millicent. I'm sure your mother would never have done such a thing, but please allow me to consult my crystal ball. It can tell us the truth."

"You mean who killed him?" one of them asked.

"Perhaps not precisely who, but it will be able to tell me if your mother was the culprit."

"Oh." They commenced looking frightened some more.

Therefore, after making several mystical passes with my hands over the crystal ball, I pretended to stare therein, and said, "'Tis murky."

"What does that mean?"

"The spirits have to settle before I can read what they want to tell me," I said softly and, I hope, mystically.

"Oh."

So they sat and stared at me as I pretended to consult the innards of my crystal ball. Its innards were the same as its outards: glass. But I'd never tell anyone that. However, I studied it closely for the sake of my clients, and then pasted on a mysterious half-smile. "You need not worry," I said in my best, most purring spiritualist's voice. "Your mother is innocent."

A couple of expelled breaths from the two Underhill girls ruffled the deep crimson cloth with which Harold had covered my table. As one, they reached into a pocket each and pulled out a dollar. I considered and rejected telling them that one dollar for the two of them would suffice, mainly because they were helping the Pasadena Humane Society.

"Thank you," came a duet of voices as Miranda and Millicent (or maybe they were Millicent and Miranda) rose from their chairs, smiling. I was glad to have helped them smile, although I don't know if I'd lied to them. I doubted it. Mrs. Underhill didn't seem like the poisoning kind of female—and I'd met a couple.

I was about to get up and search for Harold in order to give him the over-full money bowl cluttering up my tent, but another person appeared at the tent door. This person, too, looked haggard and unhappy, and stood there, wringing her hands for a second or two before approaching my table.

Mrs. Underhill. Dressed, unless I missed my guess, as Alice in Wonderland. Interesting choice.

"Mrs. Majesty?" She licked her lips and continued wringing her hands.

"Yes, Mrs. Underhill. Please let me extend my condolene she was in a blue gown, a frilly apron, with her hair tied back by a blue ribbon. Interesting mourning garb.

She stopped wringing her hands and flung one arm up in the air in a gesture of dismissal. "Yes. Thank you. However, as you've probably heard by this time, Grover wasn't a nice man. In fact, I can't think of anyone who is actually mourning his loss, least of all those of us whom he browbeat in the family or at his chemical company." As I blinked in astonishment at her, she wiped her brow. "Oh, I'm sorry. I shouldn't have said that. I'm just so...rattled."

"I'm awfully sorry. Won't you take a chair?" I gestured at the two chairs in front of my table. "How may I help you?"

She lurched forward and dashed to a chair, where she more or less wilted, assumed a seat, and commenced burying her head in the hands she'd lately been wringing. My goodness. I'd expected to have fun at this party, but I hadn't anticipated it would be so fascinating.

After a second or two of convulsive shoulder-heaving, Mrs. Underhill dropped her hands and revealed a face as pale as mine generally was, and eyes that had black circles underneath them. The poor woman was clearly upset, if not about her husband's demise, then about something that was of deep import to her.

"I'm sorry," said she, passing a hand over her eyes.

"No need to apologize," I said, meaning it. "You and your family have been through entirely too much in recent days."

She gave a moan and a sigh together and said, "You have no idea."

"May I help you somehow?" I asked, wanting to hear what she had to say. Her daughters had floored me. Maybe this woman wanted to know if they'd done in their father. That would sort of cancel all three of them, as far as I was concerned, at least in regard to Mr. Underhill's murder.

"I don't know." Mrs. Underhill commenced chewing on a knuckle of her white glove, realized what she'd done when she saw lip rouge stains on same, and slammed both of her hands into her lap. "Anything I ask you will be in confidence, won't it? I mean, you don't tell people what happens in your spiritualist sessions, do you?"

"Of course, I don't," I said in a voice pitched to soothe rattled nerves. "If I blabbed, I'd be out of business in no time at all." I gave her a smile, which she didn't return.

"Good. That's good."

A spate of silence then reigned in the tent as Mrs. Underhill scanned her surroundings trying to discern, unless I missed my guess, if anyone else could hear what was going on in it. She ultimately decided no one could.

Then she blurted out, "Did my son, Barrett, kill his father?"

Merciful heavens, as Aunt Vi sometimes says.

THIRTEEN

"Y ou think your son killed his *father?*" Incredulity, thy name was Daisy Gumm Majesty, at least just then it was.

"No. No, no, no!" Mrs. Underhill said vehemently, albeit softly. "But Grover was so *awful* to Barrett, and Barrett was trying so very hard to rescue the chemical plant from Grover's mismanagement." She sat thinking for a minute and then said, "Of course, I wouldn't really blame anyone who worked at the plant for killing Grover. He was a horrid man." She'd been staring at her hands in her lap, but she lifted her eyes and gazed pleadingly at me. "I'm sorry, Mrs. Majesty. I must sound like an undutiful and unfeeling wife, but it was the truth. Grover was a monster of cruelty to almost everyone he knew. Unless they were richer than he." She uttered the last sentence with something of a sneer, and I remembered Emmaline Castleton saying just about the same thing.

"Oh, dear," I said, unable to think of anything to the purpose to utter.

"And then there were his women," muttered Mrs. Underhill in a bitter undertone.

Goodness gracious sakes alive. Emmaline Castleton hadn't said *that* about Mr. Underhill. My eyes opened wide. "His women? You mean he had...uh...affairs of the heart with other women?"

"Affairs of the *heart*?" cried Mrs. Underhill, still bitter. "Grover Underhill had no heart. But he liked to conquer other people, and he could be charming to women who didn't know him well. Huh. Most of them found out quickly enough what a monster he was."

"Merciful heavens. I had no idea."

"Of course not. No one except those of us who knew him knew about his women, although most of the people who were close to him knew him to be an ogre. His other women were generally shocked when they found out he didn't aim to divorce me and marry them." She sneered a bit.

"Oh." I honestly couldn't think of anything else to say, which is an unusual condition for the generally voluble me. My state of uncharacteristic muteness didn't matter, because Mrs. Underhill continued without my help.

"Grover was always a stingy, cruel man, but these last two years were worse than ever. They were awful. I don't know if he was sick or just decided not to pretend he wasn't a devil any longer, but it was almost as if he were *trying* to drive his business into the ground and make people hate him. I...I don't know what was wrong with him." She sniffled and withdrew a hankie from one of Alice in Wonderland's pockets. Wiping her eyes, she said, "But please tell me Barrett didn't kill him. *Please.*"

Fiddlesticks. Another plea for absolution for a person about whom I knew nothing. Of course, I couldn't offer absolution even if I knew the entire Underhill clan, not being a priest or anything.

However, that had never stopped me before, and it didn't stop me then. I said, "Let me consult the crystal for you, Mrs. Underhill. I'm sure we can discover some answers." Liar. But never mind that.

After a few mystical passes with my dainty spiritualist's hands—I made sure always to wear gloves when gardening, and I kept my nails manicured to perfection, buffing them almost every night unless I forgot —I stared into the crystal ball as if I could actually see something in it. I felt tension radiating from poor Mrs. Underhill, so I didn't keep her waiting long.

After a few seconds of pretending, I lifted my head and smiled gently at the woman. "You have nothing to fear, Mrs. Underhill. Your son had nothing to do with his father's death."

"Or Mrs. Franbold's?" she asked with something of a squeak.

"Your son is not a killer," I said, hoping that would cover all possible situations and scenarios.

She visibly sagged in the chair and let out a huff of relief. "Oh, thank God!" she whispered. Then she reached into Alice's pocket and withdrew a five-dollar bill. "Here. Please accept this for your help. You can't imagine how relieved I am."

"But the fee for a reading is a dollar, Mrs. Underhill, and all proceeds go to the Pasadena Humane Society."

Her mouth tightened in a grimace. "In that case, take this along with the five." And darned if she didn't stuff a ten-dollar bill and the fiver into the overfilled money bowl. "Grover was even cruel to animals."

"Oh," I said, startled.

She left after that, her shoulders no longer sagging. I was glad to have eased her worry, even if I had no idea if what I'd told her was the truth. Oh, well.

Again, I lifted the money bowl and made to rise from my chair, only to be thwarted by yet another soul seeking information about the netherworld, whatever that is.

I sat, let go of the bowl and said, "Mrs. Wright! You look...amazing."

And she did. If you've never seen a tall, thin, extremely rich woman dressed as Mary, hauling a white poodle along behind her as her little white-as-snow lamb, you've missed out on a worthwhile spectacle. And that's not even taking into consideration that the poodle was a standard-sized one and much larger than your average lamb.

"Thank you. Harold Kincaid helped me with this costume. And, of course, Carlotta makes a charming sheep." She smiled fondly down upon her poodle, who didn't seem quite as thrilled with the proceedings as her mistress. I'm sure Spike would have sympathized.

"She's adorable," I said. And I guess she was, for a poodle. I preferred my dogs to look more rugged and hunter-like. Spike, for instance, was the dog for me. Although, from what I'd read, poodles were bred to be water dogs for duck hunters and so forth. Spike could do his own hunting, bless him. Well, except when he went after the neighbor's cat, Samson. Then I was more apt to curse than bless him.

"Thank you. But I'm hoping perhaps you can help me. Mrs. Underhill told me you brought your crystal ball with you this evening, and I thought perhaps if you concentrated hard, you might see something related to Evans. I'm so worried about him. He's utterly vanished, without taking a thing with him, and I'm so afraid he's met with an accident or something. And if he *did* have an accident, wouldn't someone have found him by this time? His disappearance is too mysterious to bear."

Oh, dear. Well, why not? "I can certainly use the crystal ball for that purpose, Mrs. Wright." As Mrs. Wright seated herself and her poodle, being a well-trained animal, sat obediently at her side, I asked, "Do you have any idea what Mr. Evans did during his off hours? I mean, did he frequent the cinema or go to plays or visit friends?"

"I'm not altogether sure," said Mrs. Wright, who, like most of the rich women I knew, didn't keep tabs on her servants' recreational activities.

"Hmm," said I, passing my hands over the crystal ball and trying to look spiritualistic. I gave up on that line of questioning, and stared into the ball. Then I blinked and stared harder. What the heck was going on in my crystal ball, which had heretofore only sat there, a prop in my farce of employment?

"Oh, my," said I, astounded. But really. When you're accustomed to staring into a ball made of glass and seeing nothing in it but more glass, this evening the ball seemed to be performing rather oddly.

"Oh, can you see something?" asked Mrs. Wright with much more enthusiasm than I felt at that moment.

"Um...yes. I think so." It was giving me creeping willies, too.

But darned if I didn't see, fogged over by something, a stand of pine and fir trees, wavering there in my stupid crystal ball! Whatever did this mean? Whatever it meant, I didn't like it. I felt rather as I had the one time in my spiritualistic career when an honest-to-God ghost had shown up at a séance. This wasn't fair. It wasn't right. It was...weird.

"It's showing me trees," I whispered, for once not having to feign a low, purring spiritualist voice. "I...I think they may be in a forest. They're the kinds of trees that grow in the San Gabriel Mountains. Or in the foothills. You know, near Mount Lowe."

"Oh, my goodness," said Mrs. Wright after I'd been waving my hands for a second or two and wondering what in Hades was going on with my heretofore unremarkable crystal ball. "I do believe I recall him hiking to Mount Lowe a couple of times. I know the lodge burned down, but I think he enjoyed the hike."

Interesting. Mount Lowe was a definite hike from the Wrights' mansion, but if a person were determined to hike in the foothills, he could take a red car to the end of the line in Altadena and then walk to Mount Lowe and even visit the Mount Lowe Observatory if he were so inclined. "Do you know if Mr. Evans had an interest in astronomy?" I asked conversationally.

"I don't know," said Mrs. Wright.

I ventured another question, "Is the railroad up to Mount Lowe still in operation?"

"Hmm. I'm not sure. I don't think so."

"Well," said I, "the ball is definitely showing me fir and pine trees." I squinted harder into my crystal ball, hoping in that way to make it behave. Didn't work. "Um...I think I see some kind of structure among the trees."

"Oh, dear!" Mrs. Wright clapped a hand over her mouth. "Do you think Evans is lost in the foothills somewhere?"

"I don't know. I need silence for this communication." I hoped she wouldn't take offense.

She didn't seem to. She sat there still as a carved decoy duck for another several seconds as I stared in total mystification into my crystal ball. The image of swaying trees didn't resolve into anything clearer, nor did the structure stuck in amongst them. After I'd stared for what seemed like forever, both trees and structure faded into the glass until all that was left was, well, glass. I allowed my hands to fall to my lap and gazed at Mrs. Wright. "It didn't show me anything else, I'm afraid."

"Oh, dear. I do wish the ball had been clearer."

"I do, too," I said in heartfelt sympathy.

"But perhaps that will give us a place to start. If poor Evans is lost in the forest...Well, I'm not sure what to do."

"Get in touch with the Altadena Sheriff's Station?" I suggested. "And maybe the park rangers? I imagine the Altadena Sheriff's Station knows how to get in touch with the rangers. They'll probably do it for you."

"Good idea." Mrs. Wright stood abruptly, her poodle with her, stuffed a twenty-dollar bill into the money bowl, and said, "Thank you so much, Mrs. Majesty. I think I know what to do from here. Come along, Carlotta." She and Carlotta, the extremely tall little-lamb poodle, exited the tent.

As for me, I sat in my chair, staring at my crystal ball in disbelief and unhappiness. Darn it, I hated when things I depended on went crazy on me!

A large gray hippopotamus appeared at the entrance to the tent mere seconds later. I glanced up at the vision and said, "Harold," in a weak voice.

Harold hurried over to me and plunked himself into a chair. "What's the matter, Daisy? Did another ghost appear? Good God, look at the money you're raking in! I'd better take that off your hands."

Ignoring the first part of his comment, I said, "Yes. People have been giving more than a dollar for my expertise the last couple of times. I kept trying to get up and take the bowl of money to you, but people persisted in interrupting me."

"I'll take it." Harold lifted a big canvas sack and emptied my over-full money bowl into it. Then he peered more closely at me. "Why do you look as if someone just hit you with a brick?"

After heaving a cleansing breath, I admitted, "I actually saw something besides glass in the crystal ball."

Harold's eyebrows lifted. "Oh? What did you see?"

"Trees. Pines and firs. Waving in a breeze, I guess, and with some sort of building with them. Unless it was a mysterious crystal-ball fog."

"Why the devil would you see trees?"

I shrugged. "Mrs. Wright asked me where her missing butler was. I stared into the crystal ball and saw trees. I don't understand it either." I gazed with a plea for understanding at Harold. "Honestly, Harold, all I usually see in the blasted ball is glass."

"I think you need a snack, Daisy. You're hallucinating."

"Am not."

"Are too."

We might have gone on that way indefinitely, but another person entered the tent, this one dressed as a horse, which was almost appropriate. "Daisy!" honked Mrs. Pansy Hanratty, one of my favorite people in the world. She always sounded as if she were speaking into a hollow tube or something.

"Mrs. Hanratty! You make a wonderful horse," I said, instantly forgetting trees swaying in my crystal ball, and trying not to laugh. If anyone in the world could carry off a horse costume, it was Mrs. Hanratty.

"Thank you, dear. Monty says it looks just like me." She laughed her huge honking laugh, and both Harold and I joined her. She might look and sound like a horse, even when she wasn't in costume, but she was a dear woman who performed a worthwhile service with her dog obedience-training courses.

"Mrs. Hanratty, you're a joy to know," said Harold, rising from his chair and kissing the woman on both cheeks. "Tell Daisy what you want to know, and she'll give you a forest setting."

"I beg your pardon?" said Mrs. Hanratty, baffled.

"Pay no attention to Harold, Mrs. Hanratty. He's only being silly."

"Am not."

Before I could respond in kind, Harold gave us both a finger wave and vanished through the tent flap.

"I love that boy," said Mrs. Hanratty.

"Me, too. He's one of my best friends," I concurred. Then I gave myself a mental shake and commanded myself to stop thinking about trees. "What can I do for you, Mrs. Hanratty? Want your cards read? Want to ask Rolly a question?"

"Actually, I want to know who killed that ghastly man, Grover Underhill. Is there any way you can use your skills to let us know?"

I blinked at her a couple of times. "Um...Not really, I fear. Rolly can answer specific questions about the person who's asking the question, and the cards can tell the person for whom the cards are being read something about his or her life. The crystal ball also only answers personal questions." Most of the time. I didn't say so.

"Damn," said Mrs. Hanratty. "I was hoping you could tell me who killed the son of a bitch so I could offer whoever it is asylum from the law and a lot of money. Whoever did it is a hero."

I blinked, not accustomed to such language from any of my rich clients. On the other hand, Mrs. Hanratty was a very special woman. "Oh, my. You didn't like him either?"

"Nobody liked him," said Mrs. H forcefully. "He was a brute, and he was unkind to his daughters' animals."

"Really? I didn't know that." Well, I did, but only second-hand.

"He killed their pet rabbit!" announced Mrs. Hanratty in a ringing voice. If the band weren't so loud, everyone in the ballroom could probably have heard her.

"He *killed* it?" I repeated, horrified.

"He did. And he made them take their sweet doggie to the Humane Society. *After* he kicked it downstairs."

"Good heavens!"

"You might say so. The Humane Society called me, because the poor animal—it was a Yorkshire terrier pup—had a broken leg. So I paid for its veterinary expenses, and the poor thing was eventually adopted by a nice family. But Grover Underhill was a wretched man, and whoever killed him deserves a medal!"

Well, there you go. I'd spoken to I couldn't even remember how many people that evening, and not a single one of them had a good word to say about the late Mr. Underhill.

By the end of the evening, I was kind of glad someone had bumped him off, just as Mrs. Hanratty was.

FOURTEEN

I didn't get home until nearly two a.m. on Sunday morning, which was extremely late for me, who generally trundled off to bed with my dog and a book around nine or ten. My coming home late, however, didn't negate the fact that I had to get up at seven-thirty in order to attend church with my family. If I didn't sing in the choir, I might have begged off, but there you go.

My family, unlike me, was bright-eyed and bushy-tailed that second Sunday in February. Well, Spike's tail isn't bushy, but he was as happy as ever. My eyes felt as though the lids were hanging at half-mast and someone had glued them together after throwing sand in them. I wanted to growl at my wonderful relations, unlike Spike, who only growled at stray cats and strangers. I tried to appear cheerful even as I gazed with longing at the butcher's knife with which Vi was cutting a cold baked ham.

"So tell us all about the party last night, Daisy," said Ma happily. "Who was there, and what did they dress as?"

"Oh, that's right," chirped Pa. "It was a costume party, wasn't it?"

"Mrs. Pinkerton was a gray cat," said Vi from the stove. "Harold made her costume."

A silence ensued, during which I decided I didn't really want to murder my family, in spite of not having had enough sleep. I could nap that afternoon, I told myself.

"You've about covered it," I said, hoping they wouldn't press me for details. Silly me. So I went into details. I didn't neglect to tell them about Harold being a hippo and Mrs. Hanratty a horse.

"Oh, my," said Ma. "You know, I'm not sure a horse was the best choice for her."

I squinted at my mother.

"Because she already looks like a horse?" asked Pa, who then laughed, jarring my sleepy brain into almost-overt rebellion.

"Joe!" said my mother, reproach in her voice. "I didn't say that."

"But you meant it," said my father, still chuckling.

I told myself I loved my family and didn't want to harm any member of it, especially not Pa, who was a practically perfect person.

"Here you go," said Aunt Vi. She set a platter of fried ham and scrambled eggs on the table, and I included her in my "especially not" category.

"Thanks, Vi," I said.

"But do tell us more about who attended the party, Daisy," said Ma.

So I did, in between bites of scrambled eggs, ham, and toast. Vi had even squeezed a bunch of oranges, so we had fresh orange juice to swill along with our coffee. I truly had a marvelous family. If I could survive the morning, I'd love them even more.

After I'd had a healthy glug of coffee, which didn't seem to be waking me up as well as it should have, I finished regaling my kin with a list of the party's attendees. I didn't notice the silence that had gathered about me until my mother broke into it.

"The *Underhills* attended a *costume* party? Less than a week after Mr. Underhill died at church last Sunday?" She was shocked. I could tell.

"Yes. I was surprised," I said. "At least Mrs. Underhill and her two daughters were there. I don't know if the son attended. If he did, he didn't visit my tent. The two girls were milkmaids, and the mother was Alice in Wonderland."

"Mercy sakes," said Aunt Vi, who'd finally sat at the table and begun eating her own breakfast. "I have to admit I'm surprised the Underhill family attended the party, although after learning more about the man, I'm not surprised his family isn't heartbroken that he's gone."

"Vi!" Ma exclaimed. "What an awful thing to say!"

"Well," said I, "from what I heard last night, I'd say she's right. Not a single person there had a good word to say about him, including his wife and his daughters. And you should have heard Mrs. Hanratty. Evidently, Mr. Underhill was not merely a philanderer, but he also kicked dogs and killed bunnies." I ate some ham and eggs as my family goggled at me.

"Good heavens," whispered Ma. "I had no idea."

"Me, neither," I admitted. "It was an interesting party, all things considered. The costumes were fun, and the band was good. Mr. Jackson's son played in it."

"That doesn't surprise me." Vi nodded. "I understand he even plays at the Coconut Grove at the Ambassador Hotel in Los Angeles. He must be a very good musician."

"He is," I assented, recalling when Jackson had told me his son, while allowed to play for the white folks who visited the Coconut Grove, was made to enter the grand hotel through the kitchen doors. There is no justice in this old world. Probably never will be.

"So who else was there, and what did they dress as?" asked Pa.

"I think I've mentioned just about—" And then the vision of pine and fir trees swaying in my crystal ball assaulted my memory. I couldn't admit to having seen trees in my crystal ball, so I said, "Oh, I guess I forgot Mrs. Wright. She came as Mary, and her little lamb was her white standard poodle, Carlotta, who's taller than any lamb I've ever seen."

"When have you ever seen a lamb?" Asked Vi.

It would have been a valid question had I not attended the Los Angeles County Fair at the fairgrounds built for it in the city of Pomona not long since. I freely admit to being a city girl and not knowing much about farm animals. "Last September," I told her. "At the fair."

"Oh, that's right. I enjoyed the fair," said Vi with a smile.

Sam had driven us all to the fair in his big Hudson. It was a long drive from Pasadena to Pomona, but the day had been of great interest to me, mainly because I got to see all the animals I never got to see on a daily basis. I mean, you could drive out to El Monte, which I'd once done not on purpose, and see dairy cows, but where else did you get to see goats and sheep and pigs and stuff like that? Very well, some folks in the rural parts of Altadena had chickens and horses and so forth, but Pasadena was a sophisticated city, where wildlife was confined to the occasional dog or cat.

"Anyhow, she was Mary, and her poodle was her little lamb. She must have taken the dog to one of Mrs. Hanratty's classes, because it was quite obedient."

"How nice," said Ma, who approved of obedience, both in dogs and in people.

"Does anyone know if Sam's going to meet us at church?" I asked, thinking I had some interesting tidbits of information for him, even discounting the trees I'd seen in the crystal ball.

"If anyone should know about Sam, it's you," said my mother with a twinkle in her eyes.

My own eyes still felt as if someone had tried to paste the lids together, so her merriment went unappreciated by me.

"Well, I don't," I said, sounding crabby to my own ears. Oh, dear. I really had to perk up.

"We'll soon see," said Vi. "We'd better dress for church."

That meant I had to tidy up the dining room table and wash the dishes. Feeling in as foul a mood as I could remember being in since the last time Sam and I had quarreled, I said, "Right," and stood, prepared to do my duty.

"I'll help," said Pa.

That was nice.

"I'll dry," said Ma.

That was nice, too. Neither one of my wonderful parents affected my mood one iota, but I'm sure that was my fault and due mainly to my state of exhaustion.

Nevertheless, my mother, father, and I finished our tasks in no time at all, and I retired to my room where my bed beckoned. I tried to ignore it.

Spike helped, mainly by keeping me company and being a cheerful and steadfast companion. Too bad people weren't more like dogs.

That February morning the weather was already getting warm, Februarys always being iffy in the weather department. Sometimes February days could be cold. Sometimes, as that day, they were warm. Therefore, I selected a mid-calf-length, cream-colored linen dress with a straight bodice and brown accents. Even though the weather was toasty, it was still technically winter, so I couldn't wear my comfy straw hat, but I dug around in my various hat boxes until I uncovered a cream-and-brown cloche hat that went well with my dress. Brown shoes and handbag completed my ensemble, and I was almost satisfied when I observed myself in the cheval mirror. My eyes appeared tired and baggy, so I dabbed some rice powder on the bags and decided to heck with it. Good enough was good enough. Besides, I didn't have to look at myself.

With a sigh, I led Spike from the bedroom where, lo and behold, Sam had joined the family. Spike hadn't even announced his arrival. I glowered down at my formerly faultless dog and decided I might forgive him, as my bedroom door had been closed when the intruder entered the house.

"'Lo, Sam," I said. "I need to talk to you."

"Good morning to you, Daisy. It's lovely to see you, too."

I couldn't light into him then and there, because my family stood about smiling at us. I'd give it to him later, though, for sure.

"Right," I said. "Will you please drive us to church? I'm too tired to walk."

"Happy to," said Sam, eyeing me more closely. "Late night?"

"Yes. Mrs. Pinkerton's benefit party for the Pasadena Humane Society."

"Ah. How much money did the fortune-teller make?" He headed for the front door, and my family and I obediently trailed behind him, including Spike. Spike was disappointed when I made him stay in the house when the rest of us trooped outside.

When Sam and I had first met, he'd accused me of being a fortune-teller. Fortune-telling was against the law in Pasadena, but the law didn't affect me, since I was *not* a fortune-teller. It took me a long time—years, actually—to convince Sam of that pertinent fact. The idiot couldn't perceive a difference between a tawdry fortune-teller and a profoundly solemn, if fake, spiritualist-medium. Sometimes I thought he still failed to appreciate the difference. That morning, for instance.

"My *spiritualist's* tent made a fortune, thank you very much."

"Good for you and the Pasadena Humane Society," he said, grinning like a fiend and opening the back door of his Hudson. I made a move to get into the back seat, but my parents and Vi beat me to it. Crumb.

So I opened the front door myself and slithered into the Hudson before Sam could pretend to be a gentleman. Showed him.

I know. How childish, huh?

Sam thought so, too. He was still grinning when he got behind the wheel. "I'm sure you feel better now," he said.

I huffed. "No. I don't feel better. I didn't get to bed until after two this morning, and I'm tired and grumpy."

"I'd never have noticed."

Except for a couple of chuckles from the back seat, nothing else was heard until we reached the church, which was right up the street from our house. Because I was still feeling childish, I opened my own door, hollered, "See you after church," and took off toward the door of the choir room. There I donned my choir robe, grabbed my music, and sat on a bench until I had to stand up and process into the choir stall, still grouchy. I hoped nobody would die that day during the church service, because I'd probably have a spasm.

Fortunately for me—and for everyone else in the congregation, given my mood—the service passed peacefully. Our anthem that day, "Love Divine, All Loves Excelling," was an oldie by Charles Wesley, although I think he borrowed some of the words from a play by John Dryden and Henry Purcell—don't ask me how I know that. I must have read it somewhere—but it was pretty.

As we sat in our assigned seats, Lucy Spinks leaned toward me. We sat together, Lucy and I, because we so often sang duets. I wanted to elbow her in the ribs, but restrained myself. I lifted an eyebrow in inquiry.

She whispered, "I hope nobody dies in church today."

Echoing my own precise thoughts, by golly.

"Me, too," I whispered back.

Mr. Hostetter glowered at the two of us, and we straightened in our seats and proceeded to act like little angels. Well, Lucy was taller than I, but considerably more angelic overall. I felt downright devilish that day.

After Pastor Smith had made all appropriate announcements and mentioned folks for whom prayers would be appreciated, Mr. Hostetter had the choir rise and sing our introit, the first verse and chorus of "The Battle Hymn of the Republic," in honor of Abraham Lincoln's upcoming birthday. Well, it would have been his birthday if he weren't dead. Oh, never mind. You know what I mean. It was a rousing tune, and actually perked me up for a second or two, so I'm glad Mr. Hostetter had picked it. Next week, in honor of George Washington's birthday, we aimed to sing the first verse of "A Mighty Fortress is Our God." I don't know how appropriate it was, but who cares? It was written by the original Lutheran (Martin), but I guess we share music from church to church.

The church service proceeded nicely, with no one falling ill or dying, which was a considerable improvement over last week's service. When it was over, I had a headache, probably from lack of sleep, but I still needed to talk to Sam Rotondo about what I'd learned the prior night about a variety of subjects, the main one being the poisoning of Mr. Grover Underhill. I hadn't quite figured out how to tell him about the trees I saw in my crystal ball when Mrs. Wright asked me to find her missing butler, Evans, but I'd think of something.

I joined the family in Fellowship Hall after I'd hung up my choir robe, more carefully than I'd done the week prior. It wasn't too wrinkled, so I decided not to take it home with me that day. If I decided it needed to be ironed, I'd take it home after choir practice on Thursday evening.

"Pretty anthem today," Sam greeted me.

I blinked at him, not accustomed to receiving kind words from this source. And he was technically my fiancé, too. Oh, well. "Thank you.

Pretty soon, we'll get into the Lenten season, and all our anthems will be dull and gloomy until Easter."

"Oh," said Sam, blinking at me in his turn.

"Oh, don't mind me," I said, waiving away a proffered cookie. "I didn't get any sleep last night, and I'm tired and have a headache. But I still need to talk to you. I learned quite a bit about Mr. Grover Underhill at the charity event last night."

"Great."

"Don't you dare be grumpy with me, Sam Rotondo. I also know where you might be able to look for the missing butler, Evans."

"You learned all this last night?"

"Yes."

"Do you want to just go home, Daisy? You don't look well," said Ma, eyeing me with worry.

"Yes, I'd love to go home. Thanks, Ma. I'm all right. Just really weary."

"You were up late last night," said my mother, practical at all times. "After dinner, you should probably take a nap."

That was the best idea I'd heard in a year or more. I told Ma so, and we all went home in Sam's Hudson.

FIFTEEN

S am wasn't as delighted to hear the dirt about Mr. Underhill as I
thought he should be. And he was totally unimpressed when I told
him I thought Evans was lost in the woods up near Mount Lowe.

"How do you figure that?"

Since I couldn't very well tell him I'd seen swaying trees in my crystal
ball, I said, "That's where Mrs. Wright told me he liked to hike. Maybe
he fell and broke a leg or an arm or got lost or was eaten by a bear or
something."

"All pleasant scenarios," said Sam, as sarcastic as ever.

"Yes, well, I told you where to look. It's up to you to get someone out
there to search for him," I said, fairly snarling at him.

"Calm down. I'll notify the Altadena Sheriff's Department and
they'll tell the forest rangers. If he's up there, we'll find him. Unless, of
course, he's been eaten by a bear."

"Of course." I scowled at him.

"And you say all the Underhills hated Mr. Underhill?"

"Every single one. Plus, the man was a flagrant philanderer."

"How alliterative," said Sam, making me want to smack him. I
chalked the urge up to my headache and state of weariness.

"Well, he was. That's according to his children and his wife. Widow, I mean. He also was mean to animals, according to his family and Mrs. Hanratty. He killed his daughters' bunny and broke their puppy's leg by kicking it downstairs."

Sam wrinkled his nose. "Over all, he sounds like a truly bad man."

"Sounds like it to me, too."

"Do you have any idea with whom he was philandering?"

I swear, Sam's grammar had improved tenfold since he'd met me. "Sorry. Not an idea in the world."

"Hmm. Well, thanks for the information. We'll check into it."

"Thank you."

Vi called us to the table then, and we sat down to a meal of cold ham, Boston baked beans, potato salad and pumpernickel bread. Yes. My wonderful Aunt Vi had actually made pumpernickel bread because I'd asked her to. I made myself a sandwich: ham on pumpernickel with brown mustard that was kind of spicy. Tasted really good.

"Thank you so much, Vi," I said, trying not to betray my emotions by bursting into tears. "This is so nice of you. And all because I mentioned that sandwich Sam had at Webster's lunch counter."

"You're more than welcome, Daisy," said Vi. "Anyhow, I figured you needed something to brighten your day. You've been looking like a storm cloud all morning."

That was it for me. I started to cry. "I'm so sorry! I just have *such* a headache, and am *so* tired." I wiped my tears away with a napkin and felt stupid.

But it was all right. My family—and Sam—were used to me, and I think they forgave me. Right after I'd cleaned up the dinner dishes, I downed two aspirin tablets.

Sam found me in the hallway and gave me a big hug. "You're not sick or anything, are you? You don't usually cry at the table."

"Sam Rotondo, if you're—"

"I'm not being sarcastic," he said, interrupting what might have turned into a rant. "I don't want you to feel bad. I hurt when you hurt. I love you, Daisy."

So I cried onto the lapels of his jacket for a minute or two. "Th-thanks, Sam. I'm just so tired and feel so bad."

"You're welcome. Take a good rest, and I'll bet you'll feel better."

I lifted my head and gave him a kiss. It was quite a delicious kiss, and it might have heated up some if my kin weren't in the next room. Then, as Sam moseyed to the living room and he and Pa chatted about whether or not to set up the card table and play gin rummy, I took Spike to our bedroom, removed my church clothes, climbed into bed, and slept for two and a half hours. I felt much better after I awoke from my nap. What was even better, was that I was able to get to sleep that night and slept like the dead until seven o'clock on Monday morning.

In fact, I was downright perky when I joined Pa and Spike in the kitchen for breakfast, which consisted of leftover fried ham, baked beans, and toast.

"I don't think I've ever had baked beans for breakfast before," I commented as I glanced at the part of the newspaper Pa wasn't reading. "They're good."

"The British eat beans on toast all the time," said Pa, who knew all about such things, his family having come from England in the early middle ages. I'm joking about that last part, but not about the England part.

"Huh." Although the *Pasadena Star News*'s classified ads section didn't generally capture my attention, it was what Pa had left for me, so I glanced through the postings. By golly, that morning I noticed something of interest. Darned if the Underhill Chemical Company wasn't advertising for help on their production lines. I read the notice closely, and learned that they were asking for young, healthy women to work their lines, packaging their chemicals. Which contained poison, I had no doubt. I wondered if their employees who worked the lines ever dropped dead of insidious poisoning, but wasn't sure whom to ask.

Hmm. Maybe I should toddle down to the Underhill Chemical Plant, which sat quite far south on Fair Oaks Avenue, and apply for a position as a line girl. Maybe I could nose around and discover something of use in solving the murder of the dastardly Mr. Underhill.

The chances of that might be remote, but nothing ventured, nothing gained, as the saying goes.

Therefore, after seeing my aunt and my mother off to work, going for a walk around the neighborhood with Pa and Spike, and attiring myself in a plain day dress appropriate for a young woman aspiring to stand next to a conveyor belt all day long and fill bags or bottles or boxes with poisonous chemicals, I drove the family Chevrolet south on Fair Oaks, way past Glenarm, until I reached the Underhill Chemical Plant. It was a sprawling place, with a dirt lot in which several automobiles were parked, although I also noticed a bus stop right in front of the plant. I suspected that's how most of Underhill's employees got to work, since I doubted the line girls got paid much. In those days, women didn't get paid as much as men, even if they performed the exact same job. Sometimes I wonder if that will ever change. Probably not. Not that I mean to be negative or anything.

Oh, never mind.

I left the Chevrolet in the dirt lot and walked to the front door of the plant. The big double glass doors led into a neat lobby, womanned by a person whom I didn't recognize sitting behind a desk. Not that I know everyone in Pasadena, mind you, but I had lots of friends with whom I'd gone to school. Not this girl.

"Good morning," I said, smiling at her.

"Good morning," she said, smiling back at me.

I'd thought to bring the newspaper with me, so I showed it to the girl. I'd circled the Underhill advertisement. I looked on the girl's desk, but saw no name plate. "I came to speak to someone about this job I saw advertised in the newspaper today." I tapped said ad with a nicely manicured forefinger.

"The line-girl position?" she asked, eyeing me up and down and making me feel as though I'd overdressed for this occasion.

"That's the one, all right," I said, trying to sound perky, although I'm not sure why.

"Let me call for Mr. Browning. He's the one who's interviewing applicants. In the meantime, will you please fill out this form?"

"Thank you," I said and held out my hand.

She stuck a form printed in bluish ink into it, and I wondered if the form was an example of a mimeograph. I'd have asked, but the girl was speaking into a tube-like device, presumably to someone at the other end of some kind of telephonic wire. Interesting technologies were in use in those days, and I knew nothing about any of them. Goodness gracious, but my education was limited! I'd have to visit the library again on my way home from the Underhill factory and search out information on new technologies. Perhaps the periodical section would have the most up-to-date articles. I'd ask Miss Petrie.

But that's nothing to the point. I filled out the form, which would have got blue ink all over my clean gloves had I not thought to remove them first. Therefore, I only got ink on my hands. Maybe this wasn't such a grand idea if even the forms the company used left evil residue behind. The form asked for my name, address, telephone number (if any —evidently not everyone living in the community had a telephone installed in his or her home), closest kin, and former employment history. That last question stumped me, since I had no employment history other than my spiritualist work, and I didn't think that would count for much, as it related not at all to production lines. Therefore, I left that part blank and trusted my ingenuity to come up with an answer should whoever this Mr. Browning was ask me about it. I signed my name on the bottom of the form where it was asked for and slid the paper onto the desk, since the girl was still speaking into the tube. Was that how this company communicated with its employees? Where were the telephones? They *must* have telephones. In fact, I saw one sitting on the girl's desk.

It rang, and the girl answered it. "Mr. Browning?" she said in a businesslike voice. A pause ensued, and then she said, "Yes," picked up the form I'd slid across her desk, and added, "Mrs...." She squinted at the form, although I'd printed my name legibly on the line asking for it. Perhaps she considered the name unusual, which it was, but that was no reason to squint. "Mrs. Majesty," she said at last. I got the feeling she wasn't the sharpest needle in the pincushion.

Then she jumped when I heard a voice come, loud and clear, *"Daisy?"* through the telephone.

The girl blinked at me and said, "Yes. Daisy Majesty."

I then got the feeling whoever this Mr. Browning character was to whom she was speaking knew me. I considered the few Brownings I'd ever met in my life and landed, plunk, on Robert Browning—no relation to the late poet and dramatist—with whom I'd gone to high school. He was a couple of years my senior and had graduated in the same class as my Billy. I hoped it was he, because we'd always had a friendly relationship.

It was Robert Browning! He opened the door behind the receptionist's desk a moment or two later and came at me, hands extended. "Daisy! How good to see you again."

"Thank you, Robert. It's good to see you, too." And I wasn't even lying.

"Come back here to my room. I'll have to ask you a few questions."

"Certainly."

I followed him meekly to a room a couple of doors down a long, ugly hallway, and he pushed the door open and gestured for me to enter.

"Take a seat. I have to interview you, although I'm not sure why because I've known you forever." He sobered as he took the chair behind his desk. "I was awfully sorry to hear about Billy's passing. I guess I was one of the lucky ones. I never even got off of American soil, much less made it to France or Belgium, after I enlisted."

He shook his head, and I, idiot that I am, teared up. I swear. However, the dismal truth is that I get weepy at any mention of my late, beloved Billy.

Robert noted my tears but tactfully glanced away. I'd hastened to grab a hanky from my handbag and dabbed the moisture away. "Um...I imagine that's the reason you're applying for a position here at Underhill. You need to earn a living."

Boy, you can bet I grabbed that rope and clung to it for dear life. "Yes," I said with a pathetic sniffle. "Without Billy, even though I live with my parents, I need to work. My father has heart trouble and can no longer do the job he used to do." I saw no need to tell him my mother and my aunt both had good-paying jobs, or that I made more money than both of them put together as a phony spiritualist-medium.

Robert shook his head sadly. "I'm so sorry." He glanced around his office as if he suspected spies might be lurking nearby. Lowering his voice, he said, "I doubt the Underhill production line is a good match for you. You're too smart to work on a line like that."

That was nice, and it allowed me to do a little snooping. "Oh? Why is that? Is the work tedious or difficult or something?"

"No. That is to say, the work isn't difficult, although you'd be on your feet all day, but I'm sure it's tedious." He lowered his voice still further and added, "But the truth is that Underhill, the chemical company, has been going through a lot of trouble lately."

"I know Mr. Underhill died. I was there in church when it happened," I told Robert.

I almost didn't hear his next words, he spoke so softly. "That's probably the only good thing that's happened to the company in more than a year, to tell the truth. Mr. Underhill was driving it into the ground, and he was driving all of his employees crazy in the process."

"Oh, dear. I didn't know that." Okay, so I'd just lied again. Chalk it up to snoopery. "Do you think there might be layoffs?" I'd read all about layoffs in the newspaper. Sometimes layoffs sparked riots, although it was difficult for me to imagine so staid a populace as the one living in Pasadena rioting over anything at all.

"I hope not," Robert said, although I could tell he was worried, because he had frown lines on his forehead. "Barrett Underhill, the late Mr. Underhill's son, is doing his best to clean up the mess his father left."

"Goodness. I'm sorry to hear about the problems. How many people does this plant employ?"

"Twelve hundred. Of those, over a thousand either work on the lines or in the warehouse. It's a busy place, and most of us want to keep it open for business. A lot of jobs are at stake. Plus, the chemicals we provide for fertilizer would have to be imported from other states if Underhill went under." He frowned some more. "So to speak."

"How does one transport chemicals and fertilizer and so forth?" I asked, genuinely curious.

"Train, then truck—or sometimes horse and wagon, depending on the terrain. The nearest manufacturer of the chemicals we provide is a plant in Ohio, so you can see that if Underhill folds, the entire state of California would be in the suds."

"Why's that?"

"Because transporting chemicals and fertilizer from Ohio is a lot more expensive than manufacturing the same thing right here in the state, and California produces more...well, produce...than any other state in the nation."

"Oh. That makes sense. But you say Mr. Underhill was ruining the company? Why would he do that? Do you think he suddenly went...Oh, I don't know. Crazy, or something?"

"He wasn't crazy. He was a louse."

"But why would he want to ruin his own business?"

Robert Browning heaved a deep and heartfelt sigh. "Resentment. He knew Barrett wanted to make upgrades in the equipment and spend some money on renovation. He also knew Barrett was right to do both of those things and was also a much keener businessman than he was. The elder Mr. Underhill couldn't see why he should spend money on anything but his own pleasures and comfort. Grover Underhill didn't see the point of making life easier for his employees. He'd made his bundle, and he bragged about having enough money to live on forever. When Barrett suggested the line staff should be paid more, his father threw an ashtray at him. Heavy glass thing. Made a dent in the door. Good thing Barrett ducked."

"Good heavens! I'd heard he could be...well, violent, on occasion, but I thought he only took his anger out on things like rabbits and dogs. I didn't know he abused people, too."

"Ah. So you heard about the girls' pet rabbit, did you?"

"Yes, and Mrs. Hanratty—she's the lady who taught my dog's obedience training class—told me he kicked the family dog down the stairs and she had to pay for its medical care."

"Yes. The man was...Well, perhaps it's an exaggeration, but I honestly think he was evil."

"He sounds evil to me," I said, meaning it. "Out of curiosity, has anyone ever been injured by chemicals in this plant?"

Robert's gaze paid a brief visit to the ceiling of his room. "Oh, Lord, yes. In fact, a line worker died from inhaling cyanide. Unsafe working conditions, according to the authorities, although there really aren't any oversight agencies for this sort of thing. Underhill ended up paying a huge fine and had to pay the family of the deceased a bundle in order to avoid a lawsuit."

"Mercy sakes. How much money is one life worth, anyway?"

"In this case," Robert said drily, "One hundred twenty-five thousand dollars."

Mercy sakes again! "That's a whole lot of money."

"I guess. But it was tragic, preventable accident, and it could have been avoided if Grover Underhill hadn't decided to cut all the corners he could cut in order to make himself rich."

"How sad."

"I'd say it was criminal." Robert's voice was hard and cold as ice chunks.

"So lots of people might want him dead?"

After gazing at me for a moment, as if he wondered if I were counting him among those who wanted Mr. Underhill dead, Robert said, "Yes. I suppose lots of people wanted him dead. However, I don't know who'd actually go out of their way to murder the man. That's a pretty drastic step to take."

"Could he have been accidentally poisoned somehow with a chemical from the plant?"

"My understanding is that he died of cyanide poisoning in church. Well, you said so yourself. While it's true we use cyanide in some of our products, it works fast. He couldn't have been exposed to cyanide at work on, say, Saturday, and then drop dead on Sunday. I'm afraid someone deliberately did him in." Robert didn't appear too upset by anything except that someone might possibly suspect him of doing the deed.

"I see." I sat there primly, my hands on my handbag, thinking. Finally I asked, "It's probably a stupid question, but do you know how many people working here might attend the First Methodist-Episcopal Church on Colorado and Marengo?"

With a laugh, Robert said, "Haven't a clue. Say, are you here to pump me for information, or do you want a job? You sound like the coppers who came here and bothered everyone."

"I'm sorry. I am interested in getting a job, although this one doesn't sound like a very nice one. But don't forget that I saw the man die. I'm naturally curious."

"Of course you are."

He knew I was faking, but he didn't seem to mind. With a grin, he said, "Well, then, why don't you pop by tomorrow at about eleven, and I'll show you the production floor where our line girls work. In fact, I'll take you on a tour of the plant, and then maybe we can have lunch together."

I felt myself blush. But honestly. Robert Browning, who was two years my elder, single, according to his bare ring finger, and quite handsome to boot, wanted to take me to lunch? I was flattered. And that's putting it mildly.

Out of curiosity and because he'd asked me to lunch, I said, "Say, Robert, are you married?"

"Oddly enough, no. Not quite sure why, although I..." His voice more or less choked to a stop, surprising me. "Um, I was engaged to marry Elizabeth Winslow, but..." He paused to swallow. "Well, she passed away last year."

"I'm *so* very sorry."

Oh, dear. I hadn't meant to stir up painful memories. I just wondered why he, a young, single man, wasn't married, when there were so many loose women hanging around. I don't mean loose in a bad way. Oh, bother. You know what I mean.

He heaved a gigantic sigh. "Yes, well, it was awful. She caught the influenza. The pandemic was long past, but that stuff is cruel. Elizabeth was so sick. Finally her illness turned to pneumonia, and she passed at the Castleton Memorial Hospital last November eighth. It...It...It is still painful to talk about."

"I know what you mean, and I didn't mean to dredge up awful memories." I felt like a louse, actually.

"No, no. I don't mind telling you, because you've also lost the person you loved most."

"Yes," I said, feeling blue all of a sudden. "Yes. We've both lost our loved ones. So many people have."

"Yes." He pasted on a smile and pretended to be happy once more. "But we can have a pleasant luncheon together tomorrow after I give you the grand tour, not that there's all that much grand about a manufacturing plant. Still, we can have a nice long chat. It will be good to catch up with each other."

"Yes, it will be." Pretending I wasn't embarrassed, I said, "Thank you, Robert. That sounds lovely, and I appreciate it so much." Then I bethought me of the tube via which the receptionist had summoned Robert to meet me. "By the way, what's that tube-like thing the girl at the desk used to get in touch with you?"

"Oh, that's a speaking tube. It's rather like a loud speaker." His mouth pursed into a grimace of distaste. "That's out of date, too, of course. I hope Barrett will be able to implement the changes he wants to make, if his blasted father didn't squander all the money he'll need to make them."

"Goodness. I hope so, too. Well, thanks for interviewing me. I appreciate it."

"I'm sure you do."

We both laughed as he escorted me to the lobby, guiding me with my hand on his arm. I took my leave of the girl at the desk, whom Robert called Susan, and I left the Underhill Chemical Plant.

SIXTEEN

As I'd told myself I'd do, I stopped by the Pasadena Public Library on my way home from the Underhill plant. I had a lot to think about, and I was pretty sure I wouldn't really find out anything of a crime-solving nature in the periodical section of the library, but it was worth a check. I was curious as to what modern innovations Barrett Underhill wanted to implement at the plant, and why his father had so vigorously objected to implementing them.

After a brief chat with Miss Petrie, who hadn't expected me to visit the library that day and had, therefore, tucked no books away for my family and me, I toddled to the Periodical Room, where I gazed about with bewilderment. There were so many magazines available, ranging from pure entertainment to scientific digests reporting on the latest in unpronounceable discoveries. Where, wondered I, would I find innovations in assembly line technology? Truth to tell, the subject wasn't of great interest to me except as it might help explain the death of a repulsive man who had unquestionably deserved his fate.

Nevertheless, in the spirit of detectival research, I reached for a copy of *Popular Mechanics* and a copy of *Scientific American*, gathered them in my arms, and headed to a table, where I sat and read the table of contents of each and remained completely befuddled. Mechanical stuff and I weren't the greatest of friends. Oh, boy, I wished Billy were still around. He'd been an automobile mechanic par excellence, and could have told me in a heartbeat what the newest and greatest inventions were and why they might be of use on an assembly line.

I did so miss my Billy. Oh, well. At least I didn't start snuffling in the library. I took a moment to feel sorry for Robert Browning. So many people had lost so many loved ones in the past few years.

However, after glancing at several magazines—it didn't take me long to give up on *Popular Mechanics* and *Scientific American*—I decided I didn't really care what innovations Barrett might have been interested in. Anyhow, I could ask him if I really wanted to know. I'd ask Sam if he knew. He might even answer me. Or not. I never knew about how Sam would react to me being interested in a case. In this case, however, I should think he'd be more forthcoming than usual, since...Well, since I'd witnessed the murder, darn it.

I left the library soon after my foray into the periodical section, none the wiser for my attempt at discovering the latest innovations in chemical plant assembly line mechanics. Or whatever Barrett was interested in. At least he'd wanted to pay the line girls a higher wage. That was a kind thing to want. He must have taken after his mother, since his father sounded as if he'd been sort of like a devil from the netherworld, and would have preferred having slaves rather people he had to pay.

But I didn't have much time to think about Mr. Underhill or mechanical innovations. When I entered our nice little bungalow, greeted with joy and exuberance by Spike, the cursed telephone was ringing. No one else seemed to be home—Pa was probably out beating his gums with a friend or seven—so I hurried to the kitchen and grabbed the receiver.

"Gumm-Majesty residence. Mrs. Majesty speaking." I had the part down pat, and always used my special spiritualist's voice when I answered the 'phone.

"*Daisy!*" wailed a voice I knew of old.

Good heavens, Mrs. Pinkerton's charity event had been staged on Saturday, and it was only Monday. What could have occurred to make her wail so soon after such a triumphant party? Perhaps someone stole the proceeds? If so, my bet would be on Mrs. P's stinky daughter, Stacy. I didn't say so.

Rather, I said soothingly, "Whatever is the matter, Mrs. Pinkerton?"

"It's *Stacy!*" Mrs. P howled a trifle less shrilly.

Aha! Perhaps the brat *had* stolen the charity proceeds. Rather than ask if that were so, I said in a gentle voice, "Whatever can be the matter with Stacy? I thought she was firmly attached to the Salvation Army and dedicating herself to doing good works." Even saying those words made me want to gag, but I pretended otherwise.

"She has! But that's the problem. She's gone and got herself engaged to a *private!*"

"A private?" My brain froze for a moment before understanding struck, not unlike a sledgehammer. "Oh, you mean a private in the Salvation Army?"

"*Yes!*"

Well, thought I, she could probably do worse. On the other hand, we were discussing Stacy Kincaid here, so perhaps Mrs. P had a point. I asked quietly, "Have you met the gentleman in whom she's interested?"

"Yes! And he's no gentleman!" shrieked Mrs. P.

I pulled the receiver away from my ear and shook my head. Her shriek had gone straight through my brain and, I'm sure, burrowed a tunnel through it. "Um, do you suspect him of..." Of what? Who'd want Stacy? Silly question, Daisy Gumm Majesty. "Of being a fortune-hunter or something along those lines?"

"*Yes!*"

Glad I hadn't yet put the receiver to my ear once more, I tried to lead by example and spoke softly. Mind you, I'd tried this trick time out of mind, and it had never worked yet. "What makes you think so?"

Didn't work this time, either. "He's a *rat!*"

Not, in fact, unlike Mrs. Pinkerton's first husband and father of her children, Mr. Eustace Kincaid, who'd married Mrs. P for her money. I didn't say that, either. "What makes you think so?"

"I can tell," said Mrs. P, her voice dropping to a lethal whisper. "I can *tell*."

Which didn't clear up the matter one bit, at least for me. "In what way? What makes you say that?"

"He tries to ingratiate himself. He's...he's...he's *awful*. He slithers."

Which would make him more like a snake than a rat, although I kept that thought to myself as well. It only occurred to me then that I hadn't bothered to shoo our party-line neighbors off the wire, should any of them be listening in. Oh, well. Too late now. They could be entertained for free. "Very well. He's too...oily?"

"Yes!"

"What's the gent—er, I mean, what's the man's name?"

"Percival. Terrible name."

"What's his last name?" I couldn't argue with her about the moniker, since I didn't much care for the name Percival either, although I couldn't see that his name was the poor fellow's fault, but that of his parents.

"Petrie," said Mrs. Pinkerton, making me blink. "Percival Petrie. I'm sure there's something wrong with him, Daisy. I *know* it!"

Given that name, perhaps the woman wasn't as wrong as she usually was. The very name Petrie, except when referring to my favorite librarian, conjured up extremely bad memories. I'd met a couple of truly evil Petries not long since.

"Hmm. I might be able to get some information about him, Mrs. Pinkerton," I told the woman.

"Information? Well, of course you can! I need to consult with Rolly! Soon!"

Oh, brother. What I'd been thinking was that I could make another trip to the Pasadena Public Library and ask Miss Petrie if she had a snake of a relative named Percival. She had a whole bunch of awful relations who shared her last name. They came from the bad side of the family. Miss Petrie came from the good side. Both sides had originated in Oklahoma, if anyone cares.

In what I knew to be a futile effort to make Mrs. Pinkerton understand something she didn't want to understand, I softly said, "You know

Rolly can't answer questions about anyone other than the person asking the question, Mrs. Pinkerton."

A sob smote my ear. I dared press the receiver to said ear, thinking that if she had taken to crying, she wouldn't be hollering.

"I know. I know. But please, Daisy, can't you come over and bring the Ouija board. I really need Rolly's guidance. And please bring the tarot cards, too. At least they might be able to predict chaos or happiness in my future."

Heck, even without Rolly, the Ouija board, or my tarot cards, I could predict Mrs. P's future. It would be full of hysteria over nothing and lots of good food cooked by my aunt. Well, she did have a burden to bear in the person of her daughter, but she ought to be used to Stacy by this time. I'd probably feel differently if I had a wayward child of my own, not that I ever would.

Unless Sam and I....

Pooh. Forget that.

"I can come over in about forty-five minutes, Mrs. Pinkerton. Will that be all right with you?"

"Oh, *thank* you, Daisy!" She hung up her receiver.

With a profound sigh, I did likewise.

What I'd wanted to do when I got home from the library was take Spike for a walk, build a sandwich for lunch and read for a while. However, duty—and money—called, so I put on more comfy shoes, walked Spike around the block rather than taking him for a long happy meander through the neighborhood, came home, took off my line-girl-interview dress, and looked in my closet.

The third week in February remained a trifle warmish, but it was still technically winter, so I chose to dress accordingly, in a lightweight brown-checked day dress that came down to just above my ankles. It had a darker brown belt that tied at my hip, and dark brown trim. Naturally, I'd made the dress myself. I'd made Ma one just like it, what's more. Because I had so much brown-checked fabric left over from those two dresses, I'd asked Vi if she'd like one, too, but she said she though the three of us dressing alike might be a bit much, so I made my sister

Daphne one instead. I'd given it to her for Christmas, and she'd liked it, so everything worked out all right.

After arming myself with my brown cloche hat, brown gloves, brown shoes and flesh-toned stockings, which weren't considered nearly as shocking as they once were, I gave Spike one last hug, tossed him a peanut-butter cookie, which was wrong of me, and left for Mrs. Pinkerton's house.

Once there, I endured a fit of tears from Mrs. P, called upon Rolly to tell her what he always told her—the only thing she could do for her daughter was love her, if possible (a daunting prospect, at least from my perspective)—and not to tell Stacy how much she disliked Stacy's choice in men. Rolly gently reminded her how Stacy had rebelled a couple of years prior when Mrs. P had violently objected to an infatuation of Stacy's, which had just sent Stacy storming back to the speakeasy in which the infatuation lingered. That particular evildoer, a fellow named Jinx Jenkins, had been murdered in prison not long back. He had, according to Sam Rotondo, been "shanked," a shank being a prison-made knife. Stacy had adored the low life, and it sounded to me as if she still did. Not that I should judge or anything, judgment being supposedly left up to God.

"Oh, dear," whimpered Mrs. P when Rolly mentioned Jenkins. "But how can I pretend to like this Percival fellow when I don't like him at all? I think he's as awful as that other awful man."

Rolly told her that she needn't pretend to like him, but she should be civil to him and not berate him in Stacy's presence. To do that would to drive Stacy more firmly into his arms, according to Rolly. And me, but since Rolly and I are one, that goes without saying, even though I said it anyway. Oh, never mind.

After consorting with Rolly via the Ouija board, I dealt out a tree-of-life pattern with my tatty tarot deck. I was rather disappointed to see the devil and the number of swords, including the ten and three of swords, appear in my spread, those symbols being the least happy ones in the arcana. Nevertheless, I attempted to interpret as rosy a future as I could, given the cards staring me in the face. It probably didn't matter since, even though I'd been dealing tarot for Mrs. Pinkerton for more than half my life, she still knew nothing about the tarot symbols or what they represented. Other people's deliberate ignorance was a blessing in my line of work.

If I believed in the tarot, I'd have said Mrs. P was in for a rugged road for a few months, but I don't believe in the tarot, and I didn't tell her that. And please don't remind me about those stupid trees I saw swaying my crystal ball or the ghost who popped up at one of my séances. Those were both flukes of something or other, and I *still* don't believe in spiritualism. Really. Honestly.

Oh, never mind again.

After parting with a tearful Mrs. Pinkerton, I decided to mosey down the hallway to the kitchen and have a chat with Vi, if she was in the mood for a chat.

I pushed the swing door gently, hoping to gauge Vi's mood before interrupting her. She was singing "Yes! We Have No Bananas," so I assumed her mood was happy, and entered her realm. "Hey, Vi," said I to her back as she kneaded a mound of dough on a floury breadboard.

She didn't appear to have been startled by my sudden appearance, because she smiled as she turned to me. "Good morning, Daisy! I hope you succeeded in calming Mrs. Pinkerton down some."

I sank into a kitchen chair and said, "I don't know. Evidently Stacy has become enamored of some fellow from the Salvation Army, and Mrs. P's in a twitch about it."

"Oh, don't I know it. She's been in here crying at *me*, believe it or not. I've not met the lad, so I have no opinion on the matter, but..." Her words trailed off.

"But given Stacy's usual taste, he's probably a gigolo or a punk or something of the like."

With a squint and a frown, Vi said, "I don't even know what those words mean, Daisy Majesty. I swear, you young people and your slang! It's disgraceful. In my day, we didn't use words like that."

"No, you probably had words of your own. A gigolo is a man who lives off women, and a punk is a hoodlum. That's a criminal to you, Vi."

137

"I know what a hoodlum is," Vi said with a sharp note in her voice. She glanced at the clock on the wall. "It's past noon, Daisy. Are you hungry? Mrs. P is going out to take luncheon with some of her friends and will then attend a meeting of the Women's Hospital board of directors—although I can't imagine her being of much practical use in a hospital board meeting."

"Me, either."

Vi and I both chuckled.

"But if it's not any trouble, I'd love some lunch. It's almost one, and I'm hungry."

"At least you're eating again," said Vi with a sniff.

"Let's not go into that again, please," I begged. After Billy's death, I couldn't eat. People—among them my parents, Harold Kincaid, Aunt Vi, Sam Rotondo, and several others—told me I looked downright skeletal, although I'm not sure about that. I do know I lost a good deal of weight, which hadn't yet caught up with me. That was a good thing, since women were supposed to be bone-thin and look like boys in those days. Nevertheless, it was kind of nice to feel hunger again now and then.

"Lunch is no problem. Let me get this dough into a greased bowl and slap a damp towel over it, and I'll wash up and fetch you up a special salmagundi salad. There's lots left in the refrigerator."

"Whatever is a salmagundi salad?"

"It's just a mix of chicken and eggs and lettuce. And a little bacon. I use a French dressing on mine because I always have some handy in the Frigidaire."

"I don't think you've ever served it to us at home."

Vi gave me a speaking look. "And just how do you think your family would react if I fed them a salad for dinner?"

"You feed us salads for dinner all the time."

"Not a salad all by itself. But *this* salad is a meal in itself."

"Oh." Truth to tell, I wasn't sure I wanted a mere salad for lunch, but I could always fix myself a ham sandwich at home should I still be hungry after dining on Vi's concoction.

Being hungry was the very last thing I was after I (almost) finished the gigantic salad, complete with chicken chunks, boiled egg chunks, bacon chunks, bleu-cheese chunks, and avocado chunks Vi fed me. And delicious? Oh, my goodness gracious!

"Vi, I think this would make a spectacular Sunday dinner for the family," I told her as I struggled with the last bites of bleu cheese, a delicacy we Gumms and Majestys didn't often get to eat.

"Do you really? You don't think your father or Sam would mind?"

Sam? Why was she talking about Sam as if he lived with us? Of course, he nearly did, but I still didn't approve of Vi speaking of him as if he were a member of the family. I decided I'd best not tell Vi that. "How could they possibly mind? Especially if you serve these perfectly delicious dinner rolls with the salad. Heck, there's enough meat and eggs and cheese in with the lettuce to feed an army!"

"Hmm. Well, I guess I'll have to try it. Maybe next Sunday."

"Wonderful idea!" The notion of dining on this spectacular salad again so soon pleased me greatly, and it was a satisfied Daisy Gumm Majesty who waddled from Mrs. Pinkerton's house approximately an hour and a half after I'd gracefully wafted into it.

SEVENTEEN

y gratified state lasted until I entered our Marengo bungalow, greeted Spike, and saw my father standing before me with a piece of paper in his hand. He had a slight frown on his face, which didn't seem right to me.

I rose with a grunt from petting Spike. "What's the matter, Pa?"

"I don't know. Here's a message for you. It's from the Underhill Chemical Company. Did you really go down there and apply for a job today?"

Oh, dear. I should have known I couldn't keep such a flagrant bit of nosiness a secret.

"Yes, I did. But I don't really want a job there."

Pa tilted his head and gazed at me squintily. "No. Really? I thought perhaps you were giving up spiritualism."

"There's no need for sarcasm," I told him. "I just thought I might get...well, a little information from the horse's mouth, so to speak, if I went down there and applied for the job opening I saw advertised in the *Star News* this morning."

"You don't think Sam and the Pasadena Police Department are capable of solving Mr. Underhill's murder without your help?"

Pooh. Pa was unhappy with me. I hated when that happened. My father was such an easy-going, kind-hearted man, I felt like a failure when I disappointed him. I took the message from him and read it. "Hmm. Wonder who Mr. Stephen Tiefel is."

"Someone who interviews people for the Underhill Company, I gather," said Pa.

I felt guilty and sad. Peering up at my wonderful father, I said, "I'm sorry, Pa. You're right. I should leave everything to the Pasadena Police Department. I just thought that, since I know some of the folks who work there and Miss Castleton is interested because of Mrs. Franbold—"

"Was Mrs. Franbold murdered, too?" asked my father, clearly flabbergasted.

"I don't know. Sam won't tell me one way or the other. Anyhow, I thought I might get a tip about who hated Mr. Underhill enough to kill him." Then I used my trump card; it's the one that always flummoxed Sam because he detested it, and it was the truth. "You know, Pa, quite often people are more apt to speak to me than they are to the official police. They don't fear me as they might a policeman."

"Somehow, that doesn't make me feel better about you prying into a place that uses deadly poisons, Daisy."

He had a point. But what the heck. "Well, I might as well keep this appointment. Can't hurt, and it might help, if I can get something of interest to pass along to Sam. I don't aim to get poisoned, believe me."

"I'm sure Mr. Underhill didn't aim to be poisoned either," said Pa. "He *was* poisoned, however, and I really wish you wouldn't pursue this scheme of yours to visit the Underhill plant."

Oh, boy, he was truly unhappy with me. Feeling about two inches tall, I said in a squeaky little voice, "I'm sorry, Pa. But I really think this is something I have to do."

He only shook his head. "I'm going to the Hull Motor Works to chat with Gaylord for a bit," he said.

"Want me to drive you there?"

"No, thanks. I'll take a bus."

He didn't even want me to drive him to a friend's place. I felt like crying.

Instead of doing anything so pointless, I put on some comfortable shoes and took Spike for another walk. Both Spike and I felt better when we got home.

When Sam came to our house for dinner that night, I told him about the accidental poisonings at the Underhill plant, and that the late Mr. Underhill didn't want to initiate any improvements either to the working conditions at the plant or the betterment of the folks who worked there.

Sam frowned at me from across the table. "Yes. We know that. How do *you* know that?"

I heard a snort from my father, but didn't look at him for fear I'd see more disapproval in his face. "I chatted with Robert Browning today," I said airily. "Everyone at the Underhill plant seemed to hate Mr. Grover Underhill, so you have a huge list of suspects. That must be daunting, to have so many people wanting a man dead."

"We have our ways," said Sam, dipping his fork into the delicious chicken curry Aunt Vi had prepared for our dining pleasure that night. She actually had prepared it for the Pinkertons, but she often fixed enough food for the Pinkertons and us, too. Smart woman, my aunt.

"I see," I said, and decided I'd better just keep mum about my foray into the Underhill Chemical Company. Sam would probably erupt if I told him I aimed to return to the plant the next day for an interview with a fellow about a line-girl job.

Except for discreet munching sounds, the dining room was silent for several fraught moments. I scrambled to think of anything to say that wouldn't cause either my father or Sam to get angry with me. My mind remained blank. Sam would say that's its natural condition, but that's not true.

"Delicious meal, Mrs. Gumm," said Sam at last.

I let out a long breath. Good topic. "Yes, it is. I wasn't sure I liked chicken curry the first time you fed it to us, but I love it now."

"It's one of Mr. Pinkerton's favorites," said Vi. "It has a distinctive flavor."

"Where did he learn to eat it?" I asked, thinking that topic, at least, was safe.

"He used to live in London, and I guess India has had a great impact on England's cuisine."

"I didn't know the English had a cuisine," said Sam, sounding as though he were trying to be funny.

"I don't know if that's correct," said Vi. "But Mr. Pinkerton surely does love his kedgeree and curries and so forth."

"What's kedgeree?" I asked, glad the conversation was proceeding along culinary lines.

"It's a rice-and-egg dish with smoked fish and curry flavoring. I have to admit it's not my favorite."

"Hmm. Maybe you should try it on us someday," said Pa. "Just to see what we think."

"If you really want me to, I will, but don't blame me if you don't like it," said Vi with a grin.

"I'm game to try it. Daisy?"

"Sure."

"Peggy?" Pa glanced at my mother, whose nose had wrinkled. Not an adventurous eater, my mother.

"I like the chicken curry," said Ma and, hedging her bets, added, "if you have toast and jam available for me if I don't like the...whatever it's called."

"Kedgeree," said Vi.

"Right," said Ma.

"I read in an issue of *National Geographic* that people in India often use such pungent combinations of spices in order to disguise the flavor of meat that's gone off. I guess they don't have much sanitation or refrigeration there, and..." My voice sort of petered to a stop when I realized everyone at the table had set their knives and forks down and begun staring at me. Dang. Leave it to me to spoil the conversation. "Um...I didn't mean to...Um..."

"There is *no* need for pungent spices to disguise the taste of rotten meat in this house, Daisy Gumm Majesty," said Aunt Vi stiffly.

"I didn't mean that! I only thought it was an interesting fact—Oh, never mind." I hung my head and dipped up another forkful of curry and rice.

"Sometimes I wonder about you, Daisy," said my mother, making my head sink lower.

Oddly enough, it was Sam Rotondo who saved the day. Or the dinner, anyway.

"I almost hate to admit this, Daisy, but you assisted the authorities in finding the Wrights' missing butler."

My head snapped up, and I stared at him as if he were my salvation. "You're kidding!"

"Am not."

"When did they find him?"

"Only today. This afternoon, I think. Thanks to your tip about the Mount Lowe Railroad and surroundings, the Altadena Sheriff's Station set up a search team. They found poor Evans—his first name is Daniel, by the way—being held by some bootleggers who'd set up a still in the foothills. So they not only rescued Evans, but they busted up an illegal still at the same time."

"Good heavens! Poor Evans. I'm so glad they found him," I said, flabbergasted. "I didn't know we had bootleggers in our mountains. That's kind of scary."

"It is indeed," said Ma.

"Well, they're in jail now." Sam eyed me slantwise for a moment. "I also hate to admit that you might possibly be receiving a commendation from the Altadena Sheriff's Station."

"Oh, dear gracious!" Never once did I think those wavy firs and pines in my crystal ball would lead to a result such as this. "I'm...I'm...I'm astounded."

"You're not the only one." Sam's voice was intolerably dry. At least I thought it was intolerable.

"There's no reason to sound like that, Sam Rotondo. I helped, darn it!"

"How in the world did you think to tell the police to look in that area?" asked my mother, no longer ashamed of me, I guess.

Because I'd no more tell my family I'd seen anything other than glass in my crystal ball than I'd fly to Jupiter, I said with becoming modesty, "It was actually Mrs. Wright who suggested it. I asked if Mr. Evans was used to doing anything in particular during his hours off-duty. She's the one who suggested he liked to hike in the foothills."

"But you're the one who told me," said Sam, bless him.

"Good job, you two," said Pa. I guess he'd forgiven me for being an unsatisfactory daughter, too.

"I'm so happy to hear about Evans," said Vi. "Was he injured in any way?"

"He was all right, as far as his health goes, although he was filthy and hungry and dehydrated. I'm pretty sure the bootleggers would have decided he was too much trouble and done away with him before too long. He'd been tied up there for nearly three weeks, poor sap."

Sap. What an appropriate word, given the surroundings.

"I'm so glad he was found. Poor man. I'm sure Mrs. Wright must be relieved," I said, ignoring anything to do with sap.

"He'll probably have to stay in the hospital for a couple of days," Sam continued. "He had lots of scratches and bruises. I guess the bootleggers hit him on the head pretty hard."

"Poor man! I expect Mrs. Wright will pay his medical expenses."

"I hope so. She has more money than God," said Sam.

Not precisely polite, but he was right. "You know, I've never heard about anyone building stills in our foothills before. I thought only hillbillies in the Smoky Mountains or the Appalachians had stills."

"Nope. Thanks to Prohibition, people are setting up stills everywhere. Even in their own bathtubs."

"I've heard of bathtub gin," I said. "I remember you telling me it can make you go blind if you drink too much of it."

"It's true. People need to know how to distill spirits properly unless they want to get into trouble. Health trouble, I mean. They're already breaking the law." Sam drank some of the tea Vi made because she said it went well with Indian cuisine. Couldn't prove it by me, but I liked tea, so I was happy.

The telephone rang. Our ring. Bother. After heaving a soulful sigh, I said, "I'll get it." It was assuredly for me anyway. "Be right back."

After trudging through the kitchen to the telephone, I lifted the receiver and gave my standard greeting. "Gumm-Majesty residence. Mrs. Majesty speaking."

"Daisy!" cried a voice I didn't recognize, perhaps because it was pitched at an intensely excited level. "It's Vera!"

Vera? Who was Vera? I couldn't recall a Vera in my life. Fortunately, the caller cleared up the matter of her name in her next sentence.

"It's Vera Wright, and I can't thank you enough for telling us to get in touch with the Altadena Sheriff's station! They found poor Evans. He'd been kidnapped by a gang of evil bootleggers!"

Pondering for a mere half-second or so as to whether or not I should say I already knew that, I said, "Oh, my goodness, that's wonderful news, Mrs. Wright."

"Poor Evans was brutalized by those awful men, but they've all been arrested, and the sheriff's men hacked the still where they were making illegal alcohol to bits. Evans will have to stay in the hospital for a few days, but then he can come back to us. And it's all because of *you*!"

As much as I'd liked to have taken the credit for Evans' rescue, I couldn't in conscience do so. "Actually, Mrs. Wright, you're the one who told me Evans liked to hike in the foothills."

"Yes, but it was *you*! You saw those trees in your crystal ball, and they led the search party right to him! You did it!"

Merciful heavens. Those wretched trees in that stupid crystal ball had led the search party to Mr. Evans? I wondered how. But I didn't ask. "I'm awfully glad to have been of some slight help to you, Mrs. Wright. And I'm even more glad that Evans has been found."

"Oh, yes! The poor man. Those terrible criminals had him tied up for almost three solid weeks! They hardly fed him at all, and he was dreadfully dehydrated. The sheriff's team said it was a good thing the weather has been mild, or the poor fellow might have frozen to death."

146

"Good Lord. I hadn't even thought about it being winter. I'm glad they found him before anything worse happened to him."

"I'm so grateful to you, Daisy. You saved the day. You probably saved Evans' life."

I know you probably won't believe this, but I hated being given credit for doing things I didn't do. I tried to calm Mrs. Wright's ecstasies again. "Truly, Mrs. Wright, it was your mention of the foothills that saved Evans."

"Nonsense. It was you and your crystal ball. Griselda Bissel told me you're conducting a séance at her house this coming Saturday. Is that so?"

"Yes, indeed. I'll be there with Rolly."

"Oh, good. I'll see you then! Believe me, your kindness will not go unrewarded."

My kindness? What the heck was the woman talking about? I didn't ask, figuring it would do no good. She'd pegged me as a heroine, and there didn't seem much I could do about her misconception. She'd probably reward me with money, which would be nice, even if I didn't deserve it.

"Thank you, Mrs. Wright. I'm very glad things worked out for Evans."

"The best of the best," said she, and rang off in high humor.

Well. Glad to have been of assistance even though I hadn't been really, I walked back to the dining room, where everyone sat staring at the doorway, anticipating my return.

"That was Mrs. Wright," I told them. "She thinks I'm the reason the sheriff's search party found Evans."

"I think so, too," said Sam, almost surprising the socks off me. Not that I was wearing socks.

"Good for you, Daisy!" said Pa, making me happy even if I didn't really have anything to do with Evans' rescue.

"I'm proud of you, Daisy," said Ma.

"That's wonderful, Daisy," said Vi.

Spike wagged at me. Spike always wagged at me. Therefore, I decided to take Spike's wag to heart and not try to correct my family's misconceptions about my overall assistance in helping to rescue Evans.

There was an article in the following day's *Pasadena Star News*, telling the citizens of Pasadena and Altadena all about the failed bootleggers and how they'd kidnapped a man and held him for ransom. I hadn't heard about the ransom part before I read the article. In fact, I'm sure no ransom demand had been made, or I *would* have heard about it. Were newspapers always inaccurate like this? I didn't approve. Not that the newspapers cared.

The article also said that one Mr. Frederick Kingman, a member of the criminal gang, had died overnight of a heart attack.

How convenient for him.

My life seems so very strange sometimes. Trees, bootleggers...I mean, what next?

EIGHTEEN

The next day I again made my way to the Underhill Chemical Company, this time for an interview with Mr. Stephen Tiefel, who worked in the Underhill personnel department, and for a tour given to me by Mr. Robert Browning, and then to a nice lunch. I hoped it would be nice.

To tell the truth, I was a trifle anxious about that lunch. True, we were both single people, and it was also true that we'd lost loved ones. However, I was technically engaged to Sam Rotondo, even though no one except Sam and I knew about it, and I didn't feel quite comfortable taking luncheon with another young, single male when I was, in effect, an engaged woman. Bother. I could confuse myself more easily than just about anyone else I knew.

Once more I parked in the dirt lot, noticing the same thing I'd noticed the day before: not many automobiles sat there. I again suspected most of Underhill's underpaid employees had to take a bus or walk to work. The more I learned about Mr. Underhill, the gladder I was that he was no longer cluttering up the earth. How sinful of me, huh?

Robert Browning stood next to the receptionist's desk when I entered, and he gave me a big smile. "Good morning, Mrs. Majesty. Let me take you to Mr. Tiefel's office, so that he can interview you."

"Thank you."

I smiled at the receptionist, who smiled back at me, and Robert did as he'd told me he'd do and led me through the big door, down the ugly hall, and into another room, where a bespectacled man sat behind a desk, looking worried as he stared at a bunch of papers before him. He glanced up when Robert Browning opened the door.

"Mr. Tiefel, I have Mrs. Majesty here for you to interview."

Mr. Tiefel stood. "Ah, yes. Thank you, Mr. Browning. Mrs. Majesty, please take a seat."

He waved at a chair in front of his desk, and I sat and smiled at him, not sure what to do next. I mean, it wasn't as if I applied for and was interviewed for jobs every day of my life. This was, in fact, a first for me.

"Here's Mrs. Majesty's application," said Robert, handing Mr. Tiefel a sheet of paper.

"Thank you, Mr. Browning." Mr. Tiefel gazed at the paper before him through his thick lenses, blinking several times.

"When you're through interviewing Mrs. Majesty, please give me a call, Mr. Tiefel. I'm going to take her on a short tour of the plant."

Mr. Tiefel looked up from my application and squinted at Mr. Browning. "What? Oh. Yes, I'll do that. Thank you, Mr. Browning." His gaze returned to my paperwork.

Robert Browning patted my shoulder, tipped me a wink, and left Mr. Tiefel's office.

"Oh, wait! Mr. Browning."

But Robert Browning had already shut the door behind him. Mr. Tiefel said, "Bother. I'm to take you to see Mr. Underhill after we're through here."

"Oh." Heavenly days, why? I didn't ask.

"But never mind. I'll just tell Mr. Underhill to call Mr. Browning when he's through with you." Mr. Tiefel recommenced looking at my application.

Through with me? What, precisely, did that mean? I didn't ask that, either.

It seemed to take him an awfully long time to read my application. As I'd never been employed before, except as a spiritualist-medium, I couldn't figure out what was so fascinating about my application. However, I remained sitting and smiling and waiting. After several eternities of that, I cleared my throat, and Mr. Tiefel jumped slightly in his chair.

"Oh! Uh, oh, I'm dreadfully sorry, Mrs. Majesty. I beg your pardon. I got lost in thought for a moment."

It was more than a moment. However, I only said in a voice that fairly dripped with honey and molasses and other sweet stuff, "That's quite all right. I understand there are great changes being made at the company since Mr. Underhill's untimely death."

"Untimely," said Mrs. Tiefel as if he didn't think so. "Yes. Well, that's as may be." He squinted at me through his spectacles. "So you want to work on the line, do you? Have you ever done work of this nature before?"

He ought to know. He'd been staring at my application for what seemed like hours. "No. I need a job in order to help support my family. I'm a widow." I hung my head and tried to look pitiful.

"Sorry for your loss," said Mr. Tiefel as if he didn't really mean it, although I think he would have if he hadn't been thinking about other things. "Line jobs aren't difficult, although you'll be on your feet all day, and they're tiring. You'll work from eight in the morning until six in the evening. You'll have a ten-minute break in the morning and in the afternoon, and forty-five minutes for lunch at one p.m."

Lordy, that sounded like hell to me. "I see."

"You'll have to wear a head covering and gloves. We work with toxic chemicals here, so we all have to be careful, and we require that our line girls wear face masks covering their noses and mouths."

Whooey. Greatly daring, I said, "I understand there were some problems here before, but that they've been...er, fixed."

Mr. Tiefel grimaced. "Yes. Mr. Underhill wasn't...um...Well, never mind about that."

"He wasn't concerned about the welfare of his workers?" I hazarded.

Another grimace. "You might say that." He squinted at me. "Excuse me for asking, Mrs. Majesty, but do you type or take dictation? You, er, appear to be more of an office worker than a line worker."

Surprised, I asked, "Why?"

"Er, well, your general appearance and...and grammar, and that sort of thing."

Aha. Line girls weren't well educated and couldn't expect more out of life than working at a plant bottling (or boxing or canning. I had no idea) deadly chemicals, eh? Didn't sound right to me. Then again, Billy used to accuse me of having Socialist sympathies, so I'm probably not to be trusted on these issues.

"No. I'm sorry. I never learned any useful skills in school. I'm only fit for the lines, I fear."

"I see. Come with me, please, Mrs. Majesty."

So I went with him, out the door and down the dreary hall to another office, where Mr. Tiefel opened a door and ushered me inside. To my intense shock, Miss Betsy Powell sat in a chair in front of Barnett Underhill's desk, industriously taking down shorthand in a notebook. Both Mr. Underhill and Miss Powell jerked their attention to Mr. Tiefel and me.

"I beg your pardon, Mr. Underhill. I thought you were free to interview Mrs. Majesty now. I should have knocked."

"Interview?" said Betsy Powell, her shock as great as mine. "But aren't you a—"

"I need a job," said I, ruthlessly interrupting her. Impolite, I know. But I didn't want her to blurt out anything that might reveal my true employment.

"Oh," said Miss Powell.

"Will you please leave us for a moment, Miss Powell?" asked Mr. Underhill politely. "I'd like to chat with Mrs. Majesty for a moment."

"Of...of course," said Betsy Powell, fairly leaping from her chair and dashing to the door, clutching her secretarial pad to her bosom and gazing fearfully at me the whole time.

When the door closed behind her, Mr. Underhill said, "Thank you, Mr. Tiefel. You may leave Mrs. Majesty with me now."

"Very well, sir," said Mr. Tiefel, and he, too, fled, although he didn't look scared as he did so.

After the door closed behind Mr. Tiefel, Barrett Underhill smiled at me and gestured me into a chair. "I understand you're assisting Miss Castleton in her search for Mrs. Franbold's killer, if killer there be. Frankly, I don't care who killed my father. I'm only glad he's gone, although if Mrs. Franbold was also murdered, I'd like to know who did her in. She was a lovely person, unlike my father, who wasn't."

I sat there with my mouth hanging open, trying to find words in me somewhere in order to respond to this statement. "Um...I don't think they even know yet if Mrs. Franbold was murdered, Mr. Underhill. If anyone knows, the police haven't released the information. I...Uh, I was only interested in how your plant works, mainly, and to meet people who worked with your father."

He sat back in his chair and steepled his fingers before his face. "So you're not really looking for a position on the lines here?"

Oh, dear. What to say? What to do? I decided honesty, while not always the best policy, might work in this instance. "Truthfully, no. I'm mostly just trying to help Miss Castleton, even though I don't know the cause of Mrs. Franbold's death yet. No one has told me if she was poisoned or just...I don't know. Dropped dead of a heart attack or something, I guess."

"Thank you. I appreciate your honesty, believe me."

Did he? Very well. "I'm also interested in how anyone could get cyanide in order to kill your father. I...Well, I understand he was an unpleasant man, and I haven't yet met anyone who's sorry he's gone, but still...Murder isn't very nice." Was that weak, or what?

With a huge sigh, Mr. Underhill dropped his hands to his desk, sat forward, and said, "No, I guess it isn't. Life is sure easier without him, though. He was a dreadful man, and if he hadn't died, we'd probably have had to wrest control of the company from him by force, or he'd have ruined it completely."

"My goodness. How does one wrest control of a company from the company's owner's hands?"

"We'd probably have had to vote him out of office, although that wouldn't be simple, because he owned the majority of the stock in the company. However, I'm doing my best to bring the plant back into a profitable position."

"Um...How are you doing that? If you don't mind my asking."

"I don't mind." He smiled. He had a nice smile. Not at all like his late father's wrinkled contortion that used, for him, to pass as a smile. "We have a board of directors, and, except for my father, all of the board members want to bring our equipment up to current standards and assist our staff members with monetary recompense commensurate with their contributions to the company. To bring the Underhill Chemical Company into the twentieth century, as it were."

"And that includes the girls who work on the lines?"

"If it weren't for the girls who work on the lines, the company wouldn't be able to operate at all. So yes. That includes the girls who work on the lines." Barrett Underhill shook his head. "My father was not only as miserly as Scrooge, but he was wicked. I know that sounds terrible, but it's true. If you don't believe me, ask my mother or my sisters."

I didn't have to ask them; they'd told me, without any prompting, what they'd thought of the late Grover Underhill. "I'm sorry."

"Thank you. Still, I suppose the police need to investigate his death."

"Yes."

"Even though whoever did it deserves a reward."

"Oh, my. He was really that bad?" I asked, although I'm not sure why I was aghast. Heck, if anyone deserved to be dead, it was Mr. Grover Underhill, I reckon. To hear a son talk about his father like that made me kind of sad though.

"Yes," said Mr. Underhill, not mincing words. "He was that bad. He beat my sisters and me, he cheated on my mother, he treated his employees like dirt, and...Well, he wasn't worth the space he took up on this earth."

"Oh, dear. I've heard much the same thing from others."

"I'm sure you have. Well, Mrs. Majesty, I can't give you a job on the lines—you'd hate the work anyway—but I appreciate your efforts on my family's behalf. If that's what they are. I mean, I don't want anyone to think I killed Mrs. Franbold. I aim to marry her granddaughter, for heaven's sake, but I'm not sure I want anyone to discover my father's killer."

"That's quite frank, Mr. Underhill."

"Yes, it is. It's also true." He stood. "Here, let me see you to the lobby."

Whoops! "Um...I'm sorry, but Mr. Browning told me he'd give me a tour of the plant, if it's all right with you. Do you mind calling him instead of taking me to the lobby?"

"Don't mind at all. I'll have Susan call Mr. Browning, so I'll still be taking you to the lobby, though. We still use that antiquated tube-calling system, which will also be updated as soon as possible."

"Thank you."

"Thank *you*. I appreciate your efforts to help us. Really, I do."

"You're more than welcome." I didn't know what else to say. However, I did want to know something. "Is Miss Betsy Powell your secretary, Mr. Underhill?"

"Miss Powell belongs to the stenographic pool we have here in the company, Mrs. Majesty. She's been quite rattled by the two deaths in the church we all attend, as I'm sure all the congregants were. Not pleasant Sunday jollifications."

Did he really say jollifications? I guess he did. So I said, "Indeed not," and left it at that. Guess I wasn't going to be working at the Underhill plant any time soon. That was all right by me.

So much for that. I can't say that I learned much, although having spoken to so many people who worked at the Underhill Chemical Company solidified my understanding of how much the late Mr. Underhill was loathed. Not a single person had a good thing to say about him; not even members of his family. That's kind of pathetic.

Mr. Underhill led me to the lobby and told Susan to call Mr. Browning for me. It wasn't long before Robert appeared, smiling broadly, with his jacket on and his tie straight.

"Ready for our tour?" he asked.

"Indeed, I am," said I.

Susan stared at us as if we were a couple of folks from Mars. Oh, well.

NINETEEN

Robert Browning took me to the other side of the lobby from where I'd been to offices for interviews and opened the door there. That door led to a bleak-looking corridor, along which he proceeded to lead me.

When we got to the first door on the right of the corridor, he said, "Prepare yourself. It's quite noisy in here." And he opened the door.

He hadn't been kidding. The room into which that door led was enormous, and it was full of assembly lines. They weren't the types of assembly lines I'd seen in newspapers and magazines, because those had been photographs of automobile assembly lines. These lines were long and skinny, and each one had a moving belt on it with women standing on either side of the belt, each one doing something to whatever came down the belt. All the women wore aprons, face masks, and puffy caps. Not precisely my style. I was glad I wouldn't really have to work there.

"Mercy sakes," said I, rather at a loss for words for one of the few times in my life.

He grinned down at me and said, "Here. I'll show you what we do here and how we do it." He led the way to the beginning of one of the assembly lines, where a woman seated on a tall stool, wearing what looked like motoring goggles and with a doctor's protective white mask over her nose and mouth, pulled a handle whenever a jar came up to her machine. Some kind of creamy stuff shot out of the machine every time she pulled the handle and went straight into the jar. She never missed once while I watched her, nor did she take her gaze from her task to look at Robert or me.

"Maria Gomez is the machine operator on this line," said Robert. "Hers is a more skilled job than those of the other girls on the line who, as you can see, have their own tasks to perform."

I did see. Two women stood on either side of the assembly belt directly down the line from Maria Gomez, and like clockwork, they each grabbed a jar and screwed a lid on it. One woman capped the jar I'd seen filled, and the other woman capped the next one.

"You can see we have this operation down to a fine art."

"Yes," I said, thinking there wasn't a whole lot of art to it, but it was certainly efficient.

"You'll notice that other women down the line wipe the jars—you'll also notice that they all wear face masks and gloves, because some of the chemicals we produce are caustic and some are poisonous—and so forth, down the line, until the jar reaches the end, where it's packed in a crate. Twenty-four of these jars will fill a crate."

"And then they're ready for sale?" I asked.

"No, not yet. First a line boy has to carry the heavy crate to a capping machine."

"But I thought those two women at the head of the line capped the jars."

"They do, but the caps aren't tight enough to sell to the public. We have a machine that will tighten the lids. Then the jars are put on another line where they're washed and dried and packed in another crate. Then they go to the labeling line, where more people slap gummed labels on the jars. *Then* they're ready for sale."

"My word, what a fascinating process."

"I don't know if fascinating is the word I'd use, but it's efficient and it works. But our workers deserve more money than that miserly Grover

Underhill wanted to pay them. I mean, look at them! Most of them are on their feet for eight or ten hours a day. They should get some kind of compensation for exhaustion alone, if nothing else."

I thought it was probably a good thing it was so noisy in there that the line workers couldn't hear Robert talk about their dead employer. Not that most of them wouldn't agree with him, but still....

"You'll see two lines bottling this particular jar."

"What's in that jar, if you don't mind my asking?"

"Don't mind at all. That's actually one of the medicines we package. It's a cream containing a base of lanolin with a suspension of salicylate and morphine. It's used on patients with certain painful skin conditions."

The mere mention of morphine made me wince, but I tried not to show it. Morphine's the stuff Billy took to kill himself.

"Oh, my, I didn't know morphine could be used...What do you call it? Topically? And salicylate? Isn't that in aspirin and salicylic powders?"

"Yes on both counts. But we have laboratory folks who keep doing research on such things. Most of us, including Barrett Underhill, would like to do more along the lines of medical products. Fertilizers are important, but I think we're on the brink of major medical discoveries, too."

"You mean you have scientists who work for you? Doing research on stuff?"

"Scientists and engineers. They're both kind of an odd lot, but the world needs 'em, and so does the Underhill plant."

"Oh. I had no idea."

"Yes. We're not just a poison plant." Robert's mouth screwed up into a grimace, and I got the feeling he would be glad to have the company for which he worked producing more healing products and fewer deadly ones.

"I see."

"But come along. You'll see various products in our list being packaged on the various assembly lines."

We didn't linger by any of the other lines, but I saw folks bagging fertilizer, bottling rat poison, boxing ant poison, and canning a product containing lye.

"You probably know that lye is terribly corrosive, but it has some very important uses in a lot of products, including soap."

"I think I remember my mother telling me that when she was a girl in Massachusetts, her family made soap and used accumulated ashes to make lye, although I don't know how they did it."

With a charming smile, Robert said, "Our methods of producing lye are a little more sophisticated than those used in households, but the stuff still comes from ashes. Our quantities are larger, is all."

Just as I thought my eardrums were going to burst from the hideous noise in that room, we got to the end of it, and Robert opened another door, and out we went into the corridor again. That was one long corridor. What's more, it ended in a staircase.

"Very well, now we'll go upstairs and you'll see where the brains work."

"The brains?" I asked, feeling stupid and as though I didn't personally possess one of them. A brain, I mean.

"Our scientists and engineers who do research into our products. We also have a department that tests every batch of product we package for commercial use to make sure we're following the formula correctly. We only want quality products leaving the Underhill plant."

"I had no idea this business was so complicated."

"I don't know if complicated is the correct word. Complex, perhaps."

"Yes. I see what you mean. Lots of different steps."

"Precisely."

The corridor at the end of the staircase was much less gloomy a one than the downstairs corridor leading to that gigantic assembly room. This one had windows every few feet, through which I saw men in white coats and face masks dipping sticks into various drippy things and them slathering the drips onto slides and peering at them through microscopes. Brains, indeed. I'd bet anything *those* fellows hadn't loathed algebra in high school as I had. Worse, I hadn't understood it. But upstairs in the Underhill plant were dozens of men, and even a woman or two, who had clearly not had my adverse reaction to mathematics.

"And here we have a room full of chemists," said Robert. "Some of them are research chemists and some of them are quality-control chemists."

"Oh. There's a difference?"

"Probably not really. They're all well-educated men who fancy chemistry and who love testing stuff."

"Oh. I hated algebra. I'd probably have hated chemistry, too." It was a sorry confession, but I guess each of us is born with a certain talent. Mine was for spiritualism. These guys probably excelled at mathematics and chemistry, the mere mention of which—either one—made me feel queasy.

With another laugh, Robert said, "Me, too. I was good at business management, though."

"That's fortunate for the Underhills, I should imagine."

"Indeed. But do you need to freshen up before we go to lunch, Daisy? There's a powder room—What are you staring at?"

Staring I was, by golly. There, right in front of me through one of the convenient windows Underhill had provided their herd of scientists and engineers, stood Mr. Gerald Kingston in the flesh. He held in one hand something I think is called a pipette, and he was slowly dripping liquid from the pipette into a glass thing I think is called a retort. His reason for doing so was beyond my understanding. A long tube at the end of the retort dripped liquid into a bulbous glass thing that sat over a flame. In between drips from the pipette (if that's what it was), Mr. Kingston's lips moved. I'm no good at lip-reading, but I think he was counting, probably to accurately measure the length between drips from the pipette into the retort. If that's what they were. I didn't take chemistry in school, and I've always been glad of it, although I'm sure I shouldn't be. But honestly, if algebra had driven me beyond distraction, can you imagine what chemistry would have done to my feeble brain? It doesn't bear thinking of.

However, Mr. Gerald Kingston's presence as an engineer in the Underhill factory explained a thing or two, one of them being how he and Miss Betsy Powell had met each other. When I thought back, I realized that, while Miss Powell had been a regular attendee at the First

Methodist-Episcopal Church, Mr. Kingston had begun attending services perhaps six months prior to this date.

At Robert's question, however, I started slightly and resumed walking down the corridor. "Oh, I just recognized another member of our church. Mr. Gerald Kingston. I didn't know he worked here."

"Oh, yes. He's one of our engineers, and he's an excellent product tester."

"I see. Interesting."

"Maybe. I wouldn't want the job, but these fellows don't seem to mind being cooped up in smelly offices all day long six days a week."

"The offices are smelly?"

"Not all of them. Depends on what they're working with on any particular day. I noticed Mr. Kingston wasn't wearing a face mask, so I expect he's testing something benign today." He chuckled.

Hmm. But sometimes the things he worked with weren't benign, eh? Could he have...? But why would he risk his neck in order to kill Mr. Underhill when Underhill was already under such heavy fire from his own board of directors? Nuts. It was all too much for me. I stopped thinking and walked with Robert to the stairs at the other end of the corridor. We descended those steps, walked down the dismal corridor to the door to the reception room, he opened it for me, and I sailed through, ready for my lunch.

Robert escorted me out to the parking lot where, sure enough, I learned the only folks who parked there were the scientists, engineers, and executives of the Underhill Chemical Company. Those line girls deserved a *big* raise, darn it.

"What kind of food do you like?" asked Robert as he opened the door to his Chevrolet for me to enter. His model of Chevrolet was a couple of rungs above our Gumm/Majesty Chevrolet, but I didn't care. I loved our new (to us) automobile.

"I pretty much like all kinds of food," I told him honestly. I didn't add that, no matter where he took me to lunch, I'd almost certainly get better food at home because I lived with the best cook in the entire United States of America.

"How about Mexican? There's this place called Mijares that opened a couple of years ago. I love the food, although it can be spicy."

"I've been to Mijares, and I love it," I said happily, my mouth beginning to water as I contemplated whether to order an enchilada or a taco or a tamale. Or maybe one of each. Robert was paying, after all.

I didn't mean that.

Oh, bother. I did, too, mean that.

So Robert tootled his fancy Chevrolet up Fair Oaks, made a turn on some street the name of which I couldn't see, made another turn, and we were in the parking lot of Mijares Mexican Restaurant. I pretended to be a lady and waited for Robert to open my door for me.

We walked together into the restaurant where a colorfully clad woman—she wore a Mexican peasant blouse and big flowered skirt—led us to a table for two. Robert said, "Do you have anything a little more private?"

Private? He wanted to be private with me? Hmm. I wasn't sure about this. "This is fine with me, Robert," I said with what I hoped was a winning smile.

"All right," he said promptly, gent that he was. "I was hoping we could have a quiet conversation in a more private spot, but I don't mind."

So he nodded to the waitress, who left two menus on the table, Robert pulled my chair out for me, and I sat, still smiling.

"I love the beef enchiladas they serve here," said Robert.

"I don't believe I've had one of those."

"Have two. They're small." He grinned, as if he'd made a superior joke.

I laughed a bit to make him feel good.

He shifted in his chair and appeared nervous for a second or two before he passed his hand over his face and said, "I'm sorry, Daisy. I think I lured you here under false pretenses."

"Oh?" Good Lord, he couldn't be about to declare some kind of deathless passion for yours truly, was he? No. That was too stupid a thought even to warrant a second's contemplation.

"What I really wanted—No. What I really *needed* was someone just to talk to who might understand about Elizabeth. I...I just can't seem to get over her death. I feel as though a huge chunk of me was ripped out by talons or something." He laid his hand on the table and bowed his head. "That's why I wanted to get away from the crowd. Nobody else understands. It's true I received lots of sympathy at the time of her passing, but lately...I don't know. It just seems as though I should be over the worst of my grief, and I'm not. I'm just...not." He looked as though he feared he'd said something disgraceful or embarrassing.

"Oh, dear. I'm so sorry. If I'd known, I'd have—"

"No, that's all right. You didn't know my motives." He lifted his head, tried for a grin and almost made it.

Putting my own hand over his on the table, I said, and I meant it, "You know, Robert, you don't *get over* losing a loved one. I'll never *get over* my husband's death. But in time—and I know this from experience—a scab will grow over the wound. It will still hurt, but *eventually* you'll discover that you're...Oh, I don't know. You'll discover that you're enjoying something small that you haven't thought about in months. It can be...How can I explain it? The view of the mountains or something. The feeling of basking in a tub of warm water. That sounds silly. But after a while, and it may be a long one, not every single thing in the world will remind you of Elizabeth and your horrible loss. It takes time though. I know that from bitter experience."

"I hope you're right. I can't even seem to make it through a day without thinking of her every other minute or so. And each time I think about her, my heart has such a gigantic spasm, sometimes I think I must be having a heart attack."

"I know exactly what you mean. After my Billy died, I just stopped eating. The mere thought of food made me feel sick to my stomach. And there wasn't a single moment during the day when I wasn't bogged down in a pit of grief." I hesitated for a moment and then said, "You know, I think men may be harder hit than women when they lose a loved one. Women are supposed to be weak and emotional and so forth, and when we cry, people figure it's just because we're stupid and can't hold our emotions in check. Men are supposed to be strong and not feel things and show a brave face to the world. But you *do* feel deeply, and I know it. I have a very good friend who's a widower of maybe four years, and we've talked about this same thing. When did your Elizabeth die?"

"November."

"Well, it's only barely March, for heaven's sake. Give yourself some time. It's only been four months. *Barely* four months. Four months after Billy died, I was sick as a dog, and everybody said I was starving myself to death. But I couldn't help it. It was just awful. Billy's been gone for almost two years, and I still cry when I think about him." To prove it, I wiped away a stray tear.

"After two years?"

"After two years. It will be two years in June, and my heart hurts every time I think about him and what he went through. Oh, Robert, his last few years were so terrible. He didn't deserve that." I sniffled and had to dig into my handbag for a hankie, taking my hand from on top of his. As I proceeded to wipe my eyes, a figure loomed beside our table.

I looked up, smiling, expecting to see a waiter bringing us water or something.

It wasn't a waiter. It was Sam Rotondo.

I cursed myself as an idiot for not wanting to sit in a secluded corner with Robert.

Uh-oh. Sam Rotondo's gaze locked with mine, and he frowned hideously.

Oh, dear.

TWENTY

A s I sucked in a huge breath and wished I could disappear, Sam looked down at me as if I were a squishy bug he'd just encountered on his breakfast toast and said, "Daisy."

"Hey, Sam," I said in a voice that trilled a bit and sounded unnatural.

Robert rose from his chair and smiled at Sam uncertainly. "Detective. I didn't know the two of you knew each other."

"Yes," I said. "Sam and I are...old friends. Good friends. Really good friends." Oh, dear. Oh, dear.

"I didn't know you two knew each other, either," said Sam, sharing his scowl equally between Robert and me.

"Did you come here for lunch, Sam?" I asked, trying to sound bright and cheery and failing miserably. "If you did, perhaps you can join us, because you could really add to our conversation."

Both Sam and Robert eyed me doubtfully. I sucked in a huge breath of delectably scented air—Mexican food smells *so* yummy—and said, "Robert lost his fiancée last November, Sam, and he's having a hard time handling his grief." Golly, I hoped Robert wouldn't mind that I spilled the beans like that. "So I told him about how you and I have both had trouble with our own losses."

With a confused grimace, Sam stood up straight. He had been looming over Robert and me with his hands flattened on the table. "Huh?" Typical Sam comment.

Robert didn't appear especially pleased to have his secret tossed in Sam's face, but he made a noble effort. "I...I don't know what you've been through, Detective, or what your loss was, but I...Well, I wanted to talk to Daisy about losing my fiancée, Elizabeth Winslow, who passed away last November."

"Of the influenza. It went into pneumonia, and they couldn't save her at the hospital," I added, trying to be helpful.

"Oh. Is that the truth?" Sam looked at me, not benevolently, as he asked the question.

I'd have made a face and smacked him on the arm if we weren't in a public place and I didn't feel so sorry for Robert.

"Yes, it's the truth, Sam Rotondo!" I whispered. Loudly. "What did you think we were doing?"

He didn't respond for a moment. Then he said, "Well, if that's what you're talking about, why don't you do it at a less public table?" He turned and waved to the waitress who'd just seated Robert and me. She trotted over at his imperious command.

"Yes, sir?"

"I'll be joining these folks for lunch. Can you put us in a table that's more out of the way?"

The waitress, after a split-second of looking offended—for good reason, I fear—said, "Certainly, sir. Please follow me."

So Robert and I got up and trailed Sam, who tramped after the waitress to the back of the restaurant. I felt *so* stupid. The bad part was that feeling stupid wasn't a new sensation to me.

However, after some initial conversational fumbling, and with a few interruptions from the wait staff, Sam, Robert, and I had a pretty decent chat about our various bereavements, and Robert seemed relieved to hear his wasn't a strange or out-of-the-way problem. It was a bad problem to have but not at all unusual, especially in those days after the Great War and the influenza pandemic, when it seemed as though everyone had lost at least one loved one.

In fact, as we all finished our scrumptious meals—I had an enchilada stuffed with beef and cheese, smothered with a spicy sauce, with some rice and beans on the side—Robert said, "Thank you for joining us, Detective Rotondo. When Daisy mentioned a friend who'd lost his wife not too long ago, I had no idea she meant you."

"I'm not surprised," said Sam. He didn't even sound sarcastic. "I mean, it's not something you talk about with people you're interviewing, if you're a police detective."

Robert nodded and smiled.

"It's as I told Robert, Sam. Men hold things in. Women let them out. I sometimes think women have an easier time of it during periods of grief than men do."

After gazing at me for a second with his brow furrowed, Sam said, "You mean that?"

"Of course, I mean it! I wouldn't have said it otherwise."

"She told me the same thing," said Robert.

"Huh. In that case, I think you're right."

Robert and I exchanged a smile. Sam, I noticed, appeared suspicious of our individual smiles. I sighed.

"I'd better get back to work now," Robert said after a moment of silence. "I'll drop you off by your automobile, Daisy. Unless you want to interview anyone else, of course." He chuckled.

"That's all right. I'll take her," Sam said before I could respond to Robert's offer or laugh at his joke.

"But our Chevrolet's in the Underhill parking lot, Sam," said I.

"That's all right. I...need to tell you something," said Sam. He cleared his throat, as if he were nervous. I think he was just feeling kind of like a dog in the manger, if I understand the meaning of that expression correctly.

I decided not to argue, but to submit with as much grace as I could. I held out my hand to Robert. "Thank you so much for lunch, Robert, and

I really do hope that our chat did you some good. There's no way anyone can take away the pain, but...Well, you know."

"You two helped me a lot, actually," he said. "The pain's not gone, but I don't feel so much like a fool for feeling it any longer."

"No one can help feeling grief when a woman you loved with all your heart dies," said Sam, nearly shocking me out of my flesh-toned stockings. He said it in his usual gruff voice, but he meant it. I could tell.

So, evidently, could Robert, because he lifted his napkin and dabbed at his eyes. "Thank you. Thank you both."

Sam reached for his pocket, but Robert held out a hand and stood. "This one's on me, Daisy and Detective Rotondo. You've helped me a lot, and the least I can do is treat you to lunch."

It looked for a moment as if Sam were going to argue with Robert about the meal ticket, but I poked him in the ribs with my elbow, and he merely grunted and said, "Uh. Thank you." Then he frowned at me. But that's all right. Robert felt better after chatting with the two of us, and that's what mattered. And he had more money than Sam or I did. Probably.

The waiter returned for one last visit, Robert paid him, and we rose from the table tucked away in a far corner at the back of the restaurant. We walked to the parking lot together and Robert climbed into his fancy Chevrolet. Sam and I waved him away as he took a slight turn right and headed for Fair Oaks, where he'd turn south and head back to the Underhill plant. Sam and I didn't speak as we trod to his Hudson. There he opened the door for me and I climbed in, wondering what hell he had in store for me as he took the same route Robert had taken to get to the Underhill plant and my own less-fancy-than-Robert's Chevrolet.

But he didn't scold me. Rather, he said, "Talking about that guy's dead fiancée was the only reason you two went to lunch together?" I could tell he didn't want to ask the question.

I said, "Yes."

"But he's a young, good-looking fellow, and you appear to have known him for some time."

"He was in Billy's graduating class in high school. He went on to college. He was drafted but never got off American soil during the war, so he finished college and went to work at Underhill."

"Huh."

"That's all, Sam." I put one of my hands on the one of his that was closest to me as he gripped the steering wheel. "Honest. He said he'd never been able to talk to anyone about Elizabeth. She only died in November, and he actually told me he thinks he should *be over* his grief by this time. As if anyone could be."

Sam shook his head. "Sorry if I made you uncomfortable there at the restaurant at first. I was...um...surprised to see you with another man."

"Oh, Sam, you silly person. I've known Robert Browning slightly for years. He interviewed me when I went to the Underhill plant. He knew I'd been fairly recently widowed, and he asked if I'd mind talking to him about his Elizabeth. I didn't mind."

"Until I butted in."

"Actually, I was irritated at first, but I think you helped him more than I did."

With a startled glance at me, Sam said, "You do?"

"I do."

"Oh. Well, then." And he said no more.

Because the silence became uncomfortable after a few seconds, I said, "Oh, but Sam, I learned something today at the Underhill place."

"Yeah?" He'd started frowning, but I figured that was just Sam being Sam.

"Did you know that both Miss Betsy Powell and Mr. Gerald Kingston work at Underhill's? She's in the stenographic pool and he's an engineer. He was dripping something into a glass retort when Robert took me on a tour of the plant. The lines are all downstairs, and the engineers and scientists—"

"Work upstairs. Yes. I know all that. We did interview the folks at Underhill, you know, Daisy. Trust me, we don't need your help."

"Oh." Only faintly daunted, I said, "Well, I thought it was interesting. I think, although I'm not sure, that Miss Powell and Mr. Kingston met at the plant, because Mr. Kingston started going to our church a few months ago, and he and Miss Powell seem to have some sort of romantic relationship in the works now."

"Huh."

All righty, then. "Never mind," I said.

"I won't," he said. "However, I *do* want to know what in Hades you were doing at the Underhill plant taking a tour of the place."

Whoops. I guess only Pa knew about my job interviews. "Um, I read in the classified section of the *Star News* that the Underhill plant needs to hire line girls. So I sort of applied for a job there."

"Sort of?"

"Well...Yes. Sort of. You see, I just thought it might be worth my while to go down there, talk to a few people, and..." Oh, dear. If I told Sam I'd wanted to investigate the place, he'd blow up at me. "Um, I just wanted to see the place."

"And interview for a job. Because you'd make so much more money as a line girl at Underhill's than you do as a fake spiritualist."

"Oh, very well. I was snooping. There. Are you satisfied?"

"No."

"I'm not going back," I said. "So you can save your lecture."

"Lecturing you is about as effective as lecturing a pile of rocks."

"Thanks, Sam." I felt my mouth flatten into a tight line.

"You're welcome." On the other hand, Sam had begun to grin.

Bless Sam's withered heart.

But no. I wrong the man. He had a big heart. The fact that he kept his softer emotions concealed some of the time—oh, very well, *most* of the time—didn't mean he didn't have any.

He turned into the Underhill parking lot and pulled up next to the Gumm/Majesty Chevrolet. Since he didn't kill the engine, I opened my own door. Before I allowed him to leave, I said, "You're coming to dinner tonight, aren't you?"

"If I'm invited."

I shook my head in mock annoyance. "You're always invited, Sam. I've told you that a thousand times."

Looking grumpy and slightly abashed, Sam said, "It hasn't been a thousand times."

"Has too." I leaned in and gave him a peck on his cheek. Which needed to be shaved again. I swear, the man grew hair faster than any other male human I've ever met.

"Well, then, see you tonight," said he, and he drove out of the Underhill lot. If I were to guess, he was a happier man than he'd been when he'd entered Mijares and espied Robert and me seated at that conspicuous table.

Shaking my head, I opened the door to my automobile and climbed in. Is there a way, I wondered, that a woman can ever understand the workings of a man's brain? I decided that was too complex a question for a short ride, so I ceased thinking.

As for my route, I turned north on Fair Oaks Avenue and tootled up the street a mile or two. Or maybe three. I'm not sure how far away the Underhill plant is from the Pasadena Public Library, but that's where I headed. I'd told Mrs. Pinkerton I'd ask about Stacy's beloved with another Petrie. Perhaps Miss Petrie, my favorite librarian, might have some dirt to fling about Mr. Percival Petrie, who might be of the same Petrie tree as hers or of one of its less savory offshoots. I figured, as long as I was out and about, I might as well get it over with because, sure as anything, Mrs. Pinkerton would be telephoning me in another tizzy about the same matter soon.

I had a most enlightening chat with Miss Petrie, but since our chat has nothing to do with the matter in question here, I'll go into it later.

TWENTY-ONE

The rest of that week passed pleasantly enough. I read a lot, went for a daily walk or two with Pa and Spike, read the tarot and used the Ouija board almost constantly for Mrs. Pinkerton. As I'd predicted, she telephoned me each day, and every time she called, she was either in hysterics or a tizzy or both. All her states were related to her idiot daughter Stacy and Stacy's so-called fiancé, Mr. Percival Petrie. Naturally, I also ate a good many delicious meals prepared by my very own Aunt Vi.

Then came Thursday, which was choir-rehearsal night. Sam took dinner with us that evening he generally did.

"This is wonderful, Mrs. Gumm," said he, forking a bite of beef stew into his mouth.

Typical. He always complimented Aunt Vi, who deserved it, but he wasn't awfully creative in his use of adjectives.

"Superb," said I, in an attempt to give him a hint.

"Thank you both. It's just a regular old beef stew."

"Nothing you fix is regular old anything, Aunt Vi," I told her. "You make the best of everything there is to make." Recalling the luncheon salad she'd fed me a couple of days prior, I told the table in general, "Vi's going to give us all a salamander salad one of these days. It's delicious. I can vouch for it, because she gave me some for lunch at Mrs. Pinkerton's place a couple of days ago."

"Salmagundi, Daisy," Aunt Vi said with a shudder. "I wouldn't inflict salamanders on anyone."

"Oh, that's right," I said, embarrassed. "Sorry. Salmagundi."

"Aren't salamanders those lizard-like things that live under rocks?" asked Pa as if he really wanted to know.

"I think so," said Sam. Grinning at me, he said, "Why don't you try a salamander and tell us how you like it?"

"Don't be mean, Sam Rotondo. I meant *salmagundi* salad. I misspoke. I didn't mean Vi fed me anything at all having to do with lizards."

"Ew. I don't want to talk about lizards at the table," said Ma, frowning at me.

Sometimes I couldn't do anything right even when I tried.

Silence reigned for a few minutes. I figured I'd just let it reign, since my efforts at conversation seemed destined for failure.

I regretted my decision a second later, when Pa said, "So how'd your interview at the Underhill plant go, Daisy?"

A duet of "Your *what*?" went up from Ma and Vi. What's more, they both commenced staring in horror at me. Sam merely rolled his eyes and took another bite of his stew.

Aw, shoot. "It went well, thank you. I won't be working there."

Ma at once commenced interrogating me about why I'd applied for a job, and was I trying to pry into police business, etc., etc. I only sighed and continued to eat my meal, although my appetite had fled.

"Well?" Ma asked, sounding more irked than usual. "Why did you apply for a job at the Underhill place? Are you nosing into police business again, Daisy Majesty?"

Lifting my gaze to meet hers, I sighed and said, "Just thought I'd find out what a line job at the plant is like. It's like heck. I decided to stick with spiritualism. Talking to dead people pays better than filling poison bottles, anyway."

"Daisy!" said my mother, now peeved with my honesty. Or maybe my choice of words. Because I didn't like it when my mother was mad at me, I opted to tell her a smidgeon of the truth.

"Sorry, Ma. But I promised Miss Emmaline Castleton that I'd look into Mrs. Franbold's death, and now that Mr. Underhill has been poisoned, I thought there might be a connection, and it might be at his chemical factory." Staring at Sam, I said, "Since nobody's sharing any pertinent information with me, I have to dig around on my own."

"You do not," said Sam stonily.

"I agree with Sam," said Pa, giving me a regretful smile. "Sorry, sweetie, but you always seem to get into some kind of trouble when you poke into police business."

"According to Sam, I might get a commendation from the Altadena Sheriff's Department for helping to find Mr. Evans," said I defiantly. Didn't work.

"Might. That's not because you went up into the hills and confronted a gang of bootleggers by yourself. You gave the proper authorities a tip, and *they* found Mr. Evans." Sam chewed savagely on a biscuit.

Clearly I couldn't win that night. So I just finished dinner, smiled at everyone, washed and put away the dinner dishes, bade everyone a fond(ish) farewell, and went to church for choir practice.

Bother my family.

Not that I didn't love them all.

Oh, never mind.

I wasn't precisely surprised to see Miss Betsy Powell at the church that night. After all, she belonged to various church committees. We kind of jostled each other when I was poking around the sanctuary in an attempt to figure out who might have done in Mr. Underhill. My pokery went for naught, although I did, as I said, bump into Miss Powell.

We both leaped back several inches and slammed our hands over our thundering hearts. My heart was thundering, at any rate; I don't know what hers was doing. "Oh, Miss Powell! I'm so sorry. I didn't see you there." I squinted at her. "Why *are* you here?"

Very well, I suppose my question might be considered impolite, but the woman seemed to be everywhere I went during those several weeks.

"I'm just coming from a communion committee meeting. The meeting went a little late and the front door is locked," said Miss Powell, appearing both affronted and afraid, as if she were scared of me for some reason. "So we had to come through the sanctuary. Why were you at the Underhill plant yesterday?"

Question for question. I guess that was fair. "I was interested in the line-girl job that was advertised in the paper," I said, not precisely lying.

"*You?* But you're a fortune-teller, aren't you?" she spoke the sentence with some derision.

"No," I said firmly. "I am not a fortune-teller. I'm a spiritualist-medium. And a member of the choir, which meets every Thursday evening at seven." There. That should put her in her place. And then I bethought me of the reason she was at church the same evening as the choir. She'd assisted at both communion services during which folks had dropped dead. Maybe I could determine if she'd doctored the grape juice or wafers or something.

Trying to be sly, I said, "At your meeting, did you discuss the seeming fatality of communions in our church recently?"

She stepped back a pace, as if startled, almost bumping into Mr. Gerald Kingston, who had slipped up behind her. When she jolted him, his glasses slid down his nose. As he pushed them up his nose with one hand, he held out the other one, as if he wanted to touch Miss Powell's arm, but didn't quite dare.

"Oh!" she cried. "Gerald. I didn't see you there."

"I thought I'd ask if you need a ride home from the meeting," he said meekly. Everything about Mr. Kingston was meek, as nearly as I could tell.

"No. Thank you," said Miss Powell.

Mr. Kingston seemed to wilt a little.

Hmm. What did this mean? I'd sort of begun thinking of them as a couple. Was I wrong? As much as I hate to admit it, it wouldn't be the first time.

Miss Powell turned back to me. "What did you mean by that remark?" Her voice was a trifle sharp. Not in the choir-practice way of being off-key, but in the brittle-comment way.

I shrugged. "It only seems odd that people have dropped dead during the last two communion services. I suppose it would be easy to plop poison into a communion cup of grape juice or something." Eyeing her slant-wise, I said, "You *do* work in a company that produces poisons, after all. I'm sure others in the congregation do, too."

I spared a glance for Mr. Kingston, who goggled at me from behind his glasses. "I do," said he in a softish, smallish voice.

"Are you implying that I..." Miss Powell stopped talking, pressed her lips together, and said, "Don't be ridiculous." And she stomped off.

"Miss Powell would never do anything the least bit underhand," Mr. Kingston told me in a shaky voice, standing up as tall as he could, which wasn't very. I think he was attempting to be brave. I got the feeling he was nutty about Miss Powell. At any rate, he scurried after her, uttering softly, "Miss Powell. Oh, Miss Powell."

She eventually stopped in her hurry to flee and allowed him to catch up with her. They exited the sanctuary together.

All right, that didn't go so well. Sloppy, Daisy Gumm Majesty. Mortifyingly sloppy.

So I went back to the chancel, sat in my assigned alto chair, and paid attention to the music we were supposed to learn for the next couple of weeks. The next Sunday was another communion day, so we had bread-eating hymns to learn. Our communion anthem for the upcoming Sunday was "Bread of Heaven, on Thee We Feed," which is really kind of disgusting when you think about it, so I didn't. Pretty soon we'd enter the season of Lent, and then all our hymns would be slow and dismal until Easter, when things would perk up again. Seasonal singing could be quite interesting sometimes.

The séance at Mrs. Bissel's house that Saturday went well. Mrs. Underhill was there, appearing distressed, but, when we spoke privately after the séance, I told her not to worry. The police were working on her husband's case, and none of her children was to blame.

I only hoped I was telling her the truth. She seemed happier, so I guess I did my duty well. Being a spiritualist-medium can be trying sometimes, but I do attempt to make people feel better.

~

On Sunday morning, March 2, 1924, Sam came to our house early so that he could partake of the delicious breakfast casserole Aunt Vi prepared for us.

"Delicious, Mrs. Gumm," said Sam, adhering to tradition.

"Thank you. I got this recipe from a cooking book Daisy borrowed from the library. It's called scalloped eggs, and it's from *The White House Cookbook*."

"You mean from the real White House?" asked Sam, glancing up from his eggs, which Vi served with sausage patties. Yum.

"Yes. There are all sorts of recipes in it. The White House folks eat pretty well," said Vi with a laugh.

"So do the folks in this house," said Sam, making Vi blush. My father, mother and I all nodded our agreement.

I said, "I'm glad you could use that book, Vi. I mainly wanted to see if you could create a shrimp cocktail sauce like the kind we had at the Hotel Castleton when I dined there with Harold and Miss Emmaline Castleton."

Vi gave me a speaking look. "You do travel in exalted company, Daisy Gumm Majesty."

"Yes," said Sam, sounding not pleased about it, "you do."

"Not all the time. Heck, I'm eating breakfast with you, aren't I?"

"Daisy!" said Ma.

I couldn't win. Maybe after Sam and I were married, I could say things to him without my mother thinking I was being rude. In this particular case, I was trying to be funny. My wonderful mother—and I mean that sincerely; she was a wonderful person—didn't possess an ounce of humor or imagination, which is why I couldn't get away with sly humor in our house.

"It was a joke, Ma," I said, knowing it would do no good.

"Hmph. Well, I thought it was quite rude."

Sam smirked at me. I didn't stick my tongue out at him, because I knew Ma would scold me again.

Vi saved the day when she said, "Actually, the tomato sauce recipe in the *White House Cookbook* works well for your shrimp cocktail sauce, Daisy. I just added a dollop of horseradish, and you said it tasted just like the sauce at the Castleton."

"It did!" I said, remembering, and pleased to have been of service to the entire family, who got to enjoy the results of Vi's mastery in the kitchen. "It was actually better than the one they served at Castleton's."

Vi blushed again. "Pshaw," said she, an expression she used quite often and which made no sense to me, not that it matters.

So we finished breakfast, and Ma and I washed up the dishes. Then we set out for church. The weather had turned chilly, now that it was almost springtime (I'm joking again) so we all got into Sam's Hudson for the drive to the church. That day I wore my favorite worsted suit (made by me, naturally) in a lovely green color that went well with my hair. Sam's ring would have gone beautifully with the outfit, but I hadn't dared take it from its box since I'd hidden it under my unmentionables that Christmas of 1923. Sam hadn't brought up the matter of our secret engagement, which I appreciated. There was a lot to like about the big lug, even if he did drive me crazy more often than not.

As ever, once we exited Sam's automobile and approached the church, I veered off to enter the choir room and don my robe. Because the chancel, where the choir sat, always seemed to be warmer than the sanctuary, where the rest of the congregation sat, I took off my suit jacket and hung it on the hanger upon which my robe hung the rest of the week. Then we all lined up and, when Mrs. Fleming began the organ prelude, we processed to our assigned seats.

Because I knew Miss Betsy Powell would help serve communion that day, and also because I knew she was upset with me, both for chatting with folks at the Underhill plant and for questioning her about possible poisoning of the communion elements, I'd planned ahead for this day's service. In my handbag, I had a tiny rubber envelope and an elastic band with which to secure it. Darn it, if Betsy Powell *were* murdering folks during communion, I was probably next on her list. Therefore, I aimed to take no chances. I also aimed to do something positive with regard to her villainy if she was, indeed, a villain.

Truth to tell, at that point even I didn't much care who'd killed Mr. Underhill, but if Miss Powell had poisoned Mrs. Franbold, she deserved to be punished for same. Stupid woman. Miss Powell, not Mrs. Franbold.

The choir did a spectacular job on "Bread of Heaven, on Thee We Feed," and then, after the sermon and the prayer, Pastor Smith called for us choir members to take communion. Miss Powell stood next to him and helped, holding the communion cups on a silver tray. As Pastor Smith held out the wafers for us to take, saying to each of us as he did so, "The body of Christ, broken for you," we each said, "Amen," as we were supposed to do. As I pretended to put the wafer in my mouth, I palmed it and held it concealed in my choir robe.

Then along came Miss Powell with the little glass communion cups. As we each took one—I noticed she positioned the glasses on the tray so that the communion-ee would take a specific cup, she said, "The blood of Christ, spilled for you," and we each said, "Amen" again. Then, as I knelt at the altar, I surreptitiously wrapped the communion cup in my handkerchief. I'd never be able to use *that* hankie again, the cloth-staining properties of grape juice being what they were. I tried to hide my hankie in my robe without spilling any of the juice, but that didn't work awfully well. I sure hoped grape-juice stains would come out of my choir robe with the judicious application of hydrogen peroxide.

When I regained my seat in the choir nook, I opened my handbag and stuffed the communion cup, hankie and all, into the rubber receptacle I had ready for it. Then I wound the elastic band as tightly as I could around the top of the rubber envelope, and prayed fervently that it wouldn't leak grape juice all over the insides of my handbag. Actually, I expect that was my most fervent prayer of the entire service, which just goes to show you how devout I was.

Naturally, I felt guilty.

However, my state of guiltiness didn't stay me from my purpose, which was to discover if Miss Powell had doctored either the communion wafers or the grape juice with something that shouldn't be there. Mind you, I wasn't entirely certain how to ascertain that truth, but I trusted my ingenuity.

Thank the good Lord, nobody fell down dead during communion service that day. I believe the entire congregation was fairly giddy with relief when the service ended and everyone except the choir headed for Fellowship Hall and tea and cookies. Or coffee and cookies. Or, for that matter, lemonade and a piece of cake. We Methodist-Episcopals aimed to please.

As for me, before I dared look into my handbag, I hung up my robe. I was relieved that no telltale purple stains adorned it; however, I did see that one of my fingers was sort of purple, tried to remove the purple stain with a rag that happened to be lying on one of the tables in the choir room, failed, sighed, and donned my suit jacket.

"What were you doing during communion, Daisy? Why were you fumbling with your purse?"

I looked up to see a squinting Lucy Spinks—who would become Lucy Zollinger the following Saturday—peering at me.

Nuts. I'd been hoping no one would notice. "I, er, had to blow my nose, so I was getting out my hankie." Lie, lie, lie. And in church, too. Bad Daisy.

"Oh." Lucy didn't appear terribly satisfied by my explanation, but she let the matter drop, thank heaven.

After the rest of the choir had departed the choir room, I dared open my handbag. Squinting in the poor light, I was pleased to see that, while I'd managed to ruin a perfectly fine handkerchief, none of the grape juice had spilled out of the rubber envelope. I opened it and refastened it to make sure that state of affairs would prevail throughout fellowship and the trip home.

TWENTY-TWO

S am joined us for Sunday dinner, which was a delectable roast beef with carrots, peas, Yorkshire pudding, and potatoes and gravy, followed by a white cake with coconut frosting—one of my very favorite desserts. Then, as Sam prepared to go home and the rest of us prepared to nap during the afternoon, Sam said, "I need to talk to you for a minute, Daisy."

"Sure, Sam. I'll walk you to the car." I turned to Spike, who was monitoring our conversation with wagging tail and happy mien. "Come along, Spike. You can come, too."

So Sam, Spike and I went outside. I instantly wished I'd put on a sweater, but Sam put an arm around me, so I warmed up fast.

Feeling happy and satisfied and ready for my nap, I said cheerfully, "So what do you need to talk to me about, Sam?"

"What the devil were you doing during communion? And don't tell me you needed to blow your nose, either. You stuck the wafer and grape juice into your handbag, didn't you?"

Well, blast the man! "Why were you watching me? You were supposed to be praying, drat you!"

"I know you too well. You've been prying and poking into Underhill's murder, and since he died after taking communion, you think he was poisoned, don't you? How do you expect to get the stuff you stole from the church—"

"I didn't steal anything!" I bellowed, furious. "I'm going to return the communion cup, and if you think anybody wants that grape juice back, they'll have to wring it out of my hankie."

To my utter astonishment, Sam laughed. He had a big, rumbly laugh, and nobody heard it very often.

"Anyhow," I said, calming down some. "I thought it might be a good idea to test the communion elements, since people seem to drop dead fairly often after Betsy Powell gives them their juice."

"Nobody dropped dead today," Sam pointed out.

"I know it." Sullen, Daisy Majesty. Unpleasantly sullen.

"How did you aim to get the stuff tested?"

Good question, and one for which I hadn't come up with an answer yet. Nevertheless, I said, "I figured Doc Benjamin could test everything for me."

"Poor Dr. Benjamin. I can't even imagine having you as a patient."

"That's not fair, Sam Rotondo! Just because you don't approve of the things I do, it doesn't follow that Dr. Benjamin is of a like mind."

"That's only because he's a doctor and not a policeman." Sam stopped walking and turned me around to face him. I had to tilt my head back to do so. "Listen, Daisy, there's a poisoner on the loose, and whoever it is might well have something to do with the Underhill plant. Do you know how scared I was when I found out you'd been snooping around there? If you make the poisoner—and we don't know who it is—suspicious, you might be next on his list."

"Her list," I said automatically.

"Huh?"

"I think it's Betsy Powell. I made her mad the other day when I went to choir rehearsal, so I figured she might have it in for me at communion today."

Shaking his head as if in amazement, Sam said, "For the love of God, Daisy, will you *never* learn not to irritate people you think might be deadly? If you think she's the poisoner, why, for the love of God, did you annoy her?"

"Well, I didn't mean to," I confessed. "It just kind of worked out that way."

"Why do you think she's the poisoner?" asked Sam, sounding as if he were genuinely curious.

"Well, she's the one who gave Mrs. Franbold and Mr. Underhill their grape juice, and both of them dropped dead right afterwards. In fact, I'm surprised you vaunted policemen haven't figured that out yet."

"Mrs. Franbold died of natural causes," said Sam.

My mouth fell open. "And you're only telling me this *now*?"

"You didn't need to know," said Sam. "I was hoping—which was, I admit, stupid of me—that if I didn't tell you everything, you'd leave the investigation alone. I should have known better."

"Yes," I said as Sam let me go and we resumed our walk to his Hudson. "You should have."

"But Underhill was poisoned. And I know you won't like this, and I also know you already said you wouldn't, but I want you to *promise* me you won't go back to that damned plant. They make fertilizer and so forth with deadly poisons there, you know, and I don't want anything to happen to you before we get married. Ten or so years from now."

That was actually kind of sweet. "It probably won't be ten years from now," I said, feeling a trifle embarrassed. "And I don't plan to go back to the Underhill plant ever again."

"It's a good thing, or I'd have to go down there and tell them to bar you from entering their portals."

"You wouldn't!"

"Try me." Before I could protest further, he said, "Give me that junk you got at communion. I'll have someone at the police lab test it."

"Oh. Thanks, Sam."

"Huh."

Sam had reverted to his normal state. In a way, I was glad. At least he'd stopped lecturing me. I hurried back to the house, went to my bedroom, and dug in my purse for the leather pouch in which I'd stuffed my napkin, the communion cup, and the now-soggy wafer. I decided I'd just better hand Sam the leather pouch because otherwise, things might get messy.

"Here you go," I said somewhat breathlessly. "It's all in here."

Sam undid the elastic band holding the pouch closed, peered in, grimaced, and said, "Good God."

"Yes, well, I couldn't think of any other way to take it home with me."

He said, "Good God," again, and we proceeded to his Hudson. Sam gave me a short kiss, leaned over and gave Spike a pat, and he motored off down the street. I heaved a sigh and spoke to my dog. "It could have been worse, Spike. He might have yelled at me. And he *did* offer to have that soggy lump tested for poisons."

Spike only wagged his tail.

~

The week following the first Sunday in March was a busy one for Daisy Gumm Majesty, mainly because Miss Lucille Spinks was set to marry Mr. Albert Zollinger the following Saturday, and I had agreed to make all the bridesmaids' gowns. Lucy's sister Pamela was going to be her matron of honor, but Lucy had asked me to be a bridesmaid.

Truth to tell, I wasn't a maid. I was a matron, but I don't think there's a word for that when it comes to weddings. Who's ever heard of a bridesmatron?

At any rate, women were coming and going all week long in the Gumm-Majesty household. I made pot after pot of tea, and fed the bridesmaids Aunt Vi's cookies, and it was actually kind of fun. Lucy planned to wear her mother's old wedding gown for her own wedding, which I thought was sweet. I had to do some alterations on it, since Lucy was taller and skinnier than her mother had been at the time of her wedding. Well, she still was, Lucy being tall and skinny and her mother being a wee bit shorter and plumper than she.

I considered Lucy fortunate that her mother hadn't opted for one of those Victorian-era gowns with a high-standing collar that looked as if it would choke the life out of a bride before she even got hitched. Rather, her mother had chosen a cream-colored silk chiffon mounted over a pale blue fitted bodice. The gown had a scooped neckline, short cap sleeves, a light-blue cummerbund, and a flared skirt embroidered with beaded flowers that matched those on the bodice of the gown. My addition of satin and lace below the beaded flowers looked pretty and not at all out of place.

The gown didn't precisely flatter Lucy's figure, but Lucy was long and lanky and rather shapeless, and it would have been a special gown, indeed, that would flatter her. I'm not being catty. It's the truth. I'd always been a trifle rounder than fashion called for. Lucy was the perfect shape for a straight, tubular, up-and-down dress fashionable in 1924, but she wanted to wear her mother's gown, and by gum (so to speak) I'd alter it for her so that she looked as good in it as I could make her look.

Lucy was in an exuberant mood. "Oh, Daisy, this is so exciting!"

"I know. You seem so happy with your choice, too." Mind you, I thought Mr. Zollinger was a fine man, but he was still a good deal older than Lucy, and if the war hadn't killed off so many young men, she might have made a different choice in a mate. Naturally, I didn't mention that.

Clasping her hands to her bosom, Lucy said, "Albert is so kind to me, Daisy. I know he's older, and not the most handsome man in the world, but he's truly a good and respectable gentleman."

Good and respectable. All righty, then. "I'm very happy for you, Lucy." And I was. The fact that I'd married the love of my life might mitigate my joy for Lucy slightly, but beggars, as they say, can't be choosers. Anyhow, Mr. Zollinger was alive, and my Billy had been dead for almost two years.

"Um, Daisy..." Lucy's voice trailed off.

I looked up at her, having been pinning the hem of her gown. I'd already taken in the bodice so that it wouldn't balloon out over Lucy's smallish bosom, and now I now was pinning satin and lace to the hem. When I was finished with that gown, it would be perfectly charming, as I was as excellent a seamstress as I was a spiritualist-medium. I never say things like that out loud, by the way, but I was proud of my few skills. "Yes?" I asked through the pins stuck in my mouth.

"Is...Is this difficult for you? I mean, I know it's been a couple of years since your husband passed away, but...Well, I hope this isn't bringing back painful memories. And I do *so* appreciate you helping me the way you're doing."

I thought it was kind of her to think of my possible emotional pain. I hesitated for a moment before answering her. "It's not painful. Exactly. But I do remember when Billy and I married with...nostalgia, I guess. We were *so* young and stupid."

Boy, I'd never thought of Billy and me as stupid before, but I guess we had been.

"You were?" Lucy sounded thunderstruck.

"Well...Yes. We were. I'd just graduated from high school, and Billy was working at the Hull Motor Works, and the United States had just joined Europe in the war, and we thought...We thought it was a romantic time. And it was, for about five minutes." I heaved a huge sigh.

"It's terrible what Mr. Majesty went through in that horrible war," said Lucy.

I laughed. "Mr. Majesty? Just call him Billy, please, Lucy. I can't even imagine Billy being 'Mr. Majesty.' If he'd lived, and if we'd had children and grown old together, I guess he might have become Mr. Majesty, but... Oh, he was so young and so handsome and...and I just think of him as Billy."

"I see. I hope I didn't upset you." Lucy sounded worried.

"Not at all. I still miss my Billy, but his life after the war was so hard and painful." I shook my head and felt a lump forming in my throat. I cleared it away and said, "He just wasn't the same man after he came home. It's probably a sin to say so, but in a way I'm glad he died when he did."

"Are you really?"

I grabbed the pins from my mouth and stood, pulling my hankie from my pocket as I did so. "Yes. He was in dreadful pain, and he could hardly breathe, and he just wasn't the Billy I married after he came home from that damned war. Sorry for swearing."

"Oh, Daisy, I don't blame you." Lucy had started sniffling, too, so we had ourselves a little sob-fest. Then we both laughed.

"Mercy sakes, aren't we the ones," I said, not quite knowing what I meant.

After ruthlessly wiping her eyes, Lucy said, "Yes. We are."

Then we laughed again and I finished pinning the lengthening satin and lace onto the bottom of her gown.

Except for that one isolated circumstance, I managed to keep my spirits up for the remainder of the week, in spite of everyone else's joy at Lucy's impending marriage. Or maybe because of it. I don't know. All I knew for certain at that point was that I'd always, always love my Billy, and that I wasn't quite ready to embark on another marriage, this time to the large and block-like Sam Rotondo. Even though I loved him. I really did.

Lucy was in an absolute dither at choir rehearsal that Thursday. She could hardly sit still, and Mr. Hostetter spoke to her sharply once or twice.

Leaning over, I whispered to her, "I don't even know why you bothered to come to rehearsal tonight. After all, you've got a wedding to prepare for."

"I couldn't sit still at home, and I figured I'd be better off at rehearsal, even though I won't be here on Sunday, because we'll be on our honeymoon." She giggled.

"Miss Spinks," said Mr. Hostetter. "I understand this is an interesting time for you, but the rest of the choir needs to learn Sunday's anthem."

"I'm sorry, Mr. Hostetter."

He smiled at her. "That's quite all right. I understand."

I doubted that, although I didn't say so. After all, what would an oldish man know about a young woman getting married in 1924, when half the men her age had been killed in a fruitless war? I guess all wars are fruitless, but still...Lucy getting married was not only romantic—sort of—but really rather amazing, given the circumstances. And things were worse in Europe. Hard to imagine almost an entire generation of young men being wiped off the face of the earth because of one man's greed and lust for power. I still think someone should have executed Kaiser Bill for what he did to the world.

There I go again. I'm sorry.

Anyhow, rehearsal went well after Lucy calmed down some. Our hymn for Sunday was "Forty Days and Forty Nights," to ring in (if that's the right term) the Lenten season. As I've said before, hymns for Lent are generally on the gloomy side, but I loved the music to "Forty Days" so I didn't mind it so much. If Lucy were going to be in church on Sunday, she and I would probably have sung a duet at one point or another during the anthem, but I didn't begrudge her impending absence. Heck, the girl was getting *married*!

TWENTY-THREE

After rehearsal, I asked Lucy where she and her Albert were going on their honeymoon.

"Oh, Daisy," Lucy said, clutching my arm, "he's taking me to San Francisco! I've always wanted to go to San Francisco."

"How fun! I've always wanted to visit San Francisco, too." Maybe Sam and I could go there on our honeymoon. If we ever had one.

"Me, too. I can't wait to ride on one of those cable cars. And I want to see Chinatown and the harbor, and that chocolate-company place. What's it called?"

"Chocolate?" My ears perked up, and my mouth started to water, but I didn't have an idea what Lucy was talking about.

"Some Italian fellow bought an entire city block in San Francisco in the eighteen-fifties. You know, during the Gold Rush. He began a confectionery factory. Albert says his company makes the best chocolate in the United States. He thinks Belgian chocolates are the absolute best, but I wouldn't know about that."

"No. I wouldn't either." Especially these days, when poor Belgium was still trying to recover from being mercilessly banged about by the

Germans during the way. Frankly, I wondered how Mr. Zollinger knew so much about Belgian chocolates, but I didn't ask.

"But Albert says that after Europe settles down a bit more, we might be able to take a trip to Belgium and Switzerland. His heritage is Swiss, you know. Albert says Switzerland makes excellent chocolates, too."

"And clocks and watches," I said.

"Yes. Those too. I have to admit I'm more interested in the chocolates, though."

I laughed. "I am, too. But you say there's an Italian chocolate factory in San Francisco?"

"Yes. Albert says it's the best."

Albert says seemed to be the precursor of every sentence Lucy spoke in those days. I didn't mind, though.

"Really?" Hmm. I wondered if Sam knew about this. "I don't think I've ever heard of an Italian chocolate-maker in San Francisco before. Can you remember his name?"

Lucy's brow wrinkled for a second, and then she burst out, "Ghirardelli! That's the name. I think there's even a place called Ghirardelli Square, where you can get chocolates and stuff."

I put a hand on Lucy's shoulder. "You're going to have a wonderful time, Lucy. I'm so happy for you. And for Mr. Zollinger, too. He's got a peach in you, and I hope he knows it."

"Thank you, Daisy."

We hugged each other, each of us sniffling a bit. Sentimental fools. But we couldn't help ourselves.

I'd driven to choir rehearsal because the night was cold and dark. Rehearsals got out at nine p.m., and Ma and Pa didn't like me walking home that late. Even though the church was only a few blocks from our house and I didn't mind walking, I also didn't mind not walking, and that night I was particularly happy to have the Chevrolet. I was also happy to see Sam's Hudson parked on the street in front of our house when I got home. I pulled into the driveway and entered the house via the side porch. I wanted to ask him about...Rats. I'd already forgotten the chocolate man's name.

Spike greeted me with joy and wags. Pa and Sam were sitting at the dining room table chatting and both glanced at me when I entered the room.

"Hey, Pa. Hey, Sam. What are you doing here?"

"Good to see you, too, Daisy," said Sam with immense irony.

"I didn't mean that the way it sounded. I actually wanted to ask you something."

"Good rehearsal, sweetie?" asked Pa, attempting to adjust the conversational flow so as to avoid an argument between Sam and me. Good old Pa. He was a great guy.

"Yes, it went really well. Lucy was so excited she couldn't sit still, but I love the anthem for Sunday. The rehearsal for her wedding is tomorrow night, you know."

"I know," said Pa, smiling at me.

I guess some of Lucy's enthusiasm must have rubbed off on me, because I was a little twitchy with excitement myself. "Oh, Sam! Lucy and Mr. Zollinger are going to San Francisco for their honeymoon, and they're going to visit some chocolate-guy's confectionery store. I guess there's an entire segment of San Francisco named after him."

"Domingo Ghirardelli," Sam said.

"That's it!"

"He changed his name. His real name is Domenico Ghirardelli. He changed Domenico to the Spanish Domingo."

I plunked myself down on a chair, removed my gloves and hat and plopped them onto the table. "Jeez, you'd think he'd change his last name to something pronounceable instead of his first name. I mean, Domenico is as easy to pronounce as Domingo, but Ghirardelli is just weird."

"For you. For an Italian, it isn't," said Sam. Oddly enough, he was smiling rather than frowning as he said it.

"I guess. Anyhow, I suppose anything's better than Gumm." I glanced at my father, feeling guilty. Again. "Sorry, Pa, but we really do have a laughable last name. I got teased all the time in school."

"I know, sweetie. I did, too."

"I went to school in New York City," said Sam. "Everybody had

192

strange last names. The folks who got teased the most, though, were the Irish."

"Really? Why was that?"

With a shrug, Sam said, "Beats me. I guess the Irish came over in droves during the potato famine, and everyone was mad at them for taking other people's jobs. Same thing happened in San Francisco. And then there were the Chinese. They had problems, too."

I thought about that. "We human beings aren't very nice to each other, are we?"

"Not as a rule," agreed Sam. "The Irish in New York also had a bad reputation as far as drunkenness, crime and thuggery were concerned."

"Thuggery?" I liked that word, but I think Sam just made it up.

"You know what I mean. There were a lot of corrupt Irish cops in the force during the last part of the last century." He shrugged. "Probably still are."

"That's discouraging." Some of the elation I'd absorbed from Lucy abated. "Are you going to Lucy's wedding with us, Sam?"

"Am I invited?"

"Everyone from the church is invited. Since you've taken to going to church with us on Sundays, that includes you."

"Well, then, sure. Why not?"

"Why not, indeed? If you come to the reception afterwards in Fellowship Hall, you'll get a good meal, too."

"Then I'll definitely attend. That means I'll get a good meal on Saturday and Sunday, too, as long as nobody commits any crimes I have to investigate." He appeared guilty at once. "If I'm invited to Sunday dinner here, I mean."

"You know you are," said Pa, grinning at the two of us, as if he thought we were just so adorable he could hardly stand it.

I wished he wouldn't do that. I mean, yes, Sam and I were engaged, but Pa didn't know that. Nobody knew it except Sam and me. I patted the juju I wore under my dress and thought maybe I should wear Sam's ring around my neck, too. On a chain, I mean, not the woven fabric string Mrs. Jackson had created for my juju.

Evidently Sam had thought the same thing, because when we walked out to his automobile, he reached into his pocket and withdrew a little packet. "Here. I got this for you. If you ever decided to put my ring—or Billy's, for that matter—on a chain around your neck, here's a little gold-link chain for it."

"Thank you, Sam! I was just thinking I should do that."

"Which?"

I glanced up from the golden chain I'd just unwrapped to his face. "What do you mean, which?"

"Which ring will you wear on the chain?"

"Oh." At once I thought I'd *never* take off Billy's ring from my finger. I didn't want to tell Sam that. So I said, "Well..."

"You'll wear my ring on the chain," said Sam before I could.

"Um...Yes. I think so. Just until I can get used to being engaged to you. You know, for a little while. Until—"

"Never mind explaining. I understand. It *will* be ten years, won't it?"

"I...I don't know, Sam. I'm sorry. I just...I don't know."

He could tell I was becoming emotional, so he wrapped his arms around me.

"It's all right, Daisy. I really do understand. I've had two years longer to recover from Margaret's death than you've had to recover from Billy's. If you ever can recover from losing a beloved mate."

I sniffled. "Yes. If you ever can." I recalled the conversation Sam and I had with Robert Browning at Mijares and felt sorry for all of us.

Sam left then, and I wandered back into the house in a much less buoyant mood than I'd entered from choir practice several minutes earlier.

Why was life so complicated?

Don't bother trying to answe. I'm sure you don't know, either.

However, that evening, I reached into my underwear drawer and carefully picked up the box holding the ring Sam's father had designed and Sam had given to me. I slipped it onto the golden chain and clasped it around my neck. I clutched it as I went to sleep that night.

TWENTY-FOUR

I didn't sleep awfully well that night. I guess Lucy's wedding and Sam's disappointment that I couldn't yet let myself wear his engagement ring sort of kept me tossing and turning. Spike finally got sick of my twitching and jumped down from the bed to sleep on the rug. Sorry, Spike.

In spite of my tiredness on Friday, that evening's wedding rehearsal went well. I could tell both Lucy and Mr. Zollinger were madly in love with each other, and that made me happy.

Lucy had asked an operatically inclined couple, Connie and Max Van der Linden, who'd staged *The Mikado* at our church not long back, to sing at the wedding. Connie had fully recovered from an ordeal visited upon her by another couple, not so nice, that had tried to slowly poison her. But that's another story entirely. Connie and Max both had gorgeous voices, and they sang "The Voice That Breathed O'er Eden" so beautifully, I think everyone at the rehearsal had to wipe away tears. What a beautiful song. I almost envied Lucy. Her wedding was going to be spectacular.

Billy and I had married in haste, so to speak. Not that we hadn't had a nice church wedding, but our wedding hadn't been expensive and smothered in flowers and stuff. Billy'd worn his brand-new army uniform, and I'd worn a gown I'd made myself. Our wedding had been pretty, but it was not nearly as elaborate as Lucy's was going to be. Not that it matters.

A wedding supper was then held at the Spinks' home, and I attended it along with all the other bridesmaids and groomsmen, Pastor Smith, the Van der Lindens, Mr. Hostetter, and our organist, Mrs. Fleming. Connie and I had a nice chat about another operetta the duo aimed to stage. I told her I'd enjoyed being Katisha in *The Mikado*, but she'd have to drug and hog-tie me before I'd sing in another one of their productions. She laughed.

Little did she know. I meant it. That darned operetta had nearly killed me. It *had* killed a couple of other people. I'd come to the conclusion that my unimaginative mother had been right when she'd told me she thought theater people were a bad lot. Not that Connie and Max were, but a whole bunch of the rest of them were. Look at Fatty Arbuckle. Look at William Desmond Taylor. Look at Wallace Reid. Look at…Oh, bother the rest of them. But there are examples galore, and my one experience had dampened any slight enthusiasm I'd once had for performing onstage.

The rehearsal supper was simple enough: deviled eggs, sausage rolls, little sandwiches, a fruit plate, a vegetable plate, etc. It was nice, and Connie and Max agreed to sing some more while I played the piano. We might have become slightly rowdy, but not very. Everyone laughed when we played and sang "The Cat Came Back."

"Old King Tut" was the most undignified song of the evening. Connie did an amusing thing with her hands, which she set at an angle next to her shoulders, and I'll never understand how she got her neck to do that back-and-forth thing. I've tried it in the mirror and failed miserably. At any rate, the movements looked vaguely Egyptian, and we all applauded.

I was tired but happy when I got back home. Spike was elated and not at all tired when I returned. Everyone else was in bed, and Sam hadn't come to visit, so I just washed my face, took off my rehearsal clothes, popped my raggedy nightgown over my head, and collapsed onto the bed, Spike at my side. I slept like the proverbial log and awoke refreshed and happy on Saturday morning.

That was a busy day for everyone involved in Lucy's wedding. Every single one of the bridesmaids came to my house to be sure their dresses fitted properly—they could hardly fail to, since they were in the fashionable, straight up-and-down style then in vogue. The only girl who didn't look perfectly flat in her dress was Gladys Pennywhistle Fellowes, who was in approximately the third month of her pregnancy and was beginning to show. But she didn't show *that* much. Gladys, by the way, had always awed me. She not only understood algebra when we were in high school, but she married a genius professor, Homer Fellowes, who taught at the California Institute of Technology. Still, even with all her brains, she was nice.

"I don't look fat?" Gladys asked, peering at her profile in the mirror hanging on my door and pressing her dress over her itty-bitty lump.

"Not at all. I've made your dress a little looser than the others, and anyway, you'll be holding flowers, won't you? Just hold them over your tiny little bump." I envied her that bump. Billy and I had wanted children.

Nuts.

The rest of the girls weren't in any way chubby, and they all looked swell in their blue dresses, made to match the soft blue of Lucy's satin under-dress. I'd also made everyone's hats. Well, except for Lucy, who was wearing her mother's tiara. The original lace descending from the tiara was yellowed with age, so I did make her a new veil, but I managed to find some lace that almost precisely matched that worn by her mother, so everyone was happy.

The wedding was to take place at two p.m., but the people in the wedding party had to show up at noon. I had a little sandwich made with Aunt Vi's delicious bread and some peanut butter. I was beginning to think of peanut butter as sort of a salvation food. If you didn't have time for anything else, you could always eat peanut butter. You didn't even necessarily have to spread it on bread. You could scoop it right out of the jar. Providing you remembered to buy a jarful at the local grocery store down the street, and I usually did. In those days, the grocer scooped out however much of the stuff you wanted from a wooden barrel and crammed into a jar. When the jar was empty, you could wash it out, take it back to the grocer, and he'd cram it full again.

Naturally, the ladies of the church arrived early, too, because they had to prepare the meal in Fellowship Hall that would be served to the wedding attendees after the wedding vows had been spoken. Vi brought in a roasted turkey and a baked ham, lots of her delicious dressing (not stuffing, because it wasn't in the bird) and gravy, and a superb sauce for the ham. Other ladies brought salads and side dishes and potatoes and I can't even remember what all else. Then there were the desserts, but I won't go into them. Actually, I *did* go into them, but I won't do so now.

By the way, Albert Zollinger made sure the ladies of the church were reimbursed for the money they spent in order to create such a spread. I'm sure the church ladies would have done a spectacular spread even without his generosity, but they appreciated his thoughtfulness.

The wedding, according to everyone who witnessed it, was lovely. What I could see of it from my position as one of the bridesmaids looked pretty keen. Connie and Max sang "The Voice That Breathed O'er Eden" gorgeously again. In fact, I even saw *men* in the congregation wiping their eyes during that one. The women crying was a given, so we'd all brought our hankies with us.

To tell the dismal truth, I was weepy during almost the entire service. Memories and thoughts of the future, I reckon. Mainly, I was just an emotional wreck. Happy for Lucy. Happier for Albert (not that I didn't think he was a nice guy, because I did, but I've already mentioned the paucity of younger men in the world), but also in a state of vivid remembrance.

When Lucy and Albert walked down the aisle as man and wife, with all the folks who'd served during the ceremony walking behind them, everyone stood and applauded. I guess that's what always happens at weddings, but I didn't remember the applause after my own wedding to Billy, so I was kind of surprised. However, being surprised cured me of my weepiness, so that was a good thing.

The reception following the wedding rites in Fellowship Hall was lovely. The ladies on the decorations committee outdid themselves with the white streamers and paper flowers and stuff, and the food was absolutely magnificent. What's more, one could go back for seconds if one wished. This one was stuffed to the gills after the first round at the buffet table. Anyhow, when I entered Fellowship Hall, I found my family and Sam, and we all sat together at a table close to the bride and groom's.

Since Prohibition was in full tilt—and also because we Methodist-Episcopals were, for the most part, dry as old bones—lemonade flowed like water. Albert Zollinger's best man, who was a fellow I'd never seen before, made a very nice speech to toast the couple. Then Lucy's father rose and gave another nice speech. And then Mr. Smith, our pastor, gave yet another nice speech, which ended with a titter (our pastor doesn't titter as a rule) and an announcement that Mrs. Fleming would play the Fellowship-Hall piano for waltzes and polkas after we finished our meal. Methodist-Episcopals were about as keen on dancing as they were on drinking distilled spirits, but I guess an exception was going to be made for Albert and Lucy. I was glad of it. Heck, if Pastor Smith had allowed *The Mikado* to be staged in his church, why shouldn't folks dance to celebrate a wedding?

It was fun. Just plain fun, and I danced with Sam, who waltzed rather like a wooden soldier, but that didn't matter. He even tried a polka, but we gave up after ramming into two other couples. They didn't mind, but only laughed. So we resumed our seats at the family table, and I fanned myself with my napkin, which wasn't too stained with the remains of my dinner to be non-functional.

"You two looked good together, dancing like that," said Vi, smirking slightly.

Oh, dear. I was afraid this would happen.

"Thanks."

"I can't dance very well," said Sam. Unnecessarily, in my opinion.

"You did fine," I told him. "Oh, look. There's Miss Powell waltzing with Mr. Kingston. They look mighty comfy together, don't they?"

"Who?" said Sam. "Oh, that woman who screams all the time? Is that the Powell dame?"

The Powell dame? "Are you trying to sound like *Dime Detective Magazine*, Sam Rotondo? Powell dame, my foot. Yes, that's Miss Betsy Powell, the one who had hysterics after both deaths in the church. The gentleman with whom she's dancing is Mr. Gerald Kingston. Both of them work at the Underhill plant, and I've noticed they've been hanging about together lately."

"Hmm," said Sam.

"Hmm what?"

"Nothing. Just hmm."

"Do you suspect Mr. Kingston of murdering Mr. Underhill?" I asked, moving closer to Sam and whispering so nobody else could hear.

Sam turned his big head and stared at me? "Huh? Are you nuts?"

Guess that answered my question. "Sorry I asked," I said stiffly and moved away again. He grabbed my chair and pulled it closer to him. "Stop that," I growled.

"No," he growled back, and then he grinned. The big lug.

And then it was I noticed Aunt Vi, Ma, Pa, and several other church people smiling at Sam and me, and I know that I blushed to the roots of my hair and beyond because I felt the heat creeping up my neck, into my cheeks, and so forth. Drat! Why were people so nosy?

Asked Daisy Gumm Majesty who'd just speculated about the meek and mild Gerald Kingston being a murderer.

I swear, fate doesn't play favorites, does it?

However, just about that time, I was saved from further humiliation by the arrival of Mr. and Mrs. Albert Zollinger, who must have slipped out sometime during the reception and gone and changed clothes in an office somewhere. Now they stood at the head of the table in Fellowship Hall, beaming like a couple of minor suns, all dressed up in their traveling duds.

Mr. Zollinger held up his hands, and the music and noise stopped.

"My bride, Lucy, and I want to thank you, all of you, for making this day a special one for the both of us. We'll always appreciate every one of you." And then he and Lucy turned and, holding hands, skipped out of the Fellowship Hall.

The entire congregation, or most of it anyway, followed them down the hallway, through the back door of the church, and to a waiting black automobile—Mr. Zollinger's, I presume—that had been decorated with ribbons and tin cans and all sorts of other fun rubbish. Mr. Zollinger ushered his blushing bride—clad in a brown crepe georgette dress fashioned by my very own skillful fingers as a wedding gift for Lucy—into the waiting automobile. The dress was gorgeous, with a high collar and bishop sleeves slashed to points at the wrists and infilled with cream-colored silk. It had a low waist with silver buttons lining the front from the collar and wrapping around the hips. The dress came to Lucy's mid-calf, and it was perfect for traveling via motorcar to San Francisco. I hoped. I also hoped Mr. Zollinger had extra tires in the tonneau along with the honeymoon luggage, since automobiles ran over stuff and tires went flat at the most inconvenient times.

"Golly, that's an Essex Coach," said Pa to Sam, tugging my attention from Lucy's spectacular costume to the two men in my life.

"Nice machine," said Sam, a touch of longing in his voice.

"What's an Essex Coach?" I asked.

"Hudson Motor Car Company," said Sam. "Expensive model."

"Hmm. Well, I believe Lucy's dress is nice," said I, thinking it would be just like Sam and my father to look at the car instead of the couple. Then it occurred to me that Billy, if he'd been there, would have been talking autos with them, and I sighed.

"You did a beautiful job on Lucy's dress, dear," said Ma, placing her hand on my arm, as if she understood. She probably did.

"Did you make that?" asked Vi, sounding surprised. "It's gorgeous! I thought maybe she'd gone to a Los Angeles couturier or something. It's magnificent. I knew you were a good seamstress, Daisy, but that gown is... well, it's truly lovely."

"Thanks, Ma. Thanks, Vi. I copied it from a Jeanne Lanvin dress I saw in *Vogue*, and I thought it would flatter Lucy, if anything would."

"Daisy!" said Ma.

"I didn't mean that the way it sounded," I said, thinking sometimes I couldn't win. "I just thought it would be nice for a honeymoon. It will travel well, and it's dressy, so she can wear it to hotel restaurants and dancing and stuff like that. She has other dresses for casual wear, but she wanted something special for her and Mr. Zollinger's getaway from the wedding. So to speak."

"You sound as if they robbed a bank," muttered Ma.

"I didn't mean it to sound like that. She wanted to look good, and I think I helped her look darned good."

"What are you ladies talking about?" asked Sam as the Zollingers' Essex Coach tootled off down Colorado Boulevard, trailing tin cans and making a terrible racket. I was pretty sure Mr. Zollinger, who wasn't known as a gay blade, would stop soon and remove the auto's noisy trimmings. Not, however, until they were out of sight of the church, since he was a good sport even if he was rather dull.

"The dress I made for Lucy," I told him.

"What dress did you make? Her wedding dress?"

"Well, she wore her mother's wedding gown. I only altered it for her. No, I made the dress she just left the church in. Or in which she just left the church. Myself. I made the pattern and everything."

From Sam's blank stare, I figured he didn't even know that one required a pattern before one set about sewing up a dress. I put my hand on his arm. "Never mind. They drove away in a very nice automobile, and Lucy was wearing a very nice traveling gown, thanks to me. Well, the dress was thanks to me. I don't know where her mister got the car."

Pa heaved a huge sigh. "I'm bushed. Let's go home. I'd like to nap off that meal." He gave me a huge smile. "You did a great job, sweetheart. I know you made all those bridesmaids' dresses, and helped Lucy a lot. You're a good friend to have."

So, naturally, my eyes teared up, and I felt like an idiot. I swear....

TWENTY-FIVE

The Sunday following the wedding included an exhausted Daisy Gumm Majesty. I guess all of the prior week's activities had worn me down some, because I was, as Pa had put it, bushed. Therefore, I had to drag myself out of bed, into the bathroom, then the kitchen, where we all partook of Sunday breakfast, courtesy (of course) of Aunt Vi.

For some reason, I didn't feel particularly well that morning, although I didn't mention it to anyone. I figured I'd perk up as the day progressed. Silly me.

"You look a little peaky this morning," said Ma, eyeing me critically.

Great. Just how I wanted to look. "I'm a bit tired," I admitted.

Ma leaned over and pressed her hand to my forehead. Then she frowned. "You seem a little warm to me."

"Really? Shoot, maybe I'm sick. I thought I was just tired because of all the stuff that went on last week. You know, to get ready for the wedding."

"Do you feel well enough to go to church?" asked Ma. Both Pa and Vi had commenced staring at me, and I felt kind of conspicuous.

"Of course, I'm well enough to go to church. Besides, what would Mr.

Hostetter do without me?" Glancing at three surprised expressions, I added, "That was a joke."

"Oh," said Ma. "I thought maybe you and Lucy were supposed to sing a duet today or something." I guess she remembered Lucy was no longer in Pasadena, because she said, "That's silly, isn't it? Lucy's on her honeymoon."

"Right. But I'll go to church. I love today's anthem, 'Forty Days and Forty Nights,' and don't want to miss it. Of course, if Lucy were here, we'd probably sing a duet during one of the verses, but she's not, so we won't."

"Makes sense to me," said Pa, returning his attention from my peaky face to his waffles and syrup. Have I mentioned that our back-east relations always sent us a jug of maple syrup for Christmas? Well, they did, and it was delicious.

"Wonderful waffles, Vi," said I, hoping to divert the family's attention from my state of health, which was, when I started thinking about it, a trifle under par as the golfers like to say. But I was probably just tired, so before I could think myself into being sick, I stopped thinking.

Sam arrived shortly before we were to leave for church. Spike and I met him at the door, and he stooped to give me a peck on the cheek before stooping even further to pet Spike. Sam was beginning to get his priorities straight. As soon as he straightened, he squinted at me and said, "You're looking a little peaky today. Do you feel all right?"

Criminy! Did I look *that* bad?

"Thank you. I'm fine." Snippy, Daisy. Very snippy.

"Don't bite my head off. I care about you, you know."

I slumped. "I know it. I'm sorry, Sam, but everyone thinks I look peaky today. I'm just a little tired from all the stuff I did last week and the wedding yesterday, I think."

"Very well, but if you don't feel well, you probably should stay home from church today."

"I'm going to church," I told him firmly.

"All right." He shrugged and said no more. He really was beginning to shape up. Some.

So we loaded ourselves into Sam's Hudson (not an Essex Coach, but the plain old regular variety) and Sam drove us to church.

Although I wouldn't admit it to anyone in my family (or to Sam), the longer I stayed awake that day, the worse I felt. My mother had been right about the relative heat on my forehead, I reckon, because after I donned my choir robe, and the choir sang its anthem, which went very well even without a duet with Lucy and me, I started sweating.

Now, I don't like to be sick. I'd nursed my poor husband for years before he died, and it gave me an almost crazy dislike of being ill. Of course, everyone gets sick every once in a while, and Billy's problems weren't your ordinary illnesses or anything like that, but it still took a lot for me to admit to feeling unwell.

However, right after church and after I'd taken off my choir robe and was about to head to Fellowship Hall to partake of a cup of tea—I didn't feel like eating, which was unlike me—I took a detour to the ladies' room in the very rear of the church for fear my tummy might erupt. Not a pleasant feeling, which is why I chose to use the least-popular (at that time on a Sunday morning) ladies' room.

Once I got to the ladies' room parlor, I sat on the sofa. My stomach calmed down a bit, but I still felt slightly feverish. I decided to rest a little before joining my family and, as I did my resting, I heard sobbing coming from the room leading off the parlor that contained three toilets in neat little stalls. We were very up-to-date in our Methodist-Episcopal church.

Curious, and when I was sure I wasn't going to throw up or do anything else disgusting, I tiptoed to the other room to find Miss Betsy Powell curled up in a little wicker chair with its pretty embroidered seat cover and seat back. I guess the chair had been set there for the little old ladies who couldn't stand in line, not that we ever had many lines, but we were a tremendously charitable church.

I said softly, "Betsy? Miss Powell? What's the matter? Is there anything I can do to help you?"

She jumped like a startled fawn, dropped her hands from where they'd been hankie-ing her eyes, and stared at me, her huge blue eyes drowning in tears. "What? What? Oh! It's you!"

"Is there something I can do for you? Get you some water? The doctor? Anything?"

She stared at me for a moment and then wailed (she would), "*Nooooo*! No! There's nothing anyone can do for me! I'm going straight to hell for what I've done! Oh, I can't be forgiven for this. It's impossible. Not even *God* can save me now!"

Huh? "Oh, certainly He can. God can do anything?" Well, except keep soldiers from being shot to death and people's spouses from dying of consumption, but I didn't think that was what she meant. "Here, Betsy. Come with me."

She put up a feeble struggle. "No! Leave me alone!"

"I don't think you should be alone right now. Here, the ladies'-room parlor is more comfortable than this room."

"Is anyone else there?" she asked, plainly frightened.

"No. It will just be the two of us. Nobody uses this room at this time on a Sunday morning."

"Well..."

"Perhaps if you could talk to me—or someone—about your problem, you could think of a solution."

She gave a watery, "Ha. Shows how much you know."

"True. But perhaps it will help you to talk about it."

"It won't."

Great. "I promise I won't tell a soul." I couldn't cross my fingers behind my back, but I did have certain reservations about my promise to Miss Powell that I didn't reveal to her. Maybe I'd finally discover who'd poisoned Mr. Underhill! And then, depending on who it was, I might or might not tell the police, in the form of Sam Rotondo. What the heck, if Sherlock Holmes could dispense fair justice on his own, why not Daisy Gumm Majesty?

It's probably best if you don't answer that.

I guided Betsy to a comfortable chair in the parlor and sat beside her on the sofa, where I'd more or less collapsed before. Oddly enough, I'd forgotten all about feeling sick.

"Can't you tell me what the matter is, Betsy? I'm sure it's nowhere near as awful as you think it is."

"It is," she said more firmly than she's spoken before. "I killed someone."

I regret to say I gasped, even though I'd halfway expected the words. "My goodness," I said in my mildest voice. "Well, whoever it was, I'm sure he deserved it."

After giving me a sour look, Betsy said, "It was a she, and no, she didn't."

A she? What she? When she? Who she? "Goodness. Who was it?" Oh, dear. I hoped that wasn't too blunt.

Another several sobs preceded Betsy's pitiful, "Mrs. Franbold! Oh, Daisy! I killed that poor woman, who never did any harm to anyone." She peered at me through eyes that had resumed dripping. "I'm going to hell, aren't I?"

"Not for that, you're not," I said. Even to my own ears, I sounded disappointed. "Mrs. Franbold died of natural causes."

Betsy sat up straight in her chair. "*What*?"

Dang, I wished she'd stop screeching. "She died of natural cause. The medical examiner said so."

"Then why is that detective friend of yours here every week, staring at me?"

"Um...I don't think Detective Rotondo is staring at you in particular, Betsy. He comes to church with my family because we're...friends. He's a friend of the family, I mean."

"Oh. Well, it seems as though every time I look at him, he's staring at me."

And I thought he stared at me all during church services. I guess one perceives what one wants to perceive.

"No. I'm virtually positive he's not staring at you, Betsy. I'm sorry if he's upset you, and I'm *extremely* sorry you thought you had something to do with Mrs. Franbold's death. But why would you think that?"

She sat silent for so many seconds, I wanted to reach out and shake her. At last she heaved a gusty sigh and whispered, "Because you were right about when I assisted with communion that day. I was trying to kill someone else, and I thought she'd got the wrong communion cup."

Well, that knocked me for a loop. "Whom were you trying to kill?" I asked, trying to sound merely conversational and not shocked.

Another silence ensued. Then another sigh. Finally, she said, "Mr. Underhill." And she started crying again.

I patted her shoulder and tried to get her to shut up, because the woman had just confessed to murder, only it wasn't the right one! Mr. Underhill *had* been murdered, but she hadn't mentioned him as having consumed the poison she'd wanted to give him. She thought she'd done in Mrs. Franbold, only by accident.

"Um...So you actually *did* kill Mr. Underhill? He was poisoned. The medical examiner said it was cyanide, and they thought the poison might have come from his chemical plant."

"But I *didn't* kill him! I wanted to, but I didn't. I got so scared after Mrs. Franbold dropped dead that I never tried anything like that again! Oh, but I hated that man." She'd begun to growl, and her hands clenched into fists in her lap.

Because I was quite befuddled, I only sat there in silence for a few moments while Betsy Powell fumed. Then I said, "Um...Why did you hate Mr. Underhill? Mind you, everyone I've ever spoken to who knew him hated him, including his family, but why did you?"

Her lips pinched together so tightly, lines radiated out from them sort of like the rays of the sun reflecting on a pool, only nowhere near as prettily. She didn't speak for a long time, and I feared she might not reveal her deepest secrets. And here I was so empathetic a listener. Yes, I'm being sarcastic again. Bad Daisy.

"Betsy?" I said softly. "I'm sorry. I'm sure you had a good reason to dislike him so much. Don't you think you'd feel better if you shared your burden?"

She eyed me with grave misgiving before saying softly, "You wouldn't understand."

Giving her my most comforting spiritualistic gaze, I purred, "Are you sure? I listen to people's problems all the time, and so far I've never let out anyone's secret. Some folks find my services helpful."

"You want me to *buy* your ears?" She screeched.

Oh, dear. "No, no. I didn't mean that. I don't want your money. I would like, if possible, to help you overcome this terrible burden you're carrying. I've probably heard every problem anyone's ever had, in one form or another, so I do believe I might understand and be able to help you."

The atmosphere was getting thicker and gooier with each passing second, by golly.

"Well..." She still appeared—and sounded—doubtful.

I remained silent, smiling gently and trying to look angelic. Fortunately for me, Betsy's unhappiness had driven my fever out of my head. So to speak. I mean, it was still there, but I wasn't bothered by it for the moment.

"You really won't tell anyone? Now that I know I didn't really kill anyone—although I was going to kill Mr. Underhill, which I know is an unforgivable sin—maybe I could get this off my chest."

"I'm sure God will forgive you—anyone, for that matter—for failed bad intentions. Heck, he forgives anyone who asks him." Maybe. What did I know about God? Not a whole lot, in spite of my entire life of faithful attendance at the Methodist-Episcopal Church.

"Well, then..."

Betsy Powell buried her head in her hands, and I held my breath, praying, probably sacrilegiously, that she'd spill her guts. Not literally. I continued to smile in as benevolent a fashion as I could.

At last, she blurted out through her fingers, which still covered her face, "He seduced me! He told me he loved me! He promised he'd marry me!"

It was my turn to blink and look blank. I didn't want to spoil the moment or anything, but...Huh? "Um...wasn't he a married man?" I knew, of course, that he'd been a married man, the bounder.

"Yes! But he said he'd divorce his wife and marry me. I...I...I...Oh, Mrs. Majesty, I fell in love with him. And then he *laughed* at me! And he broke my heart! And then I was ruined for anyone else, and when Mr. Kingston began paying attention to me, I didn't know what to do! I couldn't confess my evil to him, because that would drive him away. And now I don't know what to *doooooo!*"

And she turned in her chair, flung her arms around me, and darned near strangled me to death as she sobbed onto my shoulder.

Merciful heavens. I hadn't expected anything like this from the pretty-ish, forty-ish Betsy Powell. Golly, Mr. Underhill had been even more of a louse than I'd suspected, the cad.

Once I'd delicately maneuvered myself into a more comfy position, from which I could speak without inhaling or spitting on a bunch of hair and a black cloche hat, I said, "Oh, Miss Powell, I'm so sorry. That man was a complete wretch. What he did to you was a crime, and he deserved to die. And you can take comfort from the fact that, while you didn't kill him, someone else who probably had just as much of a reason to hate him as you, did kill him, and he's no longer here to plague the rest of the human race. I know God will forgive you for hating him, because you had good reason." Hmm. That sort of went against the *turn the other cheek* thing Pastor Smith was always spouting at us. Oh, well. In my opinion, you can only turn so many cheeks, and then it's time for stronger measures. Besides, if those words didn't make her feel better, I didn't know my stuff.

She pulled back slightly, thank God, and sniffled at me. "Do you really think so?"

"I know so." I sounded a good deal more positive than I felt.

"Really?"

"Yes." Firmly.

"But...but...but what about Mr. Kingston?"

Hmm. Yet another knotty problem. "I, uh, don't really know the man, but he seems quite fond of you. Do you really think he'd fault you for your one...mistake? I mean, if he's a just and kindhearted man, he'll understand."

She looked totally unconvinced. "I don't know about that. Men aren't like women. They'll do any old thing and know a woman will forgive them, but if a woman steps out of line, the entire countryside turns against her. I read about stuff like that all the time in the *Saturday Evening Post*. A man can be forgiven anything, but let a woman make one mistake, and she's banned forevermore by everyone."

Perhaps she ought to broaden her reading horizons. I didn't tell her that. "Hmm. I truly don't know what to tell you about Mr. Kingston. You know him a lot better than I do. I'm only sorry Mr. Underhill did such a wicked thing to you. I, for one, am glad he's dead." There. I meant it, too.

"Oh, Daisy! Thank you!"

Blast. She recommenced strangling me.

But that didn't last too awfully long, and by the time the two of us walked from the ladies' room to the Fellowship Hall, I'd helped Miss Betsy Powell wash her face, powder her cheeks a tiny bit to remove the major ravages of weeping, and I didn't think either one of us looked precisely like the wrath of God, although I was only guessing about that part.

TWENTY-SIX

Aaaaand, I guessed wrong. As soon as I stepped foot into Fellowship Hall that day, my entire family, Sam, and Dr. Benjamin and his wife ganged up on me. Well, that's only six people, but they felt like a gang.

"You're sick. I can tell," said Sam, always polite and gentlemanly.

I glared at him, but by that time, both Aunt Vi and Ma had a hand to my forehead, each taking opposite sides of me. "You have a fever," declared Aunt Vi and Ma in a duet.

"You're terribly flushed, dear," said Mrs. Benjamin, a worried expression on her face. She turned to her husband. "Dr. Benjamin"—she always called him Dr. Benjamin—"you need to examine Mrs. Majesty. She's clearly ill."

"I am?" I said, feeling stupid.

Dr. Benjamin added his hand to my forehead and said, "Yes."

"We'd better get you home," said Pa.

"Hmm," said I, feeling my own forehead and finding it hotter than your average frying pan over a big flame. "I guess you're right." Naturally, as soon as my illness was confirmed by everyone, I began feeling lousy. "Yes, let's go home. I'm sorry to ruin everyone's fun." And, right on cue, idiotically and typically, I burst into tears. Right there in Fellowship Hall. I *hate* being sick. I also hate crying in front of people, but oh, well.

The Benjamins followed Sam's Hudson, which carried my family and me to our home a little south on Marengo. I was feeling weak and wobbly as I walked to the front porch, even with Sam holding me up by the elbows.

For the first time since I could remember, the delicious aroma of Aunt Vi's waiting dinner didn't make my mouth water. In fact, I almost felt sick to my stomach, which isn't like me at all. Well, except for when Billy died. I couldn't eat for months after that, but this wasn't then.

"I'm going to bed," I told everyone. Then I bent to pet Spike, who was leaping and wagging and loving his family and friends being home, and I fell, plop, on the floor. I don't think I fainted exactly. I think my legs just gave out on me, something they didn't do as a rule, and which I considered mighty rude of them.

"Good Lord!" cried Ma. "Daisy! Sam! Do something!"

So Sam scooped me up from the floor and carried me through the dining room and kitchen and to my bedroom, where he almost gently laid me on the bed. "You'd better get out of those church clothes and into a nightgown or something," said he. "I'll get the doctor."

"I...I don't think I can walk," I whimpered.

"Tell me what you need, and I'll get it for you."

In the meantime, Spike had jumped on the bed and was snuggling up to me. Ordinarily, I loved it when he did that, but I was already afire, and didn't need his warm, furry body near mine to make me even hotter than I was. "Nightgown in the second drawer of the dresser." I lifted my right hand and pointed a shaky finger at the birds-eye maple dresser that used to hold both Billy's and my underthings. And Billy's morphine syrup.

Thinking about Billy and morphine made me cry some more. Boy, was I a mess!

But Sam, undaunted by plowing through ladies' underthings—probably because he'd been married and was used to such activities—did as I'd asked, and brought me a long, white cotton night dress.

"Here. I'll give you five minutes and then send in the doctor."

"Thank you, Sam."

"Huh."

Typical. However, I undressed, threw my dress over the end of the bed since I honestly didn't think I could walk to the closet to hang it up, and hunkered into my nightie. Spike looked on with interest, but his attention kept swerving to the kitchen, where delicious smells emanated. They still made me feel sick.

In approximately the five minutes Sam had promised me, Dr. Benjamin knocked on my door and entered without awaiting my answer.

"You poor thing," said he. "You don't get sick very often, but when you do, it's always bad. But I've noticed that a lot with people of your coloring." I had dark red hair and blue eyes, for whatever you want to make of that. "You'll get really sick really fast and then get really well really fast, too."

"I hope you're right about that last part," I kind of croaked.

He smiled and opened his black bag, which I knew he kept in his automobile for emergencies. This was the first time I could recall me being an emergency. Reaching in, he pulled out a thermometer case, which he opened and from which he removed a thermometer. As he shook it to get the mercury down, he said, "All right. Open up."

So I did, he thrust the thermometer under my tongue, and let it stay there for a minute or so. When he removed it, he nodded and said, "Just as I figured. You, young lady, have a fever of a hundred and two degrees. That's not good. You probably infected the whole church congregation."

"Oh, no! Did I really? But I didn't know I was sick." Tears trickled down my cheeks again.

"Don't be silly," he said bracingly. "I'm going to give you three aspirin tablets, dose you with quinine, and I'll be back tomorrow to see how you're doing. Be sure to drink lots of water. Otherwise, the fever will dehydrate you, and you might become even more ill."

"Water? Really?"

"Water. Really."

"Thank you."

"Thank *you*. If you hadn't come down with whatever it is you have,

Mrs. Benjamin and I wouldn't be partaking of one of your aunt's wonderful meals." He gave me a wink.

I loved Dr. Benjamin. He was one of the kindest men I knew.

So he gave me the three aspirin tablets, which I washed down with a cup of sweetened, milk-laden tea brought to me by my darling aunt, gave me a dose of quinine, and tucked me into bed. Ma and Pa and Sam came in to make sure I was still alive and fit to be left on my own. By that time, my eyelids felt as though they were made of lead, so I told them I'd just go to sleep now, thank you, and they all left. They took Spike with them. I missed Spike.

After the door to my room shut, I dozed off and on, listening to desultory chatter slipping into my room from the kitchen to the dining room and back again. I do believe Vi served up one of her delectable stews that day, which she always served with her flaky dinner rolls. I think, although I'm not perfectly sure, that she'd prepared a floating island for dessert. In our household floating island is a baked meringue floating in a boat of custard sauce. As a rule, I'd kill to be able to partake of a meal like that, but I was sick. Too sick to eat. Boy, what an un-Daisy-like thing to happen.

Damnation! I *hate* being sick!

Didn't matter how much animosity I held toward illness. I was sick in bed for five days. Dr. Benjamin visited every single one of those days, and so did Sam. Naturally, Pa kept an eye on me during the day, and Ma and Vi ministered to me as much as they could before and after their working hours. Vi made beef broth for me (she called it beef tea), which didn't hurt my throat too much when it went down. Sam said a Jewish lady in his New York City neighborhood claimed chicken soup could cure anything, so Vi made that, too. No matter how awful things got for me, I was blessed in my family and friends. And Sam. Sam was a true blessing, and at that time I was too weak to deny the truth.

People came bearing flowers and other goodies, which was nice. Mrs. Longnecker, our sour-dispositioned neighbor from down the street a couple of houses, even brought me some homemade ice cream, telling Ma that if I was sick, I might be able to eat ice cream if I couldn't eat anything else. That was nice of her, although I didn't feel like eating ice cream any more than I felt like eating anything else. I only drank soup because Vi and Ma made me. I followed Dr. Benjamin's advice and drank lots of water, even though I didn't want to.

Miss Betsy Powell and Mr. Gerald Kingston came by one day with a box of chocolates. Pa brought it and them in to me, and I tried to be polite and kind about them and the chocolates, but I wasn't about to eat anything Betsy gave me. She'd already tried to poison one person and had told me about it. I hadn't told Sam about her confession to me, mainly because I was so sick I forgot all about it. Then, after she came to visit, I wasn't sure what to do. She hadn't, after all, actually *killed* anyone. Besides which, I didn't blame her for wanting to do away with Mr. Underhill, the ghastly man. But now that she'd told me she'd actually tried to kill him, she might want to eliminate me, as someone who knew her worst secret.

Nuts. Life is too complicated even when one is well. When one isn't well, it's just not worth thinking about.

Still, although walking to the bathroom nearly did me in, I flushed the chocolates down the toilet. I threw them in a couple at a time and had to wait until the tank filled again before I could toss in another couple and pull the chain, but I emptied the box. I'd thought about burying them in the yard, but I wasn't equal to that task. Besides, Spike was a champion digger. Heck, dachshunds were bred to hunt badgers, according to Mrs. Bissel, and even went so far as to dig them out of their burrows. Badgers were tough customers and not known for their sweet dispositions. An ordinary chocolate was no match for a badger. A poisoned one, however... Well, the mere thought of my dog succumbing to poison made me cry. On the other hand, just about everything made me cry when I was sick. Phooey.

When Pa visited me after walking Spike and asked about them, I said I'd eaten them all. I could tell he didn't believe me, but I couldn't think of a more plausible lie. Again, that was unlike me. I know it sounds bad, but I'm generally able to lie with ease and facility.

Dr. Benjamin finally diagnosed a severe case of influenza, and kept dosing me with aspirin, quinine and sleep. The mere word "influenza" frightened people in those days, and I was no exception. Right after the Great War, a pandemic of influenza swept the world, carrying off almost a quarter of its population, so I knew it was nothing to sneeze at. So to speak. Look at Robert Browning's lost fiancée, Elizabeth Winslow, who'd died of the influenza years after the pandemic had passed.

But nobody needed to worry about me not being a good girl. I took care of myself and followed Doc Benjamin's directions to the letter. In truth, I felt so horrid, I couldn't have got out of bed and run around if I'd wanted to. All I wanted to do was sleep. I had a terribly sore throat, and pretty soon my voice deepened so much, I could have sung bass in one of the Van der Lindens' operettas.

The phone rang off the hook, in a manner of speaking, but Pa told everyone who called that I was extremely ill and couldn't take calls. I got the feeling Mrs. Pinkerton had an even worse week than I did, since she wasn't accustomed to *not* having her every need administered to instantly every time she called. I knew she was upset about Stacy's engagement to Percival Petrie, for which she had good reason although she didn't know it yet, so she was undoubtedly in hysterics that grew worse with each passing day during which I remained unavailable.

In fact, I *knew* she was hysterical, because Pa finally admitted as much to me. This was on Thursday morning, and I was finally beginning to believe I'd live through my ordeal, although there was no way I'd make it to choir rehearsal that night, and probably wouldn't be able to attend church the next Sunday. I was sorry about that, since that Sunday's anthem was "Now Thank We All Our God," a pretty hymn which, while written by a German, I liked anyway. Anyhow, that German had lived in the sixteen-hundreds and didn't have anything to do with mustard gas or Kaiser Bill.

In actual fact, when Pa told me about Mrs. Pinkerton's annoying persistence, I was sitting up in bed, my head flopping to the side occasionally as I succumbed to exhaustion. When sitting upright, however, I perused the book Miss Petrie had been kind enough to bring me from the library when she heard I was sick: *The Black Oxen*, by Gertrude Atherton. One of the reasons my head kept nodding was that this book wasn't precisely the type of novel I preferred to read. I like stuff that makes me laugh. *The Black Oxen* dealt with a truly pathetic woman who didn't want to get old. Well, I don't suppose any of us *wants* to get old, but there's not a whole lot we can do about it, unless you take Billy's way out, and that hurts other people even more than if one is taken off by the influenza.

"Do you think you can take a call from Mrs. Pinkerton next time she rings, Daisy? I hate to ask you, but she's really upset, and she's starting to...Well, she's about to make me lose my temper."

I lifted my head, which had just flopped to the side once more, and blinked at Pa. "Wow, that's not like you, Pa."

"I know, but the woman is a pest. She's really upset about something and claims she needs you desperately."

I tried to sigh and coughed instead. When I caught my breath again, I said, "She's always upset. But I think I can crawl to the 'phone when she calls." I sounded kind of like a foghorn according to Sam (I'd never heard a foghorn, so I wouldn't know), so at least the pesky woman would understand I wasn't merely avoiding her for no reason.

"Thanks, sweetheart. I don't know how you deal with her the way you do. She'd drive me batty."

"She drives me batty, too, but I'm used to her."

Right after that conversation, I decided to heck with *The Black Oxen*, set the book on the night stand, and curled up to sleep some more. Until I got that nasty 'flu, I didn't perfectly understand how weak a body could get under its influence.

The ringing of the telephone jarred me awake I don't know how much later. Since, no matter when the telephone rings, it's always for me, I attempted to brace myself. I sat up, hunched into my bathrobe, and had just stuck my feet into my slippers when Pa came to my door. I glanced up at him through bleary eyes. "Mrs. P?"

"Mrs. P," said he, sounding as if he wished it weren't.

"Be right there."

"I don't think you should get out of bed," said Pa, even though he'd asked me to take her next call.

"It's all right. I'll be fine." My voice was *extremely* deep and scratchy. Strange not to sound like one's usual self.

I dragged myself to the telephone on the kitchen wall and said, "Mrs. Pinkerton?" Pa brought a kitchen chair over to me, so I could at least sit whilst talking to the pestilential woman.

After quite a pause on the other end of the wire, Mrs. Pinkerton said, "Who is this?"

Good Lord. "It's Daisy, Mrs. Pinkerton. I've been quite ill."

"Oh, Daisy! Oh, I'm so sorry! Oh, I didn't mean to drag you out of your sick bed. Oh, I just didn't know."

Right. Even though Pa had been telling her I was sick for a week. Well, almost a week. "I have the influenza, and I'm not quite ready to work yet. I'm sorry I can't assist you immediately. Would you like me to telephone you when I'm well enough to come over with the Ouija board and the tarot cards?"

"Um...Yes, that would be nice. Um...I don't suppose I could visit you for a session? I don't want to impose, but..."

Good Lord again. She was talking to me on the telephone, hearing my voice, knowing I was sick as a dog—well, sicker than Spike—and she didn't want to impose, but she wanted to come over and have me do a special reading for her? I guess when you've never had a responsibility in your life, you sort of don't realize other people have their limits. However, I'd reached mine.

"I'm terribly sorry, Mrs. Pinkerton, but the doctor won't even allow me to have visitors." Told you I could lie when it was necessary. Darn the woman, anyhow!

"Oh, Daisy, I'm so sorry. Please take care of yourself, dear, and call me as soon as you can."

"I shall. Thank you for your understanding." Huh. Understanding? I think not.

"Get well, dear."

"Thank you."

We hung up, and I crawled back to bed.

I learned about an hour later that I'd perhaps wronged the lady. The doorbell buzzed—we had one of those twisty bells that make a grinding sound when you turn them—and when Pa went to the door, Harold Kincaid stood there with a cardboard box stacked to the brim with all kinds of things: flowers, candies, books, a beautiful silk shawl, and I can't even remember what all else.

"From my mother," said Harold as he staggered into the entryway. I know he staggered, because Pa told me so. "She even made me go to Jurgensen's and get some pickled herring, because she said fish is good for you. Don't know about that. It stinks something awful."

Pa laughed. "Thanks, Harold. The smell reminds me of my youth in Massachusetts. We down-easterners eat all sorts of things folks in California don't even know about."

"Not sure I wanted to know about pickled herring," said Harold. I heard him plop the box on the dining room table.

"If Daisy doesn't want it, I'll eat it."

"Good. Hate to have it go to waste." He and Pa both laughed at this piece of nonsense. "Is Daisy fit to be seen? I know she told Mother she couldn't have visitors, but I think that was self-defense on her part. I know my mother."

"I'm sure she'd love to see you. Go ahead. She's in her bedroom there."

I'm sure Pa pointed to my room, because Harold knocked at the door and entered without waiting for me to tell him to come in.

TWENTY-SEVEN

"Hey, Harold," I croaked from my bed. I'd managed to sit up when I heard him enter the kitchen and realized he was he. Or whatever I mean.

"Good God, you look like hell. Sound like it, too," said Harold.

"Thanks a lot, Harold. You always make a girl feel special."

"You look as bad as when you got sick in Turkey." I'd had a ghastly case of what they called Pharaoh's Revenge then, which is basically the stomach 'flu. Don't know why they called it Pharaoh's Revenge in Turkey, but they did.

"Thanks. You're so encouraging."

With a laugh, Harold said, "It's all right, Daisy. You'll get well, and then Mother can relax and give the rest of us a...well, a rest."

"Lucky me."

"Yeah, but you're used to it." He plunked himself down at the side of my bed, which dipped under his weight, and I had to grab the backboard so as not to end up on the floor. "By the way, did you manage to dig anything up about the Franbold and Underhill cases? I know you're sick, but I also know you, and I know you must have done some sleuthing before you got sick."

Aha! I could tell Harold about Betsy Powell's semi-confession and see what he said. Harold had tons of common sense, so he could advise me about whether or not to tell Sam Betsy's dark secret. So I revealed all.

Harold's eyebrows lifted. "Good God, so she really did try to poison the bastard, did she? But she didn't do in Mrs. Franbold?"

"Nope. She was trying to kill Mr. Underhill that day when Mrs. Franbold died and Betsy thought she'd managed to kill the wrong person by mistake. But Mrs. Franbold died of natural causes, and Betsy claims never to have tried to poison anyone again. So I still don't know who did in Underhill, but it wasn't Betsy. If she was telling me the truth, and I think she was. She was too miserable to lie."

That didn't make sense even to me, but never mind.

"That doesn't make any sense, Daisy," said Harold, blast him. "People can always lie. You must know that as well as anyone."

"I guess so, but I don't think she was lying."

"What about her gentleman friend?"

Shaking my head, I said, "I don't even know the man. He got mad at me for pestering Betsy about poisoned communion cups after choir rehearsal a week or so ago."

"Does he work at the Underhill plant?"

"Yes. He's an engineer. Or a chemist. Something like that. I saw him when Robert Browning—"

"The *poet*?"

"For heaven's sake, Harold, That Robert Browning has been dead for decades. No, this fellow is about Billy's age, and he can't help it if his parents named him Robert. Anyhow, he took me on a tour of the plant, and I saw Mr. Gerald Kingston doing something in a laboratory in the upstairs area of the chemical plant."

"He might have access to poisons, I suppose."

"I suppose he might, but unless Betsy Powell has told him her deep, dark secret, and she claims she's afraid to do so for fear he'll think she's a loose woman and abandon her—"

"A loose woman?" Harold interrupted me. "Have you been reading Victorian novels again, Daisy?"

"Oh, shut up, Harold. You know what I mean."

"I guess so, but I didn't think anyone cared about stuff like that any longer. This is the nineteen-twenties, my dear. Unmarried people have affairs with married people all the time these days, and nobody even notices."

I stared, appalled, at Harold. "You're joking, right?"

Harold squinted at me. Then he sighed. "You're such a sweet, innocent thing, Daisy."

"I think you're judging everyone based on your stratum of society, Harold. People in the lower echelons still care about fidelity and decency and stuff like that."

"Right. Like that bastard Underhill. He cared a whole lot."

"Well, he was in the upper classes of society—"

"New money," Harold scoffed. "He's the only one who thought he was special."

I tried to sigh and coughed instead. I was *so* tired of being sick. "Maybe you're right. Betsy Powell isn't from old money or new money or any other kind of money, and she's ashamed of herself, both for succumbing to his charms—"

"*Charms!* Name one charm that son of a bitch had."

"I can't. I didn't like him, and now I know he was a monster and am glad he's dead. But that doesn't negate the fact that Betsy Powell feels guilty for wanting to murder him, even though she didn't succeed. According to her."

"Bully for her. What about Sam? You haven't told him about this idiot woman's confession yet, right?"

"Right," came out on a fabulously deep cough. Gee, maybe I could make my fortune as a female bass. But I'd not be a bass forever, so I reckon that notion was over before it began.

"Hmm. Maybe I can find out for you if this Kingston chappie could get his hands on poison."

"How?"

"I know the junior Underhill. He'd know, if anyone would."

"I guess so. At least Emmaline's friend knows Mrs. Franbold wasn't murdered, so that cleared her friend's fiancé of murder."

"Not necessarily. Her friend's fiancé is Barrett Underhill, and her friend's father is one of the firm's head guys. And, according to everything I've heard, Underhill *was* murdered. With cyanide. Right there at your church." He squinted at me. "A whole lot of strange things happen at your church, Daisy Majesty. I wonder why that is."

"Oh, they do not." I thought of the recent production of *The Mikado*, and sidestepped a trifle. "Well, they didn't used to, until your friends came to town and decided to produce an operetta there."

With a grin, Harold said, "Yeah. Blame it on me. It's all my fault."

I whapped him on the arm. "Don't be silly. Still, it probably is your fault."

"Nevertheless, the point is that you can't rule out Barrett Underhill or Glenda's father."

"Oh. Well, I guess the younger Mr. Underhill might have poisoned his father, although I don't remember seeing him in church that day. I don't even know what the girl's father looks like."

"Kind of like a skinny dill pickle, actually," said Harold. "Tall, skinny and sour."

"You have a way with words, Harold."

"Yeah, I know."

We chatted a bit more, and then Harold left, and I went back to sleep.

Sam came to the house bearing a bouquet of flowers for me, which I thought was nice of him. His bouquet didn't hold a candle to the one Mrs. Pinkerton had Harold bring me, but Sam's was from his heart—I think he had a heart—and Mrs. P's was from guilt.

"Thank you, Sam!"

"Looks like you didn't need them," said he, glowering at the magnificent bouquet of roses, bird of paradise, baby's breath, carnations, and I don't know what all else. Sam's bouquet consisted of chrysanthemums, which I'd once mentioned to him I liked a lot. And he'd remembered. Guess the big galoot *did* have a heart.

"I like your bouquet better, Sam."

"Sure you do."

"I mean it!"

"All right. All right. What's in that big cardboard box out there on the table?"

"I haven't looked at everything. Mrs. Pinkerton sent it to me via Harold when she realized I really was sick and Pa hadn't been lying to her all week long. She sent me some pickled herring, but Pa said he'd eat it."

Sam shook his head. "That woman's a real peach."

"She can't help it. She was born rich. I think that does odd things to people. Since I'm clearly too unhealthy to go to her house, she asked if she could come here."

Sam's dark eyes opened wide, and his fuzzy eyebrows lifted. "You're joking!"

"Am not. But I told her I'd call her as soon as I could, and that the doctor had forbidden visitors. That's a lie, but she didn't need to know it."

Speaking of which, a tap came at my door just then, and Flossie and Johnny Buckingham toddled into my room. Flossie held a plate piled high with cookies.

"Oh, *thank* you!" I said to two of my favorite people. Well, Sam was a favorite, too, but in a different way.

"They're oatmeal cookies," said Flossie. "With raisins. I think they're supposed to be good for you."

"I read that oats are healthy food," said Johnny a shade doubtfully.

"She's not a horse," muttered Sam.

Johnny grinned. "Maybe not, but I still read somewhere that oats are a healthy food for people to eat."

"Thank you both. Flossie, you're a gem. And so are you, Johnny."

"Want a cookie?" asked Flossie with a bright smile.

My stomach lurched. "Not yet, thanks. I haven't been able to eat a whole lot since I got sick."

"You sound terrible," said Flossie. "You poor thing. Have you been drinking tea with honey and lemon? I think that's supposed to be good for sore throats."

"Oh, yes. Ma and Aunt Vi pour tea with honey and lemon down my throat every time they get a chance."

"Mind if I take a cookie?" asked Sam, eyeing the plate of cookies as if he hadn't eaten all day. Come to think of it, given his schedule, he might not have.

"Take two. They're small," said Johnny with a grin.

"They are not," I said. "They're huge. They look delicious, Flossie. Thank you so much."

"You're more than welcome," said she, and she lifted a corner of the towel she'd had draped over the mound of cookies and offered the plate to Sam, who took Johnny's advice and grabbed two of the delightful oat-filled rounds. After taking a quick bite, he said, "These are great." He looked at me and tilted his head slightly. "You might want to get the recipe from Mrs. Buckingham, Daisy."

Ruefully, I said, "Wouldn't matter if I did. I'd manage to ruin them somehow."

"Daisy, that's not true," said Flossie, clearly dismayed by my comment. "You taught that wonderful cooking class at the church, and you didn't ruin a single thing."

Although he was chewing, Sam managed a grunt that said Flossie was dead wrong about her assumption.

I frowned at him. "Well, I didn't ruin anything at the *class*, Sam Rotondo. It was only when I tried to reproduce one of the recipes at home that I made a slight error."

Sam still couldn't talk with his mouth full, for which I was grateful, because he might have spilled the beans. Actually, they were peas. And they were supposed to be piled on top of some hard-boiled egg slices in a little castle-shaped bread thing. Only I slipped up a tiny bit and used baking soda when I was supposed to use flour, so my efforts to feed my family suffered a humiliating defeat that evening. I preferred not to remember that dismal attempt at conquering my culinary deficiency.

"Don't you dare say a word, Sam, or I'll hit you."

After he swallowed, he held up a hand. "I didn't say a word, and I won't."

"I sense a story here somewhere," said Johnny.

"You'll never hear it from me," said Sam.

Flossie only appeared confused, so I said, "Why don't you put the cookies on the kitchen table, Flossie. I know my family will love them. I might even try one with my tea this evening."

Eyeing me critically, Johnny said, "You're losing weight again, Daisy. I think you should at least try to eat."

Nuts. Ever since I went into a decline after Billy's death and nearly starved myself to death, the entire world seemed intent upon monitoring my eating habits. "Don't worry, Johnny. I'll eat more when I get better. Listen to me. Do I sound well and healthy to you?"

"Gotta admit, you don't sound good at all," said Johnny.

"She's been sick since Sunday," Sam informed Flossie and Johnny with a frown. I guess he'd managed to eat his second cookie, since he no longer held a cookie in either hand. "Really sick. She might even be contagious still."

"Doc Benjamin said the 'flu is generally not contagious after the first couple of days," I said. "Don't worry about carrying my germs to little Billy." Frowning at Sam, I said, "Stop trying to frighten my friends away, Sam Rotondo."

With a laugh, Johnny said, "Don't worry about us. We're immune to just about everything, I think. The good Lord knows, we've been exposed to everything from the influenza to leprosy—"

Sam and I chorused, "*Leprosy?*"

Nodding, Johnny said, "Yup. But leprosy is less contagious than the 'flu. Poor person who had it lived in Africa, where the disease is more common. But it can be treated these days with chaulmoogra and resorcin and camphor."

"What in the world are...Never mind." Not that I didn't care about the cure for leprosy, because I was glad there was one, but I was already sick and didn't feel like getting sicker.

"We shouldn't talk about such things with Daisy being so ill, Johnny," said Flossie. "I do believe it was the first time I'd ever heard her chastise her husband, even though it wasn't much of a chastisement."

Johnny took it well. "You're right. Well, we don't want to wear you out, Daisy. Get lots of rest and gargle with hot salt water. It might help that croak of yours."

"Johnny!" cried Flossie. She gave him a little punch on the arm and then giggled. "Don't pay any attention to him, Daisy. He's just being mean."

I laughed, too. Sort of. Didn't sound like much of a laugh, but it was supposed to be one. "Johnny couldn't be mean if he tried, Flossie. I know all about him. He's a softie."

The exchange of glances between husband and wife would probably have been outlawed if anyone the least bit puritanical was there in my bedroom to see it. Fortunately, the only witnesses were Sam and me, and neither of us disapproved. In fact, my eyes almost started to drip again, but I forced myself not to cry.

Have I mentioned how much I hate being sick?

TWENTY-EIGHT

I stayed in bed until Sunday. Didn't even come out for meals, although my mother and Aunt Vi brought me foodstuffs on trays. I told them they didn't need to do that, because I felt like a loafer, but they scolded me and told me to stay in bed because I was sick and did I want to get a relapse and die?

Well, no. Not really.

Sam surprised me. I guess the box of stuff Mrs. Pinkerton made Harold cart over had inspired him, because he kept bringing me nice things like detective novels from Grenville's Books on Colorado Boulevard, and even some Chinese soup in a jar.

"Chinese soup?" I asked, peering at him from my mound of pillows.

"It's spicy. The guy at the restaurant says it's better than anything else he knows of for sore throats and chest congestion."

"Thank you, Sam."

I noticed he was eyeing my neck, and I wondered if my nightie had slipped or something. I pressed a hand to my front and felt the ring Sam had given me on the chain Sam had given me. I'm sure I blushed, because I felt myself get hot, and I knew I no longer had a fever.

"Well," said Sam, frowning slightly. "At least you're wearing it somewhere."

"I love it, Sam," I said in a feeble voice. I no longer croaked, but I did have laryngitis, which made me whisper whether I wanted to or not.

Sam sighed deeply.

"I love you, too, Sam," I said, and I held out my hand to him.

He took my hand and sat next to me on the bed. We didn't get all mushy or anything because the rest of my family had come home and were cluttering up the house. Besides, I still didn't feel healthy.

"I love you, too, Daisy," said he.

I sniffled.

Then Pa came to my bedroom door and said, "Dinner's ready, Sam. Daisy, do you feel like eating anything tonight, or will you stick to soup and bread and butter?"

"Maybe somebody can heat up this Chinese soup Sam brought me from..." I glanced at Sam, and he nodded, so I continued. "From the Crown Chop Suey Parlor."

"It's supposed to be good for sore throats and congested chests," said Sam. "Wish I'd known about it a week ago, because she could have really used it then."

"Really?" Pa appeared impressed, so he took the jar Sam handed him. Sam got up from the bed next to me, and they both walked into the kitchen.

I sighed, missing Sam. And he'd only been gone five seconds. Sometimes I think I'm just nuts.

However, Ma came in a few minutes later bearing a tray on which a steaming bowl of soup resided next to a bread-and-butter sandwich, which had been neatly cut into four triangles. In our house, we don't cut off the crusts, because...well, why would we?

"I don't know about this," said Ma. "Just breathing the fumes makes my eyes water."

"Oh!" Disconcerting. However, Sam had told me it was spicy. "I'll give it a try. Um...Better bring me a glass of water, if you don't mind."

"Not at all. In fact, that's a good idea." Ma vanished into the kitchen after placing my dinner tray on my night stand and returned a few moments later with not one, but two, glasses filled with water. "I don't think one's going to be enough," said she as she placed the two water glasses on the tray next to the steaming bowl.

She was right. I've never tasted anything so spicy in my entire life, and that includes the little bowls of salsa Mijares serves with their meals. Oh, but it was tasty! It sounds silly, but it felt healthy going down. I had to take two sips of water for every sip of soup, but I managed to drink all of it. The bread and butter helped quell the burn a bit, too.

Anyhow, where were we? Oh, yes. Sunday. I stayed home from church that day because I couldn't speak and still felt weak. I asked my family to please say hello to everyone for me and to please tell Mr. Hostetter I'd probably be able to attend choir rehearsal on Thursday.

Four pairs of eyes turned to glare at me (Sam was there, too), and I amended my statement. "If I'm well enough, I mean."

"Huh," said Sam.

"Hmm," said Ma.

"We'll see," said Vi.

"Sleep some more, sweetie," said Pa.

So I did.

On Wednesday of that week, I was well enough to get up, bathe, wash my hair, and put clothes on. I thought about calling Mrs. Pinkerton (who hadn't stopped telephoning the house every day or two. "Just to see how our darling Daisy is coming along." Sure.) but couldn't quite make myself do it.

Luckily for me. Miss Petrie had come by twice to bring books she thought I'd enjoy. Even more luckily for me, as I already mentioned, Sam had been prowling the stacks at Grenville's Books, and had bought the very latest murder mysteries for me.

Therefore, from Wednesday through Friday of that week, Spike and I enjoyed ourselves by sitting on the sofa in the living room, me wrapped in a nice shawl my sister Daphne had crocheted and given me for Christmas. I wore bedroom slippers on my feet, and Spike snoozed on my lap while I read. And slept. I could read for approximately forty-five minutes before I had to haul a sofa cushion closer, rest my head on it and go to sleep.

Dr. Benjamin had continued to visit me every day since the beginning of my illness, and on Friday of that week, he pronounced me well enough to take Spike for a short walk with Pa, as long as I bundled up.

"If you feel short of breath, come home instantly," he said in a serious voice. "There's still the chance you might get pneumonia, and we want to avoid that at all costs."

I felt my eyes widen. "Pneumonia? Really?"

"Really. I didn't want to frighten you, but I was worried your influenza was going in to pneumonia after the second day of your illness. You were extremely ill. Don't take any foolish chances, young lady."

"I won't," I promised, remembering all the people I used to know who were no longer with us because they'd contracted pneumonia after having the 'flu. Shoot. I knew I'd been sick, but I didn't know I'd been *that* sick.

Pa had been standing behind Dr. Benjamin, gazing at me and frowning. "Do you really think she should go outside, Doc? It's pretty cold out there still."

"As long as she bundles up, she should be all right. If she doesn't start moving soon, she'll turn into a marshmallow. I can tell her appetite has returned." He grinned at me.

I love Doc Benjamin, but sometimes he could be a trifle blunt. "I haven't been eating *that* much!" I said hotly. Well, as hotly as I could with my vocal chords still severely compromised.

"Just teasing you, Daisy," the good doctor said with a wink. "Bundle up, be sure to wear a scarf around your neck and over your ears, and don't walk far. You need to exercise a bit to regain your strength, but don't overdo it."

"May I go to church on Sunday?"

"As long as you don't try to sing in the choir. Well, you can't with that voice anyway."

I sighed. "Too true."

"But I don't think church will do you any harm."

"Thanks, Doc."

"Probably do her some good," said Pa with a wink for me. "All this pampering has spoiled her."

"Has not!" But I winked back at him.

So the days drizzled by—we got a surprise that March when some rain came. Generally we get our rain during the winter, when we get rain at all, which isn't often. Anyhow, the second Sunday since I became so ill crept up on us, and I rose to take breakfast with the family.

"Should you be up and around?" asked Ma, eyeing me critically.

"You still look peaky," said Aunt Vi, also eyeing me critically.

"Dr. Benjamin said she could go to church if she didn't overdo," said Pa, who'd been there and was reporting the truth as he knew it.

"I feel better," I said. My voice was still on vacation, but that was all right. At least Mr. Hostetter couldn't accuse me of malingering. "A little weak."

A lot weak would have been more like it, but I didn't want to admit to same. The word *pneumonia* clanged in my brain, however, and I vowed to take it easy. I still hadn't telephoned Mrs. Pinkerton. That counted as taking it easy, didn't it? I decided I'd take a nap after church and then, if I felt up to it, I'll give her a ring. She'd want me to zip over to her house instantly, but I'd make an appointment for some day later on in the week. I'd cite Dr. Benjamin's fear about my contracting pneumonia if she whined.

Sam came for breakfast, and when he saw me all dressed up and ready for church, he said, "Where do you think you're going?"

"To church," said I.

He glanced at my parents and my aunt. "Is she well enough to go to church today? She still looks sick."

"How kind," I muttered.

"Doc Benjamin said it was all right for her to go to church, as long as she doesn't overdo," said Pa.

"Huh," said Sam, and he handed me a box of chocolates. "Here," he said in his most gracious tone of voice. I'm being sardonic.

"Thank you, Sam! I won't flush these down the—"

Whoops. I hadn't meant to say that. Nobody knew I'd flushed Betsy Powell's chocolates down the toilet, except Spike, and he wasn't talking.

"Flush them?" my mother asked, looking at me strangely. "Why would you flush them?"

"Probably because they're from me," said Sam, sounding disgruntled.

"No! No, I wouldn't flush them for any reason at all. Thank you very much for bringing them to me." And right there, in front of my mother, father, and aunt, I lifted myself on my tippy toes and kissed Sam on the cheek.

His olive-toned skin turned sort of mauve. The family beamed upon us. Oh, let them beam. One of these days, I'd have to tell them Sam and I were engaged.

We had waffles with bacon and maple syrup for breakfast. Vi had a lovely chicken soup ready to heat over the stove burners when we came home from church. Vi was, I presume, still worried about my health and trusted Sam's Jewish friend in New York City regarding the healing properties of chicken soup. I'd already seen the pile of sandwiches she'd prepared for us to eat with the soup, covered with a dampish cloth and residing in the Frigidaire. She was awfully good to us, Vi was.

Because I didn't have to leave my family to put on my choir robe, the whole lot of us marched to the front door of the sanctuary, where members of the congregation who were designated as greeters smiled at us and welcomed us to the church.

"It's good to see you again, Mrs. Majesty. I understand you've been quite ill," said Mr. Jankowski, a little, bent, white-haired man with a sweet smile. "I hope you're not coming back to us too soon."

Golly. Was *everyone* going to tell me not to overdo? I'd been sleeping for two solid weeks, for Pete's sake.

"I'm feeling much better, Mr. Jankowski. Thank you."

His smile tipped upside down when he heard my whispery voice. "You don't sound well."

I shrugged and decided not to try to explain my health situation. I'd just try not to talk to anyone.

Naturally, that turned out to be impossible.

The first two people to meet our eyes when we entered the church were Mr. and Mrs. Albert Zollinger, newly returned, I suspected, from their honeymoon in San Francisco.

"Daisy!" cried Lucy a little too loudly. She glanced around with her gloved hand to her mouth as if in dismay at having made such a noise in church. Her beloved merely smiled gently at her, for which I appreciated him.

"Hey, Lucy. How was the honeymoon?"

"Gosh, you sound terrible," she said, gazing upon me with concern.

"I'm really sounding much better than I did a week or so ago. I'm pretty much well again now, but I had the 'flu."

"Well, you'd better not let Mr. Hostetter hear you," warned Lucy. "He'll be livid. Albert and I just got home yesterday, so I'm not singing today, and you've been sick so you're not singing today. He must be pulling his hair out."

"He'll be bald as an egg if he does too much of that," I said. "He doesn't have a lot of hair to begin with."

My mother said, "Daisy." But Lucy laughed, so that was all right.

"But how was your honeymoon, Lucy? It sounded perfect when you told me about it."

Folding her hands across her bosom and looking dreamy, Lucy said, "It was wonderful, Daisy. Just wonderful."

"I'm so happy for you both."

I felt a tug on my arm and realized Sam was bored and wanted us to head to our seats. So I said, "See you after church," to Lucy, and followed my family to their customary pew.

Mind you, pews weren't assigned to certain people or anything, but people tended to sit in the same places week after week. Folks could get downright argumentative if they found other folks sitting in what they considered "their" pews.

Fortunately for us, there were no such quarrels that day. Mr. Hostetter did, however, spot me. He gave me a hideous frown and stomped down the chancel steps, his choir-director's robe billowing around him.

"Mrs. Majesty. I see you're here today. When do you think you'll be able to join us in the choir?"

"Maybe I can come to rehearsal this coming Thursday," I said, smiling sweetly. I knew I sounded like a dying cat. As soon as Mr. Hostetter heard me, he said, still frowning, "Well, don't come back too soon. We don't want you damaging your vocal chords. Gargle with hot salt water. Put some lemon in it." He transferred his frown to the rest of my family. "See that she rests and takes care of her voice. We need her."

"So do we," said Ma a trifle huffily. "And we've been taking excellent care of her."

"Hmph," said Mr. Hostetter, and he whirled around and tramped back up the chancel steps.

"Of all the nerve," said Aunt Vi.

Pa chuckled.

Sam said, "He sounds as if he thinks you got sick on purpose."

"Stupid man," said Ma, which was most unlike her.

I just sighed and said, "It's nice to know they missed me."

Sam said, "Huh."

And the church service commenced. It might have been my imagination, but the choir didn't sound particularly robust that morning without Lucy and me singing. That was all right with me. I wanted Mr. Hostetter to know what a gem he had in me. Well, two gems, if you count Lucy.

TWENTY-NINE

Singing in the choir makes a church service pass by more quickly than if you're just sitting in the congregation listening. Well, and standing when you have to sing a hymn. But that morning, I couldn't even sing the hymns because my voice didn't work, and the service seemed to drag by unmercifully. I almost wished I'd stayed home and napped with Spike for one more Sunday.

But I hadn't, and the service ended eventually. Most of the choir members, including the organist, Mrs. Fleming, rushed to greet me as soon as the final amen sounded from his people again, as the old hymn has it. They were glad to see me, although they weren't delighted to hear me. I assured one and all that I was well on the road to recovery, and my family and I were finally allowed to go to Fellowship Hall for tea and cookies.

"Are you sure you're up to this, Daisy," asked Sam, being delightfully solicitous.

I gave him my warmest smile. "I'm a little weary, but I'll go to Fellowship Hall for a few minutes. It's fun seeing people again."

"As long as you don't wear yourself out. You don't need to suffer a relapse."

"True. I promise I won't make everyone late for Aunt Vi's soup."

"That's not what I'm worried about," he growled.

I patted his arm with true love and affection. "I know it, Sam. Thank you. I'm just going to take a teensy side trip to the ladies' room to powder my nose, and I'll join you in a minute or two."

"Your nose doesn't need powder," he told me, staring at said protrusion critically.

He sounded as if he meant it, and I sighed. "That's a polite way of saying I need to use the toilet," I whispered in his ear, to do which, I had to stand on my tiptoes.

"Oh. Well, don't be long." He gave my waist a squeeze and allowed me to leave his side. I opted to go to the ladies' room at the rear of the church, since I knew it wouldn't be crowded. My family—including Sam, who was becoming more and more a part of it—had stayed longer in the church sanctuary than usual because of all the people welcoming me back. Therefore, the corridor leading to the back ladies' room was deserted, and my shoes made a sort of echo-ey *click-click* as I walked. The sound and the lack of people might have been eerie had I not known every inch of that church.

I was about halfway to the ladies' room when I heard my name being called softly from a room on my left. I turned to behold Mr. Gerald Kingston smiling at me. Hmm. I smiled back, deeming it only polite to do so.

"Mrs. Majesty, could you come here for a moment? Miss Powell isn't feeling well and asked for you."

"Betsy? What's the matter with her?"

"I'm not sure, but she asked for you. I hope you don't mind. She insisted only you will do."

This seemed quite odd to me. On the other hand, most of my interactions with Miss Betsy Powell of late had been odd to one degree or another. Mr. Kingston, in his mild, meek way, appeared pleasant enough, and he showed, I thought, fitting concern that his special lady friend wasn't feeling well.

"I hope she's not getting what I had. The influenza can really knock one for a loop."

"I hope she isn't," said he, opening the door wider and gesturing for me to enter.

So I entered. The room was one used as a Sunday-school room for second-and-third-graders. I remembered it well from my childhood. We'd learn Bible verses and recite them to our teacher, and we'd get a little colored paper with the chapter and verse number printed on it as a reward. My mother and I had glued my brightly colored papers to a ribbon, which still hung in my bedroom at home, although I barely noticed any longer.

I also didn't notice Betsy Powell in the room. I turned around in time to see Mr. Gerald Kingston shut and lock the door and turn to face me, still smiling his meek-and-mild smile.

Whatever did this mean?

"Where's Miss Powell?" I asked, beginning to feel a little nervous.

"I don't know," said Gerald Kingston, reaching into his jacket pocket and revealing a syringe wrapped in cloth. He carefully unwrapped it.

Eyeing that syringe with grave misgiving, I said, "What are you doing? What's that, and why did you bring me here?"

"My dear Mrs. Majesty, you have a terrible habit of getting in my way, did you know that?"

"I what?"

"It was bad enough when you sent those sheriff's deputies into the foothills to discover my brother's still. You have no idea how difficult it was to set that thing up. Naturally, I didn't do the manual labor, being the brains in the family, but I worked out the formula for the whiskey, and that still produced a truly high-quality product. None of your bathtub gin for us. We went for quality, and we were well on our way to becoming quite wealthy, thanks to Prohibition."

My mouth fell open and my eyes goggled. That is to say, I'm pretty sure about my eyes. I couldn't see them for myself, but I was definitely stunned. "But...I don't know what you're talking about."

Oh, boy, how I wished my voice worked. I'd have screamed the entire church down if it did.

"Don't be ridiculous, young woman. You're a meddling busybody. And then, when Miss Powell told me she'd confessed everything to you, including her tawdry affair with that blackguard, Mr. Underhill, the most unworthy specimen of mankind ever to bide upon this earth, and her failed attempt to poison him during communion, I knew I had to do something about you. Your close friendship with that detective fellow makes you too dangerous for me to leave you be. You see that, don't you?"

"Wh-what?" I wish I could say I couldn't believe my ears, but I could and did. What's more, Mr. Kingston started walking toward me with that blasted syringe in his hand, tapping it with his finger and squirting a little bit of whatever was in it out, I presume to make sure it worked.

"Mind you, I realize you might already have blabbed Miss Powell's secrets to the fellow, but if you had, I'm sure the police would have picked her up for questioning by this time."

"But I wasn't even going to tell Sam about her trying to poison Mr. Underhill! And I'd *never* reveal so private a secret about their affair to anyone!" There I went, lying again.

Evidently Mr. Kingston didn't believe me, drat the man.

"Don't be silly, Mrs. Majesty. Women can never keep secrets. Now, don't worry. This won't hurt much at all, and after a second or two, you won't feel a single thing."

"Is that what you did to Mr. Underhill?"

"Of course. Only I used a different poison." He frowned. "This one is better."

"But...Does Miss Powell know?"

"About what?"

"About you killing Mr. Underhill!" It would have come out as a holler, if my voice had allowed it to. Darn and heck.

"Certainly not. She's a sweet, innocent woman."

"She tried to kill a man!" Again I tried for a scream, but all that emerged was a sort of whispery rasp. Drat it! "And she had an illicit affair with him, too!"

"That only proves her innocence. No woman with an ounce of world-liness would have fallen for the lies told to her by a fellow like that."

As he approached, syringe extended, I sidled around a desk, wishing the room was equipped with weapons. As with most Sunday-school rooms, it wasn't. But surely there must be something I could find that might stop Mr. Kingston in his murderous pursuit of me. Glancing around wildly, I didn't see much in the way of villain repellents.

"You might as well not try to run away or fight me, Mrs. Majesty. One little prick with this needle, and it will be all over for you. I'm sure your family will mourn your loss, but you've been *so* ill, I'm sure they'll chalk up your demise to natural causes."

"Is that cyanide?" I asked, thinking maybe if I could keep him talking, he'd delay his lunge, if lunge he planned.

"No, my dear. This is something else entirely. I made a mistake with Underhill. Didn't think the matter through. This will leave no telltale pink stains upon your lovely, if pallid, cheeks. You really have been ill, haven't you? If you were diabetic, this might even help you. However, insulin injected into a healthy person—"

"But I'm not healthy!" I whispered madly.

"Come, come. You know what I mean."

"Yes," I whispered, scanning the room for anything I might use to thwart his evil intentions. "I do." So much for that topic. I searched for another, less lethal one. "So you belong to a bootlegging gang?"

He laughed, sounding quite merry, which irked me. Here he was, aiming to murder me, and he was laughing? The little, mild-mannered rat. Maybe a mouse. "Heavens, no. My brother Rodney was quite the dull fellow. He was fit for nothing but manual labor, so I decided he might as well make us some money while laboring. He was a fool to kidnap the Evans fellow, because that led the police on a search. I under-stand you were responsible for that, too." He'd quit laughing and glared at me.

"I didn't mean to." Shoot, I couldn't even work up a good whisper for that one.

"You did it anyway, or so I've been told." He shook his head. "You're *such* an interfering woman."

"No, I'm not."

"Ptah!" I swear that's what he said. "At any rate, Rodney knew better than to...What is that term the gangsters use? Squeal? Yes. He knew better than to squeal on me, because he was aware of my capabilities with chemicals and so forth. To be on the safe side, however, I made sure he suffered a heart attack the evening of his arrest."

"You killed your own *brother?*" Good Lord. "Are you planning to marry Betsy Powell?"

"Not that it's any of your business, but yes. She's a sweet lady. Well, I don't suppose the term *lady* applies any longer, but I'm a forgiving man. She'll make a perfect mate for a scholarly bloke like me." He moved closer, and I continued sidling away from him.

"A murderous bloke, you mean," I whispered bitterly.

And then I spied a pile of Bibles on a shelf behind the desk.

"Now, now, now. It's not polite to call people names. Miss Powell is a most lovely and predictable woman, and just the sort of person I need to keep my house in order and cook my meals. *She* won't do outrageous things like tell fortunes or visit chemical plants on spurious errands."

"She works in one," I pointed out, still sidling. I'd reached the stack of Bibles. What I wanted was a baseball bat or a loaded gun, but this partic- ular Sunday-school room wasn't equipped with either of those items, a serious deficit under the circumstances. I did lift my arm, as if to cover my face. In fact, I wanted to be able to reach those heavy books in a hurry. This turned out to be a good thing for me to have done.

Because he lunged. I swept the pile of Bibles off the shelf. They fell with a resounding crash right in front of Mr. Gerald Kingston, who promptly fell over them, dropping his syringe. I didn't stoop to pick it up, but stomped on it, shattering it to bits. Then I ran for the door like a spooked hare.

"Come back here!" he screamed, sounding oddly like Miss Betsy Powell.

"Not on your life."

"It's *your* life in peril here!"

I heard him scramble to his feet, but I'd reached the door, unlocked it, and flung it wide. Then I bolted out of that room, hit a brick wall, and nearly bounced back into the felonious grip of Mr. Gerald Kingston.

But it wasn't a brick wall. It was Sam Rotondo. I threw my arms around him and whispered as loudly as I could, but less grammatically than I might have wished, "It was *him*! *He* killed Mr. Underwood! He killed his own *brother*! He's a bootlegger! He's a murderer!"

"Nonsense," said Gerald Kingston. "The woman's gone mad."

Sam picked me up and set me aside, then he collared Mr. Gerald Kingston. Literally. He grabbed him by the collar of his Sunday suit, twirled him around, and picked him right up off the floor. There wasn't a whole lot Mr. Kingston could do about it, since he no longer faced Sam. He tried kicking, but he only hit the wall of the church corridor.

Shaking like the proverbial aspen leaf, I told Sam, "There's a syringe in there. He was going to stick me with it. I stomped on it because he was going to kill me. It probably has...whatever he said was the kind of poison in it. He said my death would be chalked up to natural causes because I've been so ill."

Sam twirled Gerald Kingston around again and punched him in the jaw.

Bless his heart! Sam's, not Mr. Kingston's.

Miss Betsy Powell began screaming, and it was only then I realized a sizeable crowd had gathered in that corridor. Someone else was going to have to shut her up this time. I wasn't well enough to do it.

Dr. Benjamin finally had the bright idea of injecting Miss Powell with a sedative to make her stop screaming. Then the church was overrun with uniformed police officers. Sam carefully led what he called the "forensics team" into the Sunday-school room where Mr. Kingston had held me captive and tried to kill me. I'm sure the team scooped up what was left of the syringe and whatever had been in it.

∼

While we were still at the church, one of the uniforms asked, "How'd Kingston get that big bruise on his jaw? It's swelling like a balloon."

"He resisted arrest," said Sam.

The officer looked from the puny Mr. Kingston to the massive Sam Rotondo and said, "Oh." Then Mr. Kingston, without protest, was led away, I suppose to a cell somewhere at the police station. I wanted to hug Sam, but I restrained myself.

Then we all had to trek down to the police station, which sat on the corner of Fair Oaks Avenue and Walnut Street at the rear end of Pasadena City Hall, and gave statements. I was the only one with anything interesting to report, but the whole family went with me, and so did Dr. Benjamin, who thought his medical expertise might be needed. His wife, Mrs. Benjamin, declined the pleasure of visiting the station with us. Couldn't fault her for that.

My voice died completely before my interview was over, although I spilled everything I knew or had been told by Miss Betsy Powell, including her having tried to kill Mr. Underhill and thinking she'd killed Mrs. Franbold instead. I also told them what she'd told me about her sordid affair with Mr. Underhill. I felt kind of like a hoarse rat, but darn it, that woman's gentleman friend had tried to kill me. He'd already killed at least two other people.

The day didn't really get any better from then, but after a fairly harrowing afternoon we, including Dr. Benjamin, who'd stayed with us— on my account, he said. Guess he feared I'd faint from exhaustion or drop dead or something—were allowed to go home. As other people spilled their guts to the police and on the way home, my voice gained a tiny bit of volume, but I didn't use it. I was totally done in by all the goings-on that day.

Once we got home, we gathered around the dining room table for a very late dinner, although I was drooping like a wilted lily. Sam wouldn't even let me set the table. But that was all right. All we were having were sandwiches and soup, and neither Ma nor Pa minded filling in for me as far as table-setting duties went.

"Do you want your meal on a tray in your room?"

After looking from Pa to Dr. Benjamin, I realized Sam had asked the question.

I pointed at my chest and croaked, "Me?"

Wrong thing to say. Sam glowered at me. "Yes, you. You're sick. You were nearly murdered, and it's been a grueling afternoon. You probably should rest. *I'll* fix you a tray if you're worried about overworking your mother or your aunt."

Vi said, "Pish."

Ma said, "Fiddlesticks."

Pa said, "Sam, you're a caution. Daisy will be fine. She just needs to rest up a little more after we all eat."

Still frowning, Sam transferred his attention to the doctor. "Is that the truth, Doc? I don't want her to have a relapse. She looks like hell."

Well, I liked that!

"She'll be fine, Sam. Daisy's one tough cookie. Although," he added, peering at what I knew was a faded shell of my usually robust self, "she could use more rest. But she needs her nourishment, too, and I'm sure we all want to discuss what happened at church today."

My entire family, including me, nodded.

So I stayed at the table. Vi went to the kitchen to put the soup on the stove, but then she came back and sat, too. Everyone was both horrified and fascinated by the events of the day and the discovery of the villain, Mr. Gerald Kingston, of all unlikely people, so conversation rolled easily along without me having to add much to it.

"Why did you come looking for me?" I asked Sam at one point during a lull.

"You were taking forever. I was worried that you'd passed out or something."

"And the rest of us went with him to make sure you were all right," added Pa.

"And Miss Powell joined us because she said she couldn't find her young man," said Ma.

"Ha!" Boy, I wished my voice were stronger. I'd wanted that "Ha" to have some force behind it. Oh, well. "Her young man, my Aunt Fanny.

Her young man is a vicious criminal, a bootlegger and a poisoner. He murdered his own brother! Vile person. And he seemed so mild-mannered, too."

"Those are the ones you have to watch out for," said Aunt Vi as if she knew.

I didn't debate the issue with her, but I was pleased to note that most of my very best friends weren't mild-mannered, but quite vivacious. "When I read the article about the bootleg still in the *Star News*, I don't recall anyone named Kingston being a member of the gang."

"Mr. Gerald Kingston changed his last name from Kingman to Kingston, I presume so no one would connect him with his idiot brother." Sam shook his head. "I don't really think he needed to kill the man. I doubt his brother would have squealed on him." This time he shrugged. "But what do I know?"

"I'm glad our family isn't like that. Can you imagine? A murderer and a bootlegger in one family?"

"Terrible," said Ma.

"Awful," said Vi.

"We're lucky," said Pa.

I cocked my head and stared at him. "What do you mean, we're lucky? I thought we were normal."

"Where I come from," said Sam, "normal might mean an entire family of crooks. Poverty leads to lots of bad things. Thievery, robbery, burglary, even murder. At the very least it leads breaking all the laws you can think of."

"Flossie Buckingham grew up poor in New York City, and she turned out all right."

My mother, father, Aunt Vi, Dr. Benjamin, and Sam all stared at me.

"Very well," I admitted. "Flossie went through some tough times, and I guess she wasn't precisely a model citizen before she met Johnny."

"She met you," said Sam in a flat voice. "Nobody who meets you is ever the same."

I heard a snicker. I think it came from my father.

Vi rose from the table and walked to the kitchen. "Soup's hot," she called, I think in order to forestall a fight.

The chicken soup was, naturally, wonderful. The sandwiches, which had sat under their towel in the refrigerator all day long, were a tiny bit firmer than they would have been had we eaten them when we were supposed to, but nobody complained.

Dr. Benjamin left us soon after the meal was finished. He looked as if he'd like to hang around a little longer. I guess my family was more interesting than his or something.

Ma and Pa cleaned up the few dinner dishes.

After nearly being nagged to death by Sam to go to bed, I had a totally embarrassing tantrum. I burst into tears, stamped my foot, and would have hollered if my voice had cooperated. "Darn you, Sam Rotondo, I don't *want* to go to bed. That horrid man tried to kill me today, and I don't want to leave my family. I'll just sit on the sofa." I sniffled pathetically, and Sam withdrew a clean hankie from one of his pockets and handed it to me. "Thank you," whispered I. Actually, it was more of a whimper.

So Sam, still worrying about me I guess, took my arm and led me to the living room. There he sat me on the sofa and solicitously plumped pillows at my back and on both sides—guess he feared I might topple over, as I'd been doing a good deal of in recent days. Then he sat beside me, sort of squashing the pillows into me. That was okay. It was comfy. Spike dozed contentedly on Sam's lap. In years past, I might have resented Spike cozying up to the enemy, but Sam no longer counted as an enemy, bless him.

The family continued to chat as I sat there sleepily, adoring my entire family, including Sam. I don't know how long everyone droned on, but I guess somewhere along the way, I nodded off to sleep. When Sam gently laid me on my bed, I blinked a little bit, not really waking up.

"There. You'll be safe and warm now. You even have Spike to cuddle with," he whispered. He didn't whisper awfully well, I suppose because he wasn't used to doing so.

Then he leaned over and kissed me on the lips. I know I fell back into sleep smiling.

~

Eventually I got the complete use of my voice back.

Naturally, the first person I called upon after I felt well enough to work was Mrs. Pinkerton.

And *that*, as they say, is a whole 'nother story.

The End

BRUISED SPIRITS

DAISY GUMM MAJESTY MYSTERY, BOOK 11

What's that feeling you get when you think you've been somewhere and done something before? It doesn't last long, but it's jarring. I think the alienists call it déjà vu or something like that.

Whatever it's called, I suffered an instant and distinct case of it when I opened the door to my family's bungalow on South Marengo Avenue in the fair city of Pasadena, California, and beheld upon my porch Flossie Buckingham. Flossie, after a very difficult start in life as a poor girl in a dreadful slum in New York City, had moved to Pasadena with her then-lover, a gangster named Jinx Jenkins. She had once showed up at my door battered almost beyond recognition.

That particular morning—the déjà vu one—Flossie was fine. Her companion, however, looked very much as Flossie had looked that other morning a few years prior. I think she was in even worse shape than Flossie had been, because Flossie seemed to have to hold her up by an arm to keep her from collapsing onto the hard concrete of the porch.

"Flossie!" I cried, bewildered.

"Daisy, please let us come in," said Flossie in a soft voice, as if she didn't want others to overhear her. "This is Lilian Bannister, and she desperately needs your help."

My help? *My* help? The woman looked like she needed a doctor. But I trusted Flossie as I trusted few other people, so I stood back, making sure my late husband's dog, Spike, didn't jump on either Flossie or Mrs.—Miss?—Bannister.

"Come in," I said, grateful the rest of my family was out. Ma and Aunt Vi were at their daily employment, and Pa had gone out to meet some friends and chat. My father is one of those folks for whom the expression "he never met a stranger" applies. Great guy, my father.

"Can you help me, Daisy?" Flossie asked cocking her head for me to take Lilian Bannister's other arm. So I did.

Flossie and I carefully maneuvered the poor woman into the living room and over to the sofa, where we tried but failed to gently lower her. She sort of fell on the sofa with no other sound than a muffled groan and then a sob or two. I looked a question at Flossie, who appeared quite flustered, not a customary state for the gentle and loving Flossie Buckingham I'd come to know since she'd met and married my old childhood chum, Johnny Buckingham, a captain in the Salvation Army.

"May we speak in private, Daisy?"

My gaze was riveted on poor Lilian Bannister, who sagged on the sofa. Then I transferred my gaze to Flossie. "Yes. I guess so. Come into the dining room."

So she did and, with a worried backward glance at Flossie's battered companion, I joined her.

"What the heck is going on, Flossie? Who is that woman, and why did you bring her here? Someone's obviously beaten her to within an inch of her life."

"You've got that right," muttered Flossie, sounding bitter.

"I thought Johnny was the one who helped folks in distress. That's his business, for Pete's sake. I'm just a phony spiritualist."

I guess I should explain that last remark, but I'll save an explanation until lager.

"That's just it, Daisy. Johnny *can't* help her. He wanted to, but he can't."

Huh? Last I heard, the Salvation Army took in all the strays and orphans and drunkards and drug fiends and poor folk and immigrants and so forth that no one else would touch with a barge pole. "But Flossie, Lilian Bannister has clearly suffered a...a...Well, I don't know what happened to her, but she need medical help. I'm no doctor."

"She's been beaten almost to death," said Flossie, confirming my suspicion. "But Daisy, just listen to me, please. Unless you know a doctor who is absolutely true to his oath of privacy, we may even have to forego medical help."

"But why?"

"Her husband beat her to a pulp and then kicked her down the basement steps—concrete basement steps, Daisy—and locked her in. She barely managed to escape with her life. Fortunately for her, Billy and I were walking, and I spotted her nearly crawling down Fair Oaks Avenue, trying to get to Johnny's church."

"Her husband did *what*?"

"You heard me," Flossie said in a much harder tone of voice than I'd ever heard issue from her gentle lips.

Billy, by the way, was Johnny and Flossie's infant son. He'd been named after my late husband. That's probably something else I should explain later.

"But... But isn't that a crime, what her husband did to her? Can't he be prosecuted for nearly killing her?"

"He can be prosecuted for murdering her, which will probably happen if she's forced to back to him," said Flossie. "Until then, he's her husband in the eyes of the law and the church." Her mouth pinched up. "She's a Roman Catholic, and she once made the mistake of asking her priest if he could intercede and help her get away from her husband. The priest said it was her duty to abide by her solemn marital oath." Flossie jumped up from the dining room chair in which she'd been sitting and commenced pacing. "Oh, it just makes me *furious*! I've been in that woman's position, you know. Well, of course you know." She whirled around and faced me. "But I didn't have the obstacles Lily faces. I wasn't married to that horrible Jenkins man. I wasn't married to anybody! If I'd gone to the law after he'd beaten me up, they'd probably have arrested

Jinx. But the law won't arrest Mr. Bannister. They'll send her *back* to him. So will her church! You *have* to help me help her, Daisy! You *have* to!"

"Can't Johnny do *anything*?" I asked in a small voice, wishing I knew what to do.

"Johnny has to abide by the law, Daisy. If he hides her somewhere, he's liable to be arrested himself! Oh, it's all just *so* unfair!"

"Yes. Yes, I can see it is." However, that didn't negate the fact that I didn't have a clue what to do for poor Mrs. Bannister. "But... Oh, but Flossie, I can't keep her here. There's no room. And besides that, I don't think my parents would like it. They don't like breaking the law any more than Johnny does."

Flossie glared at me and I held up a hand. "Honestly, Flossie, *I* don't mind breaking the law for a just cause, and Mrs. Bannister is definitely a just cause, but—"

The telephone rang. I do believe it was the first time in years I'd been glad to hear it, generally because anyone calling the house called to speak to me, and usually to engage my services as a spurious spiritualist-medium. Not that my clients didn't think I was for real. But never mind that. I'd just been saved by the bell! At least for a moment or two.

I walked into the kitchen, followed by Spike, who loved the kitchen because it contained food. I lifted the receiver from the cradle of the wall-mounted 'phone, and spoke my typical greeting, "Gumm-Majesty residence, Mrs. Maj—"

"Daisy!" cried a voice I recognized.

Joy and hope bloomed in my heart. "*Harold!*"

"Cripes, Daisy, don't yell at me."

"I'm sorry, Harold, but I'm *so* glad you called."

"I should hope so, because I'm going to take you out to lunch today and—"

"Harold, come to my house right this minute. It's urgent. It might even be a matter of life and death."

A pause on the other end of the wire preceded Harold's puzzled, "I beg your—"

"Oh, *please* don't argue with me, Harold! I need you now."

And Harold, bless his heart, said, "Be right there," and he hung up.

Turning to Flossie, I actually managed a smile. "If anyone can help Mrs. Bannister and us, it's Harold Kincaid. I'll bet Harold even knows a discreet doctor he can call upon to tend to the poor woman."

"I've met him, but I don't really know him," said Flossie doubtfully.

"Harold is the most kindhearted, useful man in the universe, Flossie. He's actually one of my very best friends. I tell you, if he can't help Mrs. Bannister, nobody can." I thought about the wilted woman on the living room sofa and said, "We'd probably better go see how she's doing."

"Yes. Yes. I'm sorry, Daisy. But when I heard what Lily told me, you were the only one I could think of who might be able to help her."

Lucky me. "I hope your faith isn't misplaced." I meant it.

Available in Paperback and eBook From Your Favorite Online Retailer or Bookstore

ALSO BY ALICE DUNCAN

The Daisy Gumm Majesty Mystery Series

Strong Spirits

Fine Spirits

High Spirits

Hungry Spirits

Genteel Spirits

Ancient Spirits

Spirits Revived

Dark Spirits

Spirits Onstage

Unsettled Spirits

Bruised Spirits

Spirits United

Spirits Unearthed

Shaken Spirits

Scarlet Spirits

The Dream Maker Series

Cowboy for Hire

Beauty and the Brain

The Miner's Daughter

Her Leading Man

ABOUT THE AUTHOR

Award-winning author Alice Duncan lives with a herd of wild dachs-hunds (enriched from time to time with fosterees from New Mexico Dachshund Rescue) in Roswell, New Mexico. She's not a UFO enthusi-ast; she's in Roswell because her mother's family settled there fifty years before the aliens crashed (and living in Roswell, NM, is cheaper than living in Pasadena, CA, unfortunately). Alice would love to hear from you at alice@aliceduncan.net

www.aliceduncan.net

 facebook.com/alice.duncan.925

CPSIA information can be obtained
at www.ICGtesting.com
Printed in the USA
BVHW030439300321
603653BV00003B/433